THE DEVIL'S TREE

AXL MALTON

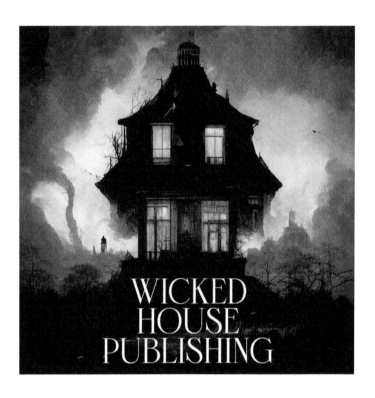

WICKED
HOUSE
PUBLISHING

The Devil's Tree
By Axl Malton

Wicked House Publishing

Cover design by Christian Bentulan
Interior Formatting by Duncan Ralston
All rights reserved.
Copyright © 2024 Axl Malton

ALSO BY AXL MALTON

Cries of Joy

Dead Man's Heart

For Haley
and our little coven of witches,
Al, Lola-Rose, and Lilly-Dot,
who forever keep me spellbound.

PROLOGUE

Alfie Weeds ran on ahead through the trees, full of excitement, desperate for his dad to follow him to see the incredible thing he had found. The woods in Wymere were vast; its pine trees started by the river Mere and didn't stop until they reached the east coast of England, twenty-two miles away. It was easy to get lost in those woods, if one was to stray too far from the path.

"Slow down," Gareth laughed. "I can't keep up with you, Alfie." Gareth tried to weave through the trees and jump over the bunches of nettles and brambles that grew on the woodland floor. He found the fact that he wasn't as fast and nimble as his ten-year-old son somewhat sobering. He had been starting to feel the aches and pains more and more in his back muscles, his knees, his shoulders – this was just another sign that he was succumbing to the sad fate that waited for us all. He was getting old.

"Come on Dad, it's this way. It's the coolest tree I've ever seen," Alfie shouted with glee from somewhere amongst the endless rows of pines.

"Be careful Alfie, I don't like going off the path."

The path was gone, and young Alfie Weeds wouldn't walk that path again.

Gareth looked back over his shoulder; how long had they been walking for? They had been at the summer fete only five minutes ago, hadn't they? There looked to be as many trees behind him as there were ahead of him. He couldn't see anything of the fete, the stalls and rides, or hear any commotion from the thousands of people that were in attendance.

It was nice to be out of the sun though, he thought; it was such a hot day and the trees had provided a welcome relief from the searing heat.

"It's here, Dad, we're almost there!"

A chill passed over Gareth and stopped him in his tracks. He looked down at his arm and noticed he was covered in goosebumps. His teeth chattered together and he struggled to catch his breath. When small gasps of air left his mouth, they floated on the breeze like small clouds of steam. He was freezing, his whole body was stiff like he had been dunked in a bath of ice. Gareth stepped forward; the effort it took was immense. The hair on his ears tickled as a voice spoke inside of him. It was a whisper, a whisper that told him things he couldn't understand and yet he felt an incredible sense of dread.

Without making a sound, he began to cry. The voice created pictures inside his head of things he couldn't bear to see, things that he had no means of escape from. For a moment, he knew he was about to do something horrible, and he even thought he might be able to stop himself if he tried hard enough. The voice seemed to laugh at this thought. It whispered to him once more. And then he knew nothing.

ALFIE CLIMBED through the gap in the thick hedgerow of brambles. It was more of a wall than a hedge. It was over six –

feet high. Anyone who came up to it would just see it as a dead end; it was so thick it was impossible to see what was on the other side. Alfie had worked his way around it, checking for an opening. It seemed to go on forever before curving out of sight. Then he found it, a gap big enough that he could squeeze through. His dad might need to make the gap bigger so he could get through, but if anyone could do it, it was his dad. The thorns were big and sharp like knives, but Alfie was careful, he slinked his small, skinny body through without touching a single one of them. He stood on the other side, taking in what was there in front of him.

He'd never seen a hedge in the woods before, so to see one like this was incredible. It went round in a large circle, creating a boundary around a deep crater that looked like it used to hold water. Alfie could see the mud in the bottom of the crater was dry and cracked. There hadn't been any rain in weeks, so the water had to have been in there before that. Alfie thought it must have dried out because of how hot it had been lately. Because of the size of it, he thought that maybe it had been a lake or an old reservoir.

"Come on Dad, it's over here!" he shouted over his shoulder.

The ground all around him was hard; the soil was black as coal. Not a single thing grew from the earth once past the border of thorny brambles. The most impressive thing in here for Alfie though, the reason he had been so desperate to bring his dad here, was the tree that sat in the centre of the old reservoir. There was a mound of black dirt, about ten feet high, and the tree grew out of the top of it. It didn't look like any of the other trees in the woods; all of those were thick with green leaves and stood tall and straight.

This tree looked dead. Its wood was white, as if it had no bark on it. Its dead branches were bare and split into twigs that looked like a thousand black veins.

A cold wind blew and made Alfie shiver. The hair on the back of his neck stood on end. He stepped closer to the edge of the empty lake and stared at the tree. He watched as its branches moved in the soft breeze. It beckoned him forward, as if mocking his fear. Twigs rattled in the wind and seemed to form shapes and faces; long, smiling faces with mouths full of black teeth.

"Dad," Alfie said, his voice stripped of its joy and now only full of worry. "I'm scared," Alfie said, and when he finally felt that he could take his eyes from the tree, he turned and ran.

He hit something and fell onto his back, propelled backward more from shock that something had snuck up on him than the impact. He looked up and felt an instant wave of relief when he saw it was his dad. Alfie held out a hand for his father to help him to his feet, but as he got closer, Alfie noticed a vacant look in his eyes, like there was no life behind them.

"Dad?"

His father stepped closer, walking with a robotic rhythm, as if he was being controlled the way a puppet is controlled by its master. His face was blank and free from any emotion. He lifted his hands; the way they were shaped made them look more like claws than hands. In one of those claws was a box cutter knife.

"Daddy?"

Alfie scurried back; he managed to claw himself away until the ground disappeared and his hand slipped down the embankment of the reservoir. He screamed in shock and tried to regain his balance. In the ensuing panic, he was sure he saw a hand rising from the boggy mud below the dead tree, a hand that was black with dirt, shiny as oil, with long fingernails that dug in and clawed grooves in the earth.

He looked forward when he heard his dad's footsteps getting closer, just in time to see his dad's hands reach out and grip his throat. Then, young Alfie Weeds felt something sharp run across his neck, and he found he couldn't breathe. His mouth filled with the taste of warm copper, and the brightness of the sun that shone immensely in the open circular space above him dimmed to black.

CHAPTER 1

The summer fete was busy. Far busier than last year when the weather hadn't been half as glorious as it was now. It looked as if the whole town had come down to get out of their homes and enjoy the fine weather. Old Maggie Colter was running the tombola, a big straw hat on her head to help shade her from the sun. She was rushed off her feet; the prizes on the table were nothing special, yet everyone queued up and pulled a ticket out of the drum. The prizes on offer consisted of a tin of shortbread biscuits, a jar of homemade jam from Webster's farm, a few board games, and the top prize, a bottle of single malt. Tony Thorne had his eye on that bottle of single malt.

He was on duty however, so he would have to watch some other lucky punter take it home. It wouldn't look good, a police officer of his standing being seen trying to win a hundred-pound bottle of scotch when he was supposed to be keeping his attention on the hundreds of people out enjoying themselves. Not that anything would happen. The most criminal thing to happen at one of these fetes was when Stuart Harland had spent all day supping beer after beer in the hot sun until he ended up trying to fight with the old man who ran the home-made crafts stall. He had jumped for him, smashed through the table, sending crocheted hats and blankets falling to the floor, as well as a bunch of delicately felted animals that were all ruined in the resulting scuffle. Tony couldn't help but smile remembering how much of a fool Stuart looked. He never came to a summer fete again. Didn't stop him drinking though.

Nope. Nothing ever happened at these fetes. Tony Thorne was just there to maintain a presence, help little kids if they got separated from their parents, and point people in the right direction when they were looking for the conveniences.

Tony watched as a man turned round from the tombola in celebration, holding the winning ticket up in the air. It was Alan Houghton, a nice man, six feet tall and as wide as a door, but the softest, gentlest man anyone was ever likely to meet. His wife, Jenny Houghton, clapped in applause with a great big smile on her face. Their little boy said, "Way to go, dad," but kept on looking toward the bright yellow bouncy castle at the end of the row of stalls.

"You go on," Alan said, and pointed down to the castle, "but don't you go anywhere else."

The boy said nothing. Just ran like the wind.

Alan picked up the bottle of scotch, turned round, and his gaze met with Tony's.

"I'll drink a glass to you, Sergeant," Alan said, raising the bottle in the air.

"An upstanding citizen might offer a glass to their hard-working police officers."

"Any time." Alan smiled, put an arm around his wife, and walked down toward the castle where their little boy was bouncing.

Tony walked to where the tree line of Wymere woods cast a heavenly wall of shade. His uniform was soaked, his beard felt wet on his face from sweat. He'd experienced hot days before, but this summer was crazy. From where he stood, he could survey the entire park. A huge expanse of neatly kept grass, usually empty, only used on weekends for the school's football team practice and the meeting every Sunday for runner's club, today held countless stalls, rides, carnival games, tombolas, a stage where a rock n' roll cover band would be performing later on. Everyone was enjoying themselves and that was good. He just wished he could do the same.

The smell of cheap burgers and fried onions blew over from the food stand. Tony's mouth watered and his stomach let out a low rumble. He checked his watch and figured he could allow himself a break. He grabbed his radio and moved it closer to his mouth.

"Ruth, I'm taking ten. You want anything?"

Static crackled. "Just grab me a water. It's hot as shit. Anything happening your end?"

"Nope. Just the same shit, only today there's a bouncy castle."

"Maybe you should have a go, might cheer you up. Miserable bastard."

Tony smiled. "I'll bring you your water."

He walked past a group of kids playing 'Ditch the Witch.' A woman dressed in a long black cloak sat on a chair suspended above a tank of water. The kids paid a pound and had three chances to throw a bean bag at the target. Hit the target, the witch dropped into the water, and the kid won a prize.

"They didn't drown witches to kill them, y'know," a young boy said. "That was a test to see if they *were* a witch. If they wanted to kill them, they would more than likely hang them, or set them on fire."

Tony shook his head. "Jesus Christ," he said under his breath. The boys took it in turns trying to Ditch the Witch.

When one hit the target, the witch dropped with a huge splash into the water, spraying everyone within six feet of the game.

"Whoa!"

Tony stopped just before walking into a man with a huge stomach. The man's white shirt was nearly transparent with the sweat it had soaked up, and was so tight every button looked as though it was about to burst open.

"Sergeant Thorne!" The man clapped Thorne on the shoulder and shook him. His hand was covered in a combination of tomato sauce and mustard; the last bite of the hot dog remained in his free hand. "Nice to see you. Great day for it, isn't it?"

"Hello, Mayor Rose. Yes, lovely day."

"So nice to see you." The mayor smiled; chunks of bread bun were stuck between his teeth. Sweat beads fell all over his reddening face.

"And you. I really must –"

A tall, slim man approached; his suit was done up immaculately, not a thread out of place.

"Sergeant Thorne." He stuck out his hand and Thorne shook it.

Then to the mayor, "Mayor Rose. Always a pleasure."

"Doctor Mahone." The mayor shook his hand. Mahone looked down at his hand and at the smear of red and yellow sauce as though someone had just handed him a fresh piece of dog shit and asked him to eat it. Mahone pulled out a handkerchief and wiped his hand clean before folding it back up and placing in his pocket. The mayor continued, "Mahone, you remember Thorne."

Not adding the *Sergeant* now, Tony noticed.

"Of course, Tony and I go way back."

"That we do," Tony said with the same lack of enthusiasm as Mahone.

"If I remember correctly, Tony was dating your daughter when she disappeared, isn't that right, Thorne?"

Tony turned to face Mahone square on.

"Yes, well, that's a long time ago now," the mayor said, shaking his head, the smile gone from his lips.

Tony stood up straight, his shoulders back and his chin up.

"Weren't you a suspect?"

Tony stepped up to Mahone. "You got something to say to me? You come out and say it."

Mahone, who stood six inches taller but was half as wide as Thorne, looked down on him and smiled.

"Okay boys, that's enough." The mayor turned to Tony. "It's been too long, we really must get together at some point —"

The mayor was interrupted by Mahone, simply shoving his hand between them.

"Mayor, I would like a word, in private, if you will."

"I've got to get on anyway. Nice to see you, Mayor." Tony walked on without waiting for the pleasantries to be done with. When he looked back over his shoulder, he saw Mahone take the remnants of the hot dog from the mayor's hand and pass it to one of the staff working at the bar to dispose of.

If there was a person in this town Tony wished he could shove in a cell and knock down a peg or two, it would be that slimy bastard.

CHAPTER 2

Matthew stopped the car. The A/C was blasting out and the idea of having to step out and join in the fun of the summer fete was not an appealing one.

"Come on Matthew," Jane said. "We've been here a month and we've not met a single person in this town. This will be a great way to meet people." She paused. "It'll be good for Tiffany too."

Tiffany lurched forward from the back seat, appearing between them both. "Is that a bouncy castle?" She gasped. "There's hook-a-duck too! Can we win a goldfish?"

Jane frowned, "I don't think they do them anymore."

"Why?"

"Because it's cruel," Matthew joined in. "You imagine being kept in a small bag, hung up all day in the sun. I'm surprised they don't end up poached."

Tiffany made a face to say that was yucky, then her eyes grew wide as she looked out the window again. "It *is* a bouncy castle, come on, let's go!"

She tried her door but it didn't open.

"Child locks." Matthew smiled.

The heat hit them as soon as they stepped out of the car. *This is how the turkey must feel as you're putting it in the oven*, Matthew thought.

Matthew Stanford walked down the stalls, taking in all the faces that looked toward him with a friendly 'welcome to the neighbourhood' smile. Small towns like these had a reputation, though. They were friendly, sure, but civility for strangers was a lot like beauty, only skin deep. He could see it in their eyes, the questions they wanted to ask, their unease at the unfamiliarity of this man who had arrived with his family not four weeks ago and no one had seen them out and about since moving day.

Matthew smiled, returned the wave of a great big man clutching a bottle of whiskey to his chest like a baby, and carried on toward the face-painting tables and game stalls. He held Jane's hand in his left, and Tiffany's in his right. Jane smiled at him. She had always wanted them to move out into the country, get away from the chaos of the city, and now they had. Matthew saw the big yellow bouncy castle at the end of the row of stalls; the decorations made it look like it was made of great yellow bricks. He looked down to Tiffany and nodded his head in the direction of the castle.

"You ready?" he said.

Tiffany jumped up and down on the spot, full of giddy excitement, and ran toward the castle. Matthew and Jane smiled at each other and followed her, hand in hand.

"It's stuff like this that makes it so worthwhile. They never have things like this in London," Jane said. "It's nice to be part of a smaller community, isn't it? Everyone knows each other and looks out for each other. The crime rate is practically zero."

"Yeah, it's great, darling. We made the right decision. Although, it will take some adjusting. The money left over from the house sale won't last forever. I'll need to find work soon."

Matthew and Jane stood with the other parents watching as children bounced and screamed with joy in the bouncy castle. Two children jumped at the same time and avoided a mid-air collision by millimetres, bringing a collection of gasps from the watching parents, followed by nervous laughs and sighs.

"I doubt you'll have a problem finding work, new build estates are being built all over the place up here. Farmland in every corner of the country seems to be being bought up and turned into houses."

Matthew grimaced. "It won't be long until it feels like we're back in the city if they carry on."

Jane shrugged. "It's awful, but people need places to live."

"Mum! Dad! Look how high I can jump!" Tiffany yelled, her long brown hair standing up on end and then falling back down over her face.

"Very good, honey!" Jane called back.

"I get that," Matthew said, continuing their conversation, "but a lot of these places in the country haven't got the infrastructure to cope with too many houses being built at once. It can lead to floods when we get too much rain because there's fewer places for water run-off, and when we're in the middle of a dry spell" – he raised his hands to indicate the sweltering heat –"we'll get droughts. The reservoir on the outside of town is already practically dry; the council will step in soon to tell us we need to start rationing. Mark my words."

"I know, love, I know. It's the kids that will suffer."

"Yeah, and they're the ones that will have to fix our mistakes."

CHAPTER 3

"Here you go. I got you two bottles."

Ruth took the water from Tony and unscrewed the cap. She had almost drunk the full bottle before she removed it from her lips. "Thanks," she said between taking gasps of air. "I needed that. Did someone turn up the thermostat, or is it just me?"

Tony smiled. "It certainly feels like it."

Ruth finished off the first bottle and put it to her side. She brushed the strands of blonde hair that had fallen from her neat ponytail back behind her ears.

Tony stood beside her and leant against her car. The metal of the bonnet burned through his trousers, so he stood straight again. He looked around, his eyes squinting against the brightness of the day. He saw Mahone walking across the field, shaking hands with those on the local council, sharing laughs and stories before moving on to the next public figure. Tony couldn't help but narrow his eyes and squeeze the bottle of water he held. Water rose to the top and spilled over his hand.

"Jesus!" he cried and shook his hand free of the drips.

"What's up, Tony?" Ruth said. "You look like someone's shit in your sandwich."

Tony shook his head but couldn't help but smile. Ruth had a way of doing that. That's why he liked her so much. Probably one of the only people he liked. He nodded in Mahone's direction. "Him. Slimy mother fucker."

"Doctor Mahone?"

"Yeah. I knew him when we were growing up. Or when *I* was growing up. He's got ten years on me, yet he never could find anyone his own age to hang around with."

Ruth shrugged. "What did he do to offend you so much? Everyone else seems to like him."

"He's arrogant. He was born into money, got his inheritance early, so lauded it over anyone and everyone he could. He loves the power of it, doesn't even try to hide it. He didn't take over at the psychiatric hospital over on Hill Top for the desire to rehabilitate those in need."

"That can't be true."

Tony shrugged and sipped his water. "There's been more than one allegation swept under the rug. Don't know how he did it, but he did." Tony reached down and picked up Ruth's empty water bottle. He screwed it up and threw it in the rubbish bin.

"Hey!" Ruth said, her arms spread wide in a *what the hell are you doing?* gesture.

"What?"

"Plastic recycles, you fucking caveman." Ruth bent and pulled the crushed bottle out of the bin. The plastic crinkled as it expanded in the heat, trying to get back to its original shape. "There are recycle bins all over the place, you know."

Tony put his hands up and cringed awkwardly.

"Let's take a walk. Don't want any drunks to cause a scene whilst we're stood gassing."

Tony and Ruth made their way through the stalls and past

the beer tent, then headed toward the games. That's where most of the kids hang out. Tony knew most were fine and innocent, but teenagers will always be teenagers, no matter where they grew up. Small towns, big cities – all the same. Just a different size playground.

Tony walked toward a gang of five. He knew the faces of the kids, had seen them hanging around the high street, loitering outside shops hoping for some gullible sucker to buy them beer because they forgot their ID.

"You boys behaving today?" Tony asked. Ruth stood by his side, having disposed of the plastic water bottles in the correct green bins.

"Yes, officer," one boy said. "We're having loads of fun."

"Good boys. Let's keep it that way."

The boys nodded and smiled, standing in a perfect huddle like a group of angels, as if butter wouldn't melt in their mouths.

Ruth tugged on Tony's sleeve and pointed down the line of games. The witch fell into the water tank and splashed the group watching; gangs of children stand grouped together beside every game stall waiting their turn. At the end of the row, moving through each group, was a woman.

Tony lifted his hand on to his brow to shield the sun, hoping to make out who the woman was. She grabbed a kid from each group, roughly, but from what Tony could see, it wasn't aggression. It was panic, the kind of frantic panic you get when you've lost something or you're running out of time for something important.

The woman let go of one kid and moved on to the next group. Tony looked at Ruth and they both moved toward the woman. Before they got within five metres, she looked up and saw them. Tony saw the worry etched into her face. He could also see now that it was Caroline Weeds, who looked a decade older than her thirty-eight years.

Caroline ran toward them, her dress lifted up in one clenched fist to help her run faster. "Officer Thorne, I'm so glad I've found you!"

"What is it, Caroline?"

"Have you seen my husband, Gareth? He was stood on the stall with me all day, then Alfie wanted him to go check something out in the woods, we were busy, but Alfie looked so excited and Gareth can never say no to him."

"And they haven't come back?"

Caroline shook her head and wrinkled her brow. "No... well, I don't know. They could have, they could just be around here somewhere and I just can't find them. But it doesn't feel right, Tony, Gareth would have come straight back to me and more than likely brought Alfie with him. Some people let their thirteen-year-olds run wild but we don't. The world ain't safe enough –"

She was starting to babble. Tony Thorne had been a police officer long enough to know that when people were worried, they could talk for hours unless you stopped them. It was a coping mechanism, it kept the mind too busy to form possible nightmare scenarios. He put his hand on her shoulder and interrupted her mid-flow.

"Caroline. What I want you to do is make your way to the medical tent." he pointed to the big white pole sticking up in the air on the other side of the field, "Tell them your husband and child are lost. They will do a call out on the speakers. Try not to worry, there's a speaker every hundred metres on this green, so wherever they are, they'll hear it."

Caroline nodded and the first of what would be many tears started to fall from her eyes.

Chapter 4

When the speakers overhead started calling out in a calm, monotone voice, Jane's first response was to make sure she got eyes on Tiffany. Tiffany was all smiles, bouncing in the castle with a dozen other kids around her age. Jane allowed her heart to slow down and manged to keep from pressing her interior panic button. Matthew grabbed her arm, making her jump.

"Jane, listen."

'Gareth Weeds and Alfie Weeds, please report to the medical tent.'

"I hope they find them," Jane said.

"I'm sure they'll turn up," Matthew agreed, trying not to feel panicked. "In a town like this, I imagine it's hard to go too long before someone sees you and passes the message along."

Matthew called Tiffany to come out of the bouncy castle and she did as she was told without an argument.

"Can I get my face painted, Daddy?" Tiffany asked, gripping her parents' hands. "Pleeeeaaassseeeeee."

Matthew and Jane shared a look and then smiled down at her.

"Yes."

Tiffany celebrated and pulled them along toward the stall where a queue of five girls and boys waited patiently for their turn.

Matthew's t-shirt was darkening around his arm pits and a spot had started to darken in the centre of his chest. "God, it's hot," he said, flapping his shirt to catch a breeze underneath.

Jane's eye widened as if she just remembered something important she had forgotten. She reached into her handbag, fumbled around through all the junk that gathers naturally over the years in any mother's handbag. The days when she could open up a purse and only find a small wallet, a compact, and a stick of lipstick were long gone.

"Here," Jane said, pulling out a tin of factor fifty sunscreen. "Let's get you topped up, Tiffany. We need to keep plenty of this on so you don't burn. I couldn't bear the guilt if you got burnt because of my forgetfulness."

"I'll take some of that too, my neck feels like it's on fire."

"Jesus!" Jane cried when she looked. "That's gonna blister. You'll need some lotion on that tonight, take some of the sting out of it."

"No kidding."

Matthew sucked his teeth and winced as the first sprays of sunscreen hit his reddening skin. Then the coolness became soothing.

"I've never known a summer to be so hot for as long as this," Jane said.

"Global warming, it's real, and it's happening now," Matthew said.

There was a disturbance at the head of the line. There was no rushing around or screaming, nothing that would instinctively induce panic, but the fun and the joy that seemed to float in the air was changing. Turning darker somehow.

Matthew thought it might just be him, but when Tiffany squeezed his hand so hard her knuckles turned white, he knew she felt it too.

Moving down the line of children with their parents was a police officer. Only young, fresh out of the academy by the look of it. The fear in his eyes did nothing to alleviate some of the panic leaking into the atmosphere.

"'Scuse me," the officer said, holding a photo in his hand. "Have you seen either of these two?"

Matthew and Jane looked at the photo. It was of a tall man, skinny as a rake with big, rimmed glasses on a long nose. His hair was thinning, white patches of his scalp grinning through where a few weak strands of hair were brushed over to try and cover the bald spots. A young boy, about ten years old, stood by his side with a smile from ear to ear. He wore a polo shirt and shorts, but his trainers were the most noticeable item of clothing. Bright red with yellow smiley faces on the side.

"Sorry, no. We've not seen them," Matthew said, almost apologetically. "We'll keep a good look out though. Do you think they're hurt?"

The officer grimaced. "The man is Gareth Weeds, he's the manager of the local supermarket. It's not like him to disappear like this. His wife's worried, but I'm sure they'll turn up just fine."

"Oh, hey," a voice came from behind them. Matthew turned around and saw a man with a baseball cap with cartoon fire printed on the peak. His face was bright red from the heat, and sweat was dripping down his apple-shaped cheeks. "I saw Weedy going into the woods with the kid. Alfie, isn't it? Constable Westlake."

"That's right, sir." Westlake confirmed.

"Yeah, they went in over an hour ago. They looked fine to me. Alfie was desperate to show his dad some tree he could climb and Weedy went along, happy as always. That guy can't say no to anyone, never mind his own son. He once gave me a refund on a DVD because I said I didn't like the movie." The man burst into a giant laugh. "You believe that? He's a good guy though, despite being a bit of a pushover. He'll turn up. Not like him to be more than two metres away from his wife. I thought she had an invisible leash on him all this time." The man laughed again.

"Thank you, sir. You've been very helpful." Constable Westlake gave a straight smile to Matthew and Jane, then walked off, talking into his radio.

"That kid's going to have a heart attack before his twenty-fifth birthday if he's getting that stressed out over a dad and his kid going for a walk through the woods," Matthew said.

"I don't know. Something just doesn't feel right here. It's as if –"

Before Jane could finish her thought, a high, tooth-grinding scream cut through the park, forcing the hundreds of people there into silence, as if a switch had been flicked. Everyone turned to face the same way. Jane looked behind her, where the woods started. She moved forward, keeping Tiffany's hand tight in hers. As they weaved through the crowd, Jane saw some people backing away, others putting hands to their mouths and covering their children's eyes. When she reached a clearing, she saw the man from the picture – Weedy, the man in the fire-rimmed cap had called him – stood at the tree line. The look on his face was that of fear and great confusion.

Although it was hard to be sure through all that blood.

His hands were out in front of him, and he looked down at them as if they were an alien appendage that didn't belong to him.

The crowd of people stood looking at him without saying

a word; the police officer that had spoken to Matthew and Jane like a deer caught in headlights.

A woman pushed past Matthew forcefully. She was sobbing, frantically questioning everyone but getting no answers.

"What's happening? Is it Alfie? Are they okay? Where have they been –"

She stopped dead in her tracks, one of her feet suspended in the air with just her toes on the ground like someone had pushed pause on the remote that controlled her. She looked at Weedy, then her hands shot up to her face.

"What have you done?" she screamed. Her voice carried along the dead atmosphere; the pain and panic in it sent goose-bumps up Jane's arms. "Where is he?! Where's my boy?"

Weedy started crying, his bloody hands still stuck out in front of him. His shirt that had been white that morning, was now mostly red; drops of blood dotted his shorts and smeared up his legs. Jane felt sick, and everyone in the crowd was verging on panic.

"I don't know what I did," he said. "I don't know what happened." He took a step toward the crowd and everyone gasped and stepped away.

An officer with a jet-black beard pushed past Jane and approached with one arm raised, showing Weedy the empty palm of his hand. The other was clasped to the taser gun in his belt.

"Weedy, it's Sergeant Thorne, hands behind your back please," the officer said. "Do it, now."

Weedy stood, crying, shaking his head, staring at his hands in disbelief. "I don't know what I did. I don't remember. I think he's dead, I think I killed him!"

"Hands behind your back, now!" Officer Thorne shouted.

Weedy lifted his hands and gripped his hair, he pulled on it and started screaming. Jane felt a stab in her chest. His scream was as heartbreaking as his wife's. He dropped to his knees, then the officer and two of his colleagues surrounded him, dropped him face down, and cuffed him.

The gathering crowd formed a semi-circle around the officers as they made the arrest. Caroline Weeds dropped to her knees and screamed for her son.

CHAPTER 5

There was a rare silence in the police station. The few officers who handled calls and distributed information to patrol cars were sat at their desks, not saying a word to one another. The town of Wymere suffered its bouts of crime like most towns, thefts, robberies, assaults – but rarely murder.

The only occasion where such a horrible crime such as this had happened was when a man had barricaded his wife and two young children into their home. That man had lost his mind, thought a mutated virus was going to take over the world. He was responsible for murdering four people at a supermarket, as well as his own infant daughter. Most of the officers sat in this station had dealt with that case, and it had taken a year for them to be able to put those images to the back of their minds. Tony Thorne had been in charge of that case; it was the worst in his ten years as an officer.

Now, there was this. Now, he had to wrap his head around a father killing his own son. He knew there was a word for it, but couldn't remember what it was. He looked it up: *filicide*. Now that a case like this had happened, no one in town, or on the entire police force for that matter, quite knew how to take it. The man responsible for all those murders years ago had gone insane. Gareth Weeds had not.

Despite the body of young Alfie Weeds not yet being found, the amount of blood his dad was covered in left no one under the illusion that the boy was still alive. But people could hope, just as Caroline Weeds was doing. The last Tony heard, she was still sat on the outskirts of the woods, waiting for the search teams to finish their sweep and bring her back some news, news that wouldn't crush her soul and take away her reason for living. But, life didn't bring what people hoped for, it watched the people hope, listened to their wishes, and then shattered them, destroying that hope to make the pain all that harder to bear. Tony knew this, and Caroline was about to learn it, too.

"He talking?" Ruth said, making Tony jump as she approached him from behind. Tony was looking through the one-way glass. Weedy sat at an empty metal table; his eyes looked smaller, like a pair of shirt buttons, without his glasses to magnify them. He was sobbing, but all of his tears had been shed. Now the bloodshot redness of those eyes glistened under the harsh yellow light coming from the halogen bulb above him.

"He's talking, but not saying much," Tony replied.

Ruth nudged him once more and he looked down at the cup of coffee she held in her hand. "Thanks," he said, and took the coffee gratefully. It'd been five hours since the fete came to an abrupt and disturbing end, and this was the first thing that wasn't bile to go into his mouth.

"No problem." Ruth stirred her coffee. "He not telling you where the kid is?"

"He says he doesn't know. He hopes Alfie's still alive, or that's what he says. Just keeps on saying he doesn't remember anything. He was walking through the woods because Alfie wanted to show him this tree he found. Next thing he knows, he's walking out of the woods covered in blood with everyone staring at him."

"You believe him"

Tony shrugged. "He does. I've known Weedy since I was a kid, he's never shown an ounce of aggression that entire time. Didn't do well in school, suffered from the attention of a few bullies, but he made it to adulthood and did well for himself. Manager of the supermarket, married to Caroline, who's nice enough." Tony stopped and shook his head, as if disbelieving what he was seeing before him. "Most of all, he loved that kid. Adored him. Worshipped the ground he walked on. Why would he do this?"

"I don't know, Tony, but what I do know is that his clothes are going to come back from forensics with a match for Alfie's blood, along with the blood-covered box cutter we found in his pocket. He may be this harmless man to everyone on the outside, but no one can say for certain that is what he' truly like. He could have been repressing things for years and then one day" – she snapped her fingers –"boom, like that he decides to fuck shit up."

"I don't buy it. It doesn't fit."

"People do crazy things. Who knows, maybe the heat drove him to it? Dehydration is more than possible in temperatures like today, with that comes hallucinations, confusion – you name it."

Tony sipped his coffee and winced. "I'm not putting the motive of a young boy's murder down to it being hot, Ruth."

Now it was Ruth's turn to shrug. "Just a theory, Tony."

Tony sipped his coffee again, but the rising acid in his stomach told him that was enough. He threw it in the bin in the corner of the room and gestured to Ruth. "Come on. Let's see if we can get any further with him."

They stepped into the room. Weedy looked up at them as

if they were monsters who had just stepped out of his bedroom closet.

Ruth sat down. Tony hit the record button on the Dictaphone set to the side and sat down in the chair next to Ruth. He looked at Weedy, whose eyes were darting from Ruth to Tony in quick succession. Weedy's hands were tight fists on top of the table, bound together with handcuffs. The plain grey prison issue tracksuit hung loosely on his slim frame.

"Have you found him?" Weedy said, breaking the silence. "Have you found my boy?"

Tony said nothing to this. Hoping that Weedy would keep talking until he said what they wanted to hear.

"I don't know what happened. I remember, he was so excited to show me this tree that he wanted to climb, he was so excited by it... I remember walking into the woods because it was so damn hot stood out in that field all day, I thought I was going to burn to a crisp, but when I walked through the tree line, the shade was so cool..." Weedy paused. "Then it was cold," he said, looking down at his hands with a frown of deep confusion. "It was like water had been thrown over me, like cold water shock. Remember when we would jump in the river as kids, the spring air would be so warm and mild we thought the river water would be the same, but we'd jump in and the breath would just get sucked right out of us? Remember?"

Tony kept his stare on Gareth Weeds with a hard intensity.

Weedy looked back down at his hands. "Well, that's what it was like. Then it all went black." Weedy started to cry. Tears began spilling from his eyes once more. "The last time I looked at my boy's face, he was smiling. That big, toothy, ear-to-ear smile that made him so adorable. If I've done anything to him..." His words fell away into deep sobs.

Ruth nudged Tony with her elbow and raised an eyebrow. *What now?* it said.

Tony took a deep breath. "Gareth. We haven't found Alfie yet –"

"So, he could still be alive?" Weedy interrupted.

"That's not what I'm saying. What I am saying is that we have got a dozen police officers and even more civilian volunteers out there in those woods searching. We also have a mother sat desperately waiting for news on the whereabouts and wellbeing of her son. If you can tell us where he is, and what you did to him, you'd save prolonging her heartbreak. Now's the time, Gareth. Come on. Tell us where he is."

Gareth shook his head and sobbed wildly. He smashed his clenched fists into the table with a flash of frustrated anger that startled Ruth and Tony, forcing them to flinch backward. "I DON'T KNOW!" he screamed. Gareth laid his head in his folded arms on the table and cried, repeating over and over again: "What did I do? What did I do?"

CHAPTER 6

The house was still new to Matthew and Jane, and required some getting used to. It was a detached stone cottage that sat on several acres of grassland, bordered by centuries-old dry-stone walls that were probably as old as the house they now called home. It was a far cry from the city home they had moved from, where the constant noises out their window had been blaring car horns and idling car engines. Now the noises had been replaced with near silence, only a dash of hooting owls and the distant bleating of sheep.

The agent who sold them the house gave them a brief history lesson. "*This is one of the oldest houses in the town. It is believed that hundreds of years ago, this was the mayor's house of the time.*" Matthew and Jane didn't need the history lesson to persuade them. They were already sold.

Tiffany sat curled up on the sofa watching her favourite Tom and Jerry cartoons. Matthew and Jane had tried to talk to her when they got in, hoping to ensure that what had happened at the fete hadn't mentally scarred her. She said she was fine, and the tone of her voice was steady and calm; to anyone else in the world it would have been believable. In fact, they would have believed that she was so 'fine' with it, that it would have been a concern in itself. Matthew and Jane knew better than most though, as any parent does when it comes to their own children. It was all in the eyes. Tiffany's were a beautiful green. When she really was fine, they were bright and shimmering like emeralds in the hot sun. When she wasn't fine, they dulled, like the spark that made her wonderful had been smothered.

"Do you think she'll be okay?" Jane said.

Matthew looked at Tiffany when he spoke. "Yeah. She'll be fine."

"I don't know, Matthew, it was quite frightening, seeing that man like that. There was so much blood."

"It'll bring a lot back for her, but she's young, she'll forget about it soon enough. She just needs to make a friend."

Jane frowned. "I don't know where you're getting your medical advice from, but the trauma she's gone through can have a lasting effect on her mental well-being. If we don't treat this right now, she'll be suffering with the memories into her adult life."

Jane was getting angry now, her voice was rising, and Tiffany looked over at them, instantly calming her down.

Matthew put his hand on Jane's shoulder and moved her away, taking them on a walk to the kitchen.

"You can't suffocate her. Kids' brains work different, she just needs time to watch some cartoons, make some friends, and play out in the countryside, then she'll forget all about it. Trust me, Jane."

Jane put a pod into the coffee machine and clicked the flashing green button that spurred it into action, making a loud grinding noise before the liquid poured out. The cup beneath it filled and the pod popped out; she chucked it in the bin and made another for Matthew, adding two spoons of sugar and a splash of milk to his.

Jane looked at the blue sky outside the kitchen window; the sun was working its way down but still shone with a dazzling brilliance. She shielded her eyes so she could make out the stone cottage that sat by the tree line a few hundred yards away.

"Do you think they've got any kids?"

Matthew walked over to Jane and looked out the window with her, raising his hand to shelter his eyes. "Didn't even think anyone lived there."

"Someone does, I saw them in the window the other day. They were looking over at us."

"Weird," Matthew laughed. "What are they watching us for?"

"Oh, I don't know, maybe because we've been here a month and haven't taken the time to introduce ourselves to our only neighbour for five miles?"

"What do you want to do, take over a fruit basket and a 'we're your new neighbour's' card?"

"Is that such a bad idea?" Jane said.

Matthew stood with his hands open wide and almost laughed. "I suppose not."

"You don't think I'll do it, do you?"

Matthew raised his hands. "I'm saying nothing."

Jane smirked. "Right, that's it. I'm going to make a basket up and take it over to introduce ourselves." She looked up at the clock on the wall. "It's a bit late, I'll do it tomorrow."

Matthew walked over, put his hands on her shoulders and kissed her cheek. "Again, I'm saying nothing."

CHAPTER 7

It was getting late. The sun was almost down for the day; the clock read ten p.m., which meant Tony had done a fourteen-hour day. Weedy had been put back into his cell on suicide watch. He'd torn his t-shirt into rags and tried to stuff it down his throat so he'd suffocate. It took three officers to pin him down and pull the rags out. He wept after, repeating only that he couldn't understand why he would hurt his son. He couldn't take the torment of it. He was hit with a sedative and placed in a new cell.

"Any more of that, I say we send him up to the nuthouse on Hill Top," Officer Westlake had said. Tony Thorne liked Westlake's enthusiasm, but worried that the young man saw the world through a very narrow scope, where everything was black and white.

"Just remember, Westlake, that we don't know what's gone on yet. Let's keep professional. And by that, I mean neutral."

"How am I supposed to stay neutral after that? He was covered in blood and we all know it's his son's."

"Because it's our job," Tony snapped back, using the authoritative tone he saved for newbies like Westlake.

Westlake rolled his tongue over his teeth and shook his head. "Yes, sir," he said, but the words came out reluctantly. "As you say."

Tony watched Westlake walk away and understood his frustration entirely. He couldn't help but feel mad at Gareth Weeds himself, infuriated and sickened by what the man had most likely done to his own son. Sending him to Hill Top Psychiatric Hospital would probably be the course of action when all this was concluded. After all, it would take someone with a seriously blurred grasp of reality to murder their own child.

Tony had given up on getting anything out of Gareth. If he had anything he wanted to say, he'd have said it by now. All they had to do was wait for the body to turn up.

Tony wanted to get out and help look for the boy. He knew all too well what it was like to search those woods for a body. He knew the contradicting feelings that finding that person could conjure up. Relief that they'd been found and could be put to rest, and complete devastation that the person you loved the most was gone forever.

For his own experience of it, he was stuck in limbo. He had been deprived of any sense of closure. His old girlfriend, Sophie Rose, had been declared dead, although a body had never been found. They found evidence of her blood; there was lots of it and it was all in one place. There was an old reservoir in the woods. It was hard to get to; a natural wall of brambles and briars three feet thick surrounded it. There was so much blood, medical professionals had deemed it too much blood to lose for a person to be able to survive, especially in the middle of the woods without medical intervention. The search went on for months and months, but nothing was ever found.

"Tony?" It was Ruth.

"Hey," Tony said, giving her a tired smile.

"Why don't you go home? Weedy's not going to give us anymore, and I've just heard from the search team, they're about to pack up for the night."

"They find anything?"

"Nothing."

"Shit." Tony's head dropped so his chin rested on his chest. He pushed his fingers through his beard and scratched.

"Go home. You've been here too long. Get some rest, I think tomorrow's going to be another long day."

"You want to help the search tomorrow?" Tony asked.

"Sure. You?"

Tony nodded. "Okay, see you in the morning."

"I thought your shift didn't start until twelve?" Ruth said, frowning at Tony.

"I'd rather come in early. Help with this, and help find Alfie."

Ruth looked at him with a hand on one hip and one eyebrow raised as if that was enough to draw out the truth from him. "Things still bad at home?"

"Good night, Ruth" Tony waved, avoiding having to answer that. He'd been through enough today; he couldn't dredge up his home troubles too.

CHAPTER 8

Caroline Weeds sat on a picnic bench in the park, opposite the woods where officers searched for her boy. The stalls that had been full of crafts and tombolas, souvenirs and bric-a-brac, had all been packed away and folded down. The game stalls stood empty; the prizes that had been displayed so enticingly were now packed away in locked containers. The fairground rides that had been put on at the expense of the town, were powerless. The runaway train rollercoaster was as still as a statue, sad and depressing without the flashing, multicoloured lights showing the way around the track.

Caroline sat with her hands in her lap, her cheeks stained with tear tracks. She wasn't crying anymore. She wasn't even sure if she felt sad anymore. A numbness had overtaken her, blocking out any feeling from taking hold. Her face was blank and expressionless, her eye lids never blinked, she just sat and stared at the trees, waiting for the inevitable to come and bring with it the ultimate heartbreak. Maybe then she'd feel something.

The air was warm, despite the sun making its hasty retreat

toward the horizon, as if it, too, were desperate to turn its back on this day and start a new tomorrow. The sky was a deep blue, readying itself for the black that would take over.

An officer stepped out of the woods and Caroline's heart skipped a beat. She got to her feet and stood still, wringing her hands together.

Tell me, she wanted to say.

Tell me you found my boy. Put an end to my misery.

The officer, as if reading her thoughts, only shook his head. The rest of the search team began emerging from the woods, all with solemn, regretful looks on their faces, like a child knowing they were bringing disappointment back to their parents.

"I'm sorry, Mrs. Weeds. We couldn't find him. We'll be back out tomorrow, first light."

A single tear rolled down the crease of her nose. "I just want my boy back. My little boy."

CHAPTER 9

J ane had fallen asleep with Tiffany curled up beside her on
the sofa. Tom and Jerry cartoons rolled on in an endless
loop on the TV. It was pitch-black outside; the stars were
twinkling on a black canvas beside a moon that was almost
full.

Jane woke suddenly at the sound of a loud crash; her reaction made Tiffany wake up and look at her mum as if she had
just punched her in the face.

"Sorry, love, your dad must be working in the basement,"
Jane said, trying to rub away the heaviness of her eyelids.
Matthew had been obsessed with wanting to turn the dirty,
rundown basement into a man space. Jane had argued that he
had the garage for that, but he said the garage was for work,
the basement was for pleasure. Jane let him have it without
further argument; she didn't want to spend her days down in
the basement, no matter how nice he made it.

Jane checked her watch and saw it was nearly eleven.
"Jesus Christ," she said, sitting up. "What the hell is he playing
at, starting work at this time?"

Tiffany shrugged and let out a huge yawn. Her eyes moved

back to the TV where she watched Jerry hiding from Tom in a pond, using a hollow reed to breathe the air above the water without being seen.

Jane watched the TV too, but what she enjoyed more was the genuine smile that crept along Tiffany's lips. "Come on, let's get you to bed," Jane said, leaning in and kissing Tiffany on the cheek. "I'll deal with your father later."

Jane took Tiffany up to bed and settled her in. The night was warm, cool enough to bring a great relief from the heat of the day, but it was still too warm to sleep with a full feather duvet. Jane covered her daughter with a thin blanket instead, then Tiffany snuggled up with a cuddly toy.

"Night, sweetheart, see you in the morning." Jane kissed Tiffany's forehead and stroked her long brown hair from out of her face. "Love you."

"Love you too, Mum." Tiffany smiled, then closed her eyes.

Jane walked over to close the curtains, and she noticed that the house two fields over had a light on in the window. It glowed a bright yellow in the darkness. There was a dark shape, hard for Jane to make out at first because of the tiredness in her eyes, but she soon realised that it was the silhouette of a person. Whoever lived there was standing in the window looking toward her. Jane couldn't take her eyes off them, they were stood so still, just watching.

"Are you going to turn off my light?" Tiffany said sleepily. And then Jane realised, with an unwarranted bite of fear, that the person looking over could see her just as much as she could see them. Jane flung the curtains shut and turned to put her back to them. She felt breathless; her heart pounded and the tiredness in her eyes was replaced with adrenaline.

"What's the matter, Mummy?"

"Nothing, sweetheart," Jane said, then wiped her face with both of her hands. "Right, see you in the morning." She forced a smile, but couldn't shake the uneasiness that the sight of their neighbour had put in her.

"Love you, darling." Jane switched off the light and pulled the door half-closed, allowing some light from the hallway to filter into Tiffany's room.

THE BASEMENT WAS GOING to look great when it was finished. As a builder, Matthew knew how to turn a shithole like this into something modern and usable. It was a good-size space, one big room the size of the entire floor plan of the house. There were stone pillars, four in total, but he liked them, it would give the place a bit of character. The surrounding walls were made of the same stone. The house had been built hundreds of years ago; some of the foundation stones were the originals used when it was first built, making it somewhat of a place of historic importance, really. It was a shame to cover them up, but the plan was to frame out the walls with timber, board it up, plaster, and paint. It would bring a modern design, whilst keeping the original stone pillars to mix in some of the old.

The basement was bright; Matthew had fitted several temporary site lights until the wiring was completed. There was a long work bench he'd set up for cutting the timbers; he'd got most of them into place so nearly every wall was complete.

He heard the basement door open and footsteps descend the stairs.

"Honey?" It was Jane. "Matthew, sweetheart, it's nearly the middle of the night. I think the chop saw will have to be retired for now."

Matthew grimaced. "Sorry, love. I'm not going to be much longer, just finishing some bits off."

Jane nodded and looked around. "Wow, I've got to say, you've really made some progress down here."

"Yeah, well, I don't mess around, you should know that. When I want something done, I do it."

Jane smiled, leaned into his chest, and held him. "I love you," she said.

"'Love you too." Matthew kissed her head and she looked up at him. They kissed longer than they had in weeks. The stress of the move and trying to find work had taken all their energy; Matthew thought that maybe now they could finally get back to being them again.

"Don't be long," Jane whispered, and planted her lips softly on his.

"'I won't," Matthew said with a smile and slapped her bum as she walked away. Jane laughed and skipped up the stairs.

He took a deep breath and tilted his head sharply to the side so his spine let out an audible crack. He put his hand to where the sun had caught him on the back of his neck. It was hot to the touch, and the skin felt strange under his fingers; it seemed to wobble, like he was pressing a bubble. He pressed harder and winced. He sucked his teeth at the sudden sharpness of pain that bolted through him. A warm liquid oozed down his neck and he realised he'd just popped a blister.

Matthew grimaced. "Mother fucker." He touched the sunburn again in reaction to the pain, but that only increased it. He grunted in frustration, picked up a hammer from the work bench and threw it at one of the stone walls, knocking a stone loose. The hammer dropped to the concrete floor by Matthew's feet with a loud clang. Then he went upstairs to put some after-sun on his neck.

CHAPTER 10

T ony Thorne got home well after eleven. His lower back
and his legs were sore from the long day. His skin was
burning so hot he envisioned steam hissing off it when he had
a cold shower later.

The streets were quiet as he drove home from the police
station; he couldn't remember passing a single car on the drive
back. Then again, his mind wasn't as focused on the road as it
should have been. Instead, all he could see was Gareth Weeds'
face, full of distress and misery, but it was the confusion that
really stood out. He believed that Gareth was telling the truth,
he didn't know what he had done. But how was that possible?
The tests they'd put him through had come back negative for
alcohol or narcotics, not that Tony thought for one second
that Gareth Weeds would take anything stronger than aspirin.

Tony's house sat at the middle of Manor Drive, a quiet
suburban street that ran a mile long, with detached houses
spaced evenly. The ultra-manicured lawns outside every house
were usually lush green without a blade out of place, but now
they were all covered in burnt-brown patches where the grass
had dried out and burned. As he mounted the steps to his

front door, Tony reminded himself to water the grass after his shower.

"Hey," a soft voice greeted him as he walked in.

"Hey," Tony said. "How was your day?"

Sarah, Tony's wife of nine years, paused the TV and put her glass of wine on the coffee table. A bottle sat there, almost empty. She stood and walked toward him. "Never mind my day, how was yours?"

"You heard, huh?"

"Of course I heard, it's all anyone's talking about. Is it true? They're saying he killed his son." Sarah put her hands on Tony's shoulders. He struggled to bring his head up to look at her.

"It looks that way."

Sarah dropped her hands from him. She had hoped he might fall into her, give her a hug, and let her stroke his hair, give him comfort after a shitty day. That was just the drink pickling her brain, making her believe she had a marriage like on one of those TV shows she liked to watch, where husbands come home smiling, pleased to see their wives, maybe give them a kiss, ask how they are, maybe even fuck 'em once in a while.

"Did he say why?" Sarah's voice was a little harder now than it had been when Tony had walked in.

"Just that he doesn't remember. He went into the woods, came out covered in blood, and doesn't remember a thing in between."

"Well, that's horse shit."

Tony shrugged. "That's all he said."

"I hope you went in hard on him. The whole town wants him crucified for this –"

Tony held up his hand to stop her. "I'm beat. I'm gonna grab a cold shower, then I need to water the grass. If this drought carries on, there's not going to be any grass left."

Tony started walking up the stairs, leaving Sarah stood, hands on hips, with her mouth slightly ajar.

"Where did you find the body?"

Tony was almost at the top of the stairs; he winced at the tiredness burning in his thighs, making every step a great effort. "What?" he called down.

"Alfie, Gareth's son, where did you find him?"

"Didn't. There's going to be a full search tomorrow. Two teams. There's a group coming from the city with a few drones, they can get a bird's eye view of the woods, which makes it easier to map out where we've searched already. They're also equipped with thermal imaging. Although, I don't think we'll be finding any warm bodies in those woods."

"You're doing a full search?" Sarah's voice came out almost strangled.

"Yeah," Tony snapped sharply. "I need to have a shower, talk later."

Tony disappeared into the bedroom on the right. Sarah felt her knees go weak, they shook, and for one short moment, she thought she might collapse to the floor right there. When she took several deep breaths and forced the strength back into her legs, she made her way back over to the sofa. She sat, picked up her glass with shaking hands, and drank the mouthful that was left. Then she picked up her phone and dialed a number she hadn't dialed in a long, long time.

"Sarah?" a man's voice answered. "Why are you calling? We said never to –"

"They're searching the woods. They're going to find her."

"Calm down," the voice said.

Sarah's hands shook; panic and fear made tears well in her eyes. "I know it, I feel it in my bones. They're going to find her; they're going to find Sophie."

CHAPTER 11

The engine of Doctor Mahone's Jaguar purred like it was fresh off the production line. Most people had their vehicles serviced once a year; some waited until the magic ten-thousandth mile clicked by on the odometer. Not Mahone. He had his Jaguar serviced every six months. A valet came to Hill Top Psychiatric Hospital every Monday and Friday to clean it inside and out; the exterior paint was buffed and waxed to give the perfect mirror finish. The leaping Jaguar that stood proudly on the front of the bonnet gleamed in the early morning sun. God, did he love that car.

Mahone pulled into his personal parking space at the hospital. The car park was quiet, a twenty-year-old Nissan Micra and a Peugeot, owned by the nursing staff that had worked the night shift, sat at the opposite side of the lot. Mahone looked at the cars and shook his head indignantly.

Have a little pride, he thought. Was it really that hard? Clean your car, keep the body and engine in good order, and it'll last twice as long. People were lazy, they treated everything as though it would last forever without taking any time or care to look after it, and then they were surprised when it conked out and they had a huge bill to pay. It was all about planning. Do things properly, do things *right,* and there'd be nothing to worry about.

Mahone never cut corners; his possessions were kept exactly how he wanted them. Everything was an extension of himself. His car, his Armani suits, that were dry cleaned after every wear, the women he chose to accompany him to social events, all had to be *right* and *proper.* He had no interest in a relationship; he knew nobody would meet his standards on a long-term basis and that was fine. He didn't need anyone.

He shut the car door. Even that sound gave him pleasure, the way the inner lining cushioned the door as it swung into place before the handle clicked shut. Magic. He grabbed his briefcase from the back seat, locked the car, and did a swift walk around to check for any scrapes or chips that may have occurred to the body as he drove to work. Of course there were none, but he needed to be sure in case Ben, the valet, found it too difficult to wash a car and managed to scratch it whilst not paying attention.

He was about to head for the main door when a cat jumped onto the bonnet of his Jag. It meowed at him. It was a stray, he knew, because of the way its fur looked patchy and unclean. The left side of its mouth was swollen, from a tooth infection he surmised. He moved closer, and when he saw the muddy paw prints over the shiny black paintwork, a small bubble of rage rose up his throat, curling his face into a grimace.

The cat meowed again. It walked toward the windshield and then back toward the shiny leaping Jaguar emblem. Its teats were full and drooping so low they almost grazed the paint work. It must have had kittens recently.

Mahone hissed at it through clenched teeth. The cat stepped back, its ears flattened against its skull, and it hissed back at him in retaliation. It raised one paw, ready and alert to fight back.

"Get back, you feral bitch! *Hissss!* Get out of here before I make a hat out of you!" He swung his briefcase toward it and the cat jumped back with its claws splayed. It hissed back at Mahone before running off down the side of the hospital where the bins were kept.

Inspecting the area where the cat had been, Mahone removed a handkerchief from his breast pocket and rubbed at the footprints. Ben would be here in less than an hour, but if Ben saw it in this state, he might think it was acceptable not to do a thorough job.

Mahone gasped when he saw the thin white line where the cat's claw had dug into the paintwork as it jumped back from him. He rubbed at it with his handkerchief but the white line still remained. He grimaced and forced himself to take a deep breath.

"I'm going to kill that fucking cat!" he promised himself, and he didn't doubt that he would. He could lay rat poison and stuff it in a fresh full side of salmon, but that seemed too easy. Too impersonal. It was as though the cat had done it on purpose, the sheer *audacity* of the foul thing to jump on his car was incredulous!

Ben would have to buff it out or the whole car would have to be re-sprayed. In a foul mood, Mahone finally stepped inside the hospital.

CHAPTER 12

"Are you getting to work in the basement today?" Jane asked Matthew. She had her back to him, frying bacon in a pan, two slices of bread popped up from the toaster a perfect shade of light brown. Matthew sat with Tiffany at the table.

"That's the plan. I've managed to get all the walls studded, just about, then I can put the plaster board up, feed through the electrical wires for the sockets, and get the whole thing plastered and painted."

"Ooh," Jane said with real excitement. "What colour you having down there?"

Matthew pursed his lips and gave it some thought. "Not sure. I'm thinking something light to brighten it up a bit. There's only the one small window and that hardly lets any light in at all."

"It'll be great when you've finished." Jane plated up three plates of bacon, eggs, and toast, and handed them to Tiffany and Matthew; she remained standing to eat hers.

"What about you, what are you doing today?" Matthew asked with a mouthful of bacon. He managed to catch a dribble of grease that ran down his chin before it fell on his shirt.

"Well, I was thinking about how we haven't introduced ourselves to the neighbour. After that awful event at the fete yesterday, I think it would be a good idea to get to know people in this community, especially those that are a stone's throw away from us."

"Good idea," Matthew agreed.

"Can I come?" Tiffany said. She had cut her toast into soldiers and was dunking them into a runny yolk one by one before stuffing them into her mouth.

"Yes, absolutely. I thought we'd bake some cookies and take them over. What do you think?"

Tiffany nodded exuberantly and went to work on finishing the rest of her breakfast as fast as she could.

Matthew, who had already finished, wiped his mouth with a piece of kitchen roll and pushed his plate away from him. "Golden that, love, best way to start the day."

"I aim to please," Jane said and winked at her husband.

Matthew smiled in return. "Right, I'm going to get started. I'm hoping to get plenty done today. If I don't come up for air and see you before you go, have a good day with the neighbour." Matthew kissed Jane on the cheek and then went back round to squeeze Tiffany from behind and plant twenty kisses on her head, making his daughter burst out in a fit of giggles.

"Love you," he said.

"Love you too," Jane and Tiffany said in unison.

When he had gone, Jane cleared the plates and put them in the sink. "Right then you, whilst I'm clearing up, you go get changed, and by the time you come down, we'll get started on those cookies."

"Yes!" Tiffany dropped down from the kitchen stool and ran upstairs to her bedroom.

Matthew skipped down the basement steps. He was so eager to get the stud walling finished. After that, the plaster boarding would be easy, then he could mark out where all the plug sockets and light switches needed to be, and pull the wires through ready for the electrician to come and wire them up. Matthew knew how to do it himself, but not well enough that he would risk setting the house on fire where his wife and kid slept.

He measured twice and cut once; all of the timbers he cut fit perfectly and the last wall was almost complete. He measured the last one, measured again, but when he set it against the wall to screw it in place – such is any builder's luck when they felt they were on a roll – one of the old stones was jutted out in an awkward angle, meaning the timber couldn't sit flush. For a cowboy, this wouldn't be too much of an issue, but Matthew liked things to be right.

"Sonofabitch," he muttered, and put the cut timber on the bench. He inspected the stone and saw the dented chip where he had thrown the hammer at the wall last night in his small surge of anger. He didn't want to disturb the wall too much, but thought he could prise out the stone, clean it off, and re-bed it with some fresh cement. The cement that held it in place was old and cracked; it wouldn't take much.

He grabbed the lump hammer from his tool bag and hit the stone, sending sparks and fragments of stone chips across the room. He hit it again and again. The easy job that he thought *wouldn't take much* had, all of a sudden, become a laborious chore. Sweat began to roll down his face; his white shirt clung to his body. After a dozen hits, his arms were beginning to tire, his breathing was laboured, and the thought of getting out the electric jack hammer crossed his mind.

"One more," he said.

He swung the hammer; chunks of cement crunched to dust under his boots. When the hammer hit, the stone flew from the wall, and he jumped back to avoid a broken foot and choked a shout in his throat.

Matthew laughed, wiped the sweat from his forehead with the back of his arm, and dropped the hammer onto his work bench at the far side. A cold breeze hit his face and carried with it a damp, sickly-sweet smell that was both pleasing and rancid at the same time.

He looked at the black hole that now stood in his wall, at least three-feet wide. Because of the darkness of it, he could only guess how deep it went. A shiver rolled slowly down his spine and his skin burst out into gooseflesh. He stared into the hole, his eyes played tricks with him. He thought in flashes that the hole went on forever; he could have put his whole arm in there and still not touch the end. A thought stuck into his head that if he put his arm in there, he might not get it back. Something would grab it, a stone would fall and crush it, pinning him in place. All these thoughts were ridiculous, and he knew it, but still, he couldn't shake the dreadful sense of fear that prickled at the corners of his mouth, stopping the smile he was so desperate to spread across his lips.

"Stop being such a pussy," he said to himself. He hit his chest with a fist, a silverback gorilla showing his masculinity, and trudged over to the hole in the wall. The protests that started in his feet moved up to his knees and as he got closer, he felt weak, as though his legs were about to buckle from underneath him. He leaned his neck to one side until it cracked, sniffed, coughed, grabbed his 'package' to ensure it was still there – it was, although not as *there* as it normally was, his ball bag had shrivelled away like a drawstring purse.

After conjuring up the gusto he needed, he put his hand through the hole. Sweat rolled down his cheeks. He licked his lips and tasted the saltiness on them. His heart thrummed like a jack hammer in his chest. His hand explored the hole thoroughly, touching other stones, bits of broken cement, and chunks of timber. It was cold in the hole, colder than what he thought it should be –

Thud.

He hit something hard. Something wooden. His breathing stopped. For what felt like hours, he held his breath. He hit the thing again and was met with another dull *thud*.

Matthew put his second hand in, his mind already gone blank; he wasn't thinking about what he was doing, he was just *doing,* as one simply breathes without thinking about it. When he got the thing out of the wall, he discovered it was a wooden box. It was three feet in length, two feet wide and the same in depth. It was covered in dust, and when he set it on the work bench and wiped the dust away, he saw the wood was a rich dark colour, or had been before time had aged it.

His heart slowed and the unsettling feeling he had dissolved into mild embarrassment. He checked the box over, running his hand along the joints to each corner. He found the crack that showed where the lid ended and the box began; dust had filled the gap and cemented itself in place. He tried with his fingers to pry the lid off and felt a fresh prang of stupidity prickle the back of his neck where the sunburnt blister had burst.

Happy that no one was watching him, he searched for his hammer, hoping he would be able to bury the claw section under the lid and lever it open. The claw hammer was with his tool belt, hung on a six-inch nail that he'd pounded into the wooden beam that ran floor to ceiling at the bottom of the stairs.

He put the claw in the gap carefully; a box this old might hold value even if there was nothing inside it. It needed a clean and a polish, but if he damaged the integrity of the grain, it would be worthless. He leaned on the hammer, the lid creaked, and he felt a small but definite movement. In his excitement, he pushed harder on the hammer, and the claw came out of the crack, knocking a chunk out of the wood and sending him and the hammer tumbling.

"Sonofabitch!" he yelled. In the application of pressure, he'd caught his finger on the edge of his work bench; the fingernail had a thin outline of blood growing thicker and thicker the longer he looked at it. Then, he noticed the fingernail was sat slightly askew on the nail bed.

That's why it hurts so damn much, he thought. He'd torn his fingernail from the nail bed. He grabbed at it with his other hand; the nail came away easily, only sticking right at the last. He yanked it and threw the glob of blood and nail to the floor. The red mess of gore that was his nailbed, throbbed as blood pulsated from the tear in the delicate flesh.

He winced and sucked his teeth, letting out a tirade of foul language: "Mother fucker, son of a cock sucking –"

He held his finger in his other hand, then grabbed a clean rag and wrapped it around the wound. He turned, saw the box on the bench through a haze of red that wasn't really there.

"Fucking stupid box!" he said, sounding like a petulant child. He grabbed the box, mad at the inanimate object, as if it had pre-planned his injury and had in fact been entirely to blame for the incident.

"You can go back in the fucking wall!"

As he brought the box toward his face, preparing to throw it back in the black hole in the stone wall, a waft of rancid, putrid decay stung his nostrils, making him gag. It was the last straw. He threw the box in the hole and balanced the stone back in loosely, making sure it sat straight as it was supposed to. He was glad he put it back, he'd board over it and it could stay hidden for another hundred years.

His finger didn't stop hurting until later, when he put the first board into place.

Chapter 13

His shift didn't start that day until noon, but home was the last place Tony Thorne wanted to be. He got up at seven, showered, brushed his teeth, put on a fresh set of police uniform, and went downstairs. He'd a have a coffee and then split, hoping to avoid the inevitable run-in with Sarah. Things never did work out the way you hoped, did they?

Tony's hope was that Sarah would have been fast asleep on the sofa, nursing the hangover she undoubtedly had after passing out from wine consumption, meaning he could just sneak out to work without seeing her. To his surprise, she was already in the kitchen.

He stopped as he reached the bottom of the stairs and saw her sat at the kitchen table. A fresh pot of coffee was on the side; the aroma that met his nostrils told him it was fresh, 'proper' coffee, and not the instant stuff.

"Got the good coffee on?" he remarked.

"Does the job better," Sarah replied. Her hair was up in a messy bun, she had swollen bags under her glassy, bloodshot eyes. Without make-up, she looked ten years older than she was.

Tony raised his eyebrows and said nothing. He was tired of telling her he hated being married to a drunk, to be met with the usual rebuke that she was tired of being married to someone who was never there. He poured the coffee into a cup. They hadn't argued last night, they hadn't shared warm words of comfort with one another, either. The atmosphere in the air, however, was one that suggested an argument was right on the cusp.

"I thought your shift didn't start until twelve?" Sarah said, sipping her coffee with a headache-induced frown.

"It doesn't, but I want to get in on this. We need to find that boy, he's out in those woods alone."

"You don't think he's alive, do you?"

Tony shook his head as if shaking off a hit. "He's still out there, dead or alive, and he deserves to be brought home. Jesus, Sarah."

"I didn't mean..." Sarah put her hands to the sides of her head and rubbed at her temples. "Argh!" she grunted. "You always make out like I'm such a bad person, that I always mean the worst. I just don't want you to burn yourself out or become obsessed with this one."

Tony walked over to the table where Sarah sat and stood opposite. He didn't want to pull out a chair and sit down, because he knew that he'd be walking out that door any minute.

"What do you mean, 'this one'?"

Sarah looked at Tony with hard eyes. "You know what I mean."

"Say it, then." He put his hands on to the tabletop, balled into fists. He bent over so his eyes were level with Sarah's.

"When it was... her. She was lost in those woods and you searched day and night for weeks and weeks. Months even. Even a year after, you would go searching for anything that they might have missed. You were eighteen years old when she went missing, and you were obsessed with trying to find someone who..."

"Who what? Who was dead?"

"Of course Sophie's dead!" Sarah shouted.

"You think I don't know that? It's been eighteen years. I know Sophie's dead, okay?! I just wanted to bring her home. I needed closure and I never got it."

Sarah, realising she had got to her feet when she shouted, sat back down.

"I wish you had found her, maybe then you could have moved on. Maybe then we could have had kids, maybe then we could have been happy!"

Tony said nothing. He stood up straight and lifted his coffee to his mouth.

"You never stopped loving her," Sarah continued. "That's the truth of it. If Sophie Rose hadn't gone missing, we probably never would have got married. I was nothing to you while she was alive, and after she was gone, I was just someone to fill a Sophie-shaped hole in your life because, at the time, I seemed like a better option than being alone. Isn't that right, Tony?" Tears began to gather in Sarah's eyes; after the first dropped, the rest began to follow more easily.

"That's right," Tony said, and he felt shame at the venomous way the words came out.

When Sarah dropped her head to the crook of her arm and began to sob, he wanted to go over to her and rub her back. Tell her he was sorry, he never meant to hurt her. Tell her he didn't want her to be upset and he didn't mean what he'd said. But it would have been a lie. Instead of doing those things, he poured his coffee out into the sink, grabbed the keys to his Ford, and left.

The front door closed behind him; he walked across the dry patchy grass to his car on the driveway. The heat of the day hit him like a brick wall, and he was glad he remembered to water the grass before going to bed or it might all be dead by the end of the day. That sun bore down hotter than hellfire. He was about to step into his car when he got a whiff of one of life's most identifiable smells. Dog shit. Tony lifted his shoe so it was sole up and saw a great big smudged shit all over it, deep in every crack.

He looked up and saw old Maggie Colter waving over at him, her big chocolate Labrador by her side.

"I'm so sorry, Sergeant Thorne!" she shouted over. "Did Dexter poop on your lawn again?"

"He sure did," Tony replied through gritted teeth, managing to keep the polite, pleasant tone to his voice, thanks to years of police training. "If you could try and keep him on your lawn that would be great, failing that, just pick it up as soon as he's done it."

"I forgot my bags; I was just about to go back inside and get them."

Tony was sure she was bullshitting him, but it was hard to call out a woman who was closer to eighty than seventy, for spouting a pack of lies.

"Next time, try and remember. My shoes will thank you."

"Sorry again!" She waved at him before going back into her house.

Tony went to the hose pipe and washed off his shoes before getting in the car and heading into town.

CHAPTER 14

That stray – *piece of shit* cat, had been the start of what would turn out to be an extremely frustrating day for Doctor Ian Mahone. He waved a dismissive hand to Helen on the front desk, a gesture she knew all too well to mean *not now*. He walked down the corridor. The breakfast room was half full of the "more stable" patients, who liked to get up early; they were eating breakfast whilst watching the morning news broadcast.

The search for young Alfie Weeds goes on today. It is strongly believed that he is in the woods where he was last seen entering with his father, who, so we're told, is still in custody. Despite the people gathered with placards spreading words of hope and prayer, nobody is optimistic of a positive outcome here. As always, if anyone has any information related to the where-abouts of Alfie –

Mahone moved past the doorway and heard no more. He had too much on his own plate to concern himself with, besides, he knew as well as everybody else in this damn town that the boy was dead. It was just a matter of time before they found the body.

His office was at the end of the main hall. The sound of his polished Gucci shoes was soft and quiet on the lush red carpet; the walls were a brilliant white, without a stain or a blemish to be seen. If a stain were there, it *would* be seen, for the hallway was lit with drop down lights every four feet. No other hallway in the building looked like this; the rest were the usual drab, hospital hallways one was used to seeing. The walk to Mahone's office had to be different.

Once in his office, his mood and temper began to return to satisfactory levels, and he started his day. His office was painted a rich, deep red; the desk with his top-of-the-range Apple computer, was made from dark walnut. Bookcases lined the walls either side of him and behind his chair, which looked more like a throne. On the wall behind his desk hung degrees and doctorates in psychology, medical science, chemistry – he majored in everything he could. He wanted to be the best. And that's what he was. The best.

After checking through his emails and refining the itinerary for the day, he pressed the button for the intercom.

"Helen?"

"Yes, Doctor Mahone?" Helen replied.

"Tell Lucy to come to my office, it's time to begin the medication rounds for the patients on the psychiatric ward."

There was a pause.

"Helen, acknowledge," he snapped.

"Er–yes, Doctor. It's just that Lucy, erm –"

"Lucy what? Spit it out, God damnit!"

"She's not here yet."

Mahone sat back in his chair. He checked his Rolex and saw it was nine-fifteen. Lucy's shift started at nine.

"Alert me upon her arrival," he said into the intercom.

"Yes, sir."

CHAPTER 15

It had been a hard night. Watching someone in so much despair, seeing their heart break right before your eyes, was the hardest thing to bear witness too. If she could help alleviate that in any way, she would. She didn't care how long it took.

Lucy had worked a twelve-hour shift the day of the fete. A fourteen-hour shift, really, considering she got to the hospital an hour early to help Tammy Dean with the patients that were early risers, and then it took her an hour to leave because Gerald, the wonderful Gerald who was full of so many stories, had so many things he needed to tell her before she left.

When she finally got to her car, she could practically feel the touch of her mattress, the coolness of her bed sheets. She wanted to get back to her crummy apartment and go to sleep, ready to do it all again the next day. Only, when she turned the key in the ignition and got the car started (successfully on the second attempt), the radio told her all about what had happened at the fete, and that there was a police-led search of the woods to help find little Alfie Weeds.

They were asking for anyone willing to volunteer to get

down to the park where the fete was held. So, even though her knees were crying out and the tendons in her neck and shoulders were taut and aching, she indicated right instead of left, and went to help find Alfie Weeds.

Caroline Weeds had been sat on a picnic bench, waiting for news to come. Lucy helped her first, giving her a cup of tea and what most human beings need in times of grief: a hug. Then, she spent three hours in the woods. Her feet throbbed from the swelling in her tight nurse's shoes. The thin pleather proved to be no protection from the stones and logs she walked over. But she couldn't have slept that night knowing she did nothing to help.

So, when she woke up this morning, with every muscle in her body chastising her for putting it through so much in one twenty-four-hour period, she hadn't realised she'd slept through her phone alarm. It was as the light of the day filtered through her curtains and hit her in the face that she realised. She bolted upright out of bed, throwing her covers to the floor. Naked, she ran to the bathroom, where she had peeled off her nurse's uniform. She gave it the smell test – it passed, barely – then put it on. No tights, it was too hot for tights. She grabbed her phone and saw it was 9:05. "Shit!" Grabbing her keys from the nightstand, she ran to her car. It was a fifteen-minute drive to Hill Top. Mahone was gonna be pissed.

She pulled into the car park and closed her eyes despairingly when she saw Mahone's Jaguar sat in its space, gleaming in the morning sun. She parked her VW Golf, the wheel bearings letting out a tooth-grinding squeal as she turned into the space. She lifted the handbrake and jumped out, running for the front door.

The automatic doors parted ways. Lucy barely had a foot in the door when Helen, Mahone's lap dog, said, "You're late! Ian is not happy. He expects you in his office immediately!"

Lucy shrugged, lifted her hand, and extended her middle

finger, smiling while she did it for good measure. Helen's mouth dropped open in disbelief.

Lucy laughed and made her way down the hall to the locker room. Mahone was bad, and she was in no doubt she'd get an ear full when she saw him in the next five minutes, but Helen was something else. Mahone treated her the same awful way he treated everyone else and yet, she would lick his car clean if he asked her to. Lucy thought it sad, and a little pathetic, that when Helen spoke about Mahone in front of others, she referred to him by his first name. *Ian is not happy!* If she did that in front of him, he'd tear her a new one. Doctor Mahone or just Doctor, would do fine.

She put her handbag in her locker.

"You're late," a voice full of joy said from behind her.

Lucy turned round and saw it was Tammy Dean.

"Hey Tammy, yeah, I know. Had a late one helping out with the search, slept through my alarm."

Tammy shook her head and reached out to rub Lucy's shoulder. "He's going to be so pissed, you know he's a complete fucking Hitler, don't you? I know you've not been here that long, but it doesn't take a genius to work it out."

"Yeah, I know. Not that I've ever really had a conversation with him."

Tammy smiled. "You will today. He picks different nurses every week to accompany him on his rounds. Today, you'll get to see all the real headcases, the criminally insane patients on the restricted access ward." The smile on Tammy's face grew wider.

"Why does he pick different nurses?" Lucy asked, unable to hide her curiosity.

Tammy pinched the bridge of her nose and laughed as if Lucy was being naïve. "Because he doesn't want any one nurse getting too close to what goes on back there. There's a rumour that he takes backhanders from some of the big pharmaceutical companies to test out new drugs on the patients he has here."

Lucy frowned. "Why would they choose the patients here?"

Tammy shook her head. "Why'd you think? Half of the psychos in this place are lost causes. Just a drain on the system. Nobody cares about them, they'd be in jail if they weren't completely fucking tapped." Tammy poked a finger against her head to demonstrate. "Mahone can test drugs on them and who are they gonna tell? If they did manage to tell anyone, who would believe 'em?"

"But surely someone would know that this was happening? The council, the mayor, the police?"

"The police don't do shit. This is a small town where being a police officer means patrolling for drunks at summer fetes and speed trapping outside the primary school. As for the council and the mayor? Mahone's got them in his back pocket. Who's to say he's not giving them a piece of the pie?"

Lucy checked her watch. "Shit, I'm so late. You really think he's doing that?"

Tammy shrugged. "It's possible. No one's ever in there with him long enough to find out. Anyway, I had to cover a night shift after you left yesterday, so I'm going home to sleep for the next sixteen hours. Enjoy the day! Pah!" Tammy barked a laugh and slapped Lucy on the back as she left.

Lucy ran to Mahone's office at the end of the hall. She stopped by the door, leant against the wall, and took several deep breaths, readying herself for the onslaught. Why she put herself through this stress, she didn't know. She looked down the hall and saw a face poking out from around the rec room door. Then a hand came out and waved at her. It was Gerald. He was smiling, that Cheshire cat smile with half as many teeth as he should have, and his big brown eyes so full of joy, it was like looking into the eyes of a child. Then she remembered why she put herself through this, because of people like Gerald, who relied on people like her to keep them safe and help give them a good life when the rest of the world had forgotten about them.

Lucy waggled her fingers back at Gerald, then mimed for him to go back in the room. Mahone didn't deal with the healthier patients in the hospital, he dealt with the patients with the *really* big problems. She felt sorry for them, because they had to deal with Mahone, and if what Tammy told her was right, they were having drugs they didn't need pumped into their systems. Lucy hoped to God that wasn't true.

She knocked twice on the door, waited for the 'Enter!' and then opened the door.

Mahone was stood in the centre of the room. His hands were clasped behind his back, his white lab coat hung over his shoulders, and the look in his unblinking eye was that of diluted rage.

"You're late," Mahone said, breaking the silence.

"I'm sorry, I was out all night helping in the search and –"

"And nothing! Whatever you do in your own time should not affect your work. It is unprofessional. We have a duty, and to fulfil that duty, we need to be on time and in order! Is that clear?"

Lucy held her hands in front of her, her fingers twitching against one another nervously. "Yes, Doctor."

Mahone walked around her. The smell of his aftershave was strong, not too strong, just the right amount to make anyone take notice.

He stopped walking when he moved behind her. He leant in close enough so she could feel his breath tickle the hairs on the back of her neck. "What are those?" he said, his tone harsh and low.

"What?" Lucy said, not knowing what he was referring to.

"These!" he hissed. His hand shot up to the side of her

face and gripped the gold hoop earring between his thumb and forefinger.

Lucy realised that in her rush to get ready, she had forgotten to take them out. The gold hoop earrings her mother gave her when she finished school. They weren't expensive or anything, they weren't even that nice really, but Lucy loved them because her mum had liked them enough to give them to her.

"This is not uniform. I know you have a good rapport with some of our easier patients, but the ones on my ward are... different, shall we say? A lot of them are unpredictable, unstable... it would only take a second and –"Mahone pulled on the hoop. Lucy let out a choked scream. "They could rip your ear lobes off in one swift move."

He pulled a bit more; Lucy was sure she could hear the skin tearing. It felt like he was dragging a burning hot scalpel across her ear. She yelped once more but it didn't stop him. He leaned in closer, the edge in his voice sharper, more sinister than before. "Maybe next time, you'll remember. Next time, you'll get to work on time without these wretched things in your ears. What do you think Lucy, do you think this will help you remember?"

"Argh!" Lucy yelped.

"Hmm? I didn't catch that?" Mahone pulled again.

"Yes," she yelped, and he let go.

Mahone walked back to his desk, and sat in the chair behind it. He didn't look up at her, he simply worked his way through the papers on his desk. Lucy stood, holding both hands up to the side of her head; she touched her ear and a fresh stab of pain shot through it. She'd cry if he weren't there.

Mahone looked up from his desk at Lucy and frowned, as if confused as to why she was there. "Go on then," he said. "Go back to the locker room, sort yourself out, and get back here. We start rounds in fifteen minutes."

Lucy looked at him, dumbfounded.

"Go on!"

Lucy turned and ran out the door. Once out into the hall, she looked at her hand and saw fresh droplets of blood in her palm.

Chapter 16

Town was getting busy. The cafés were putting their boards out on to the pavement, offers of 'Full English – £5.99, the coffee is on us!' and 'Come for the tea, stay for the scones!' The shops were opening, the barbers, the supermarket, although, who'd be managing it today, Tony didn't know.

He turned off Main Street and headed down King's Road toward the station. Lemmy's Bar and Grill faded by on his right and he thought he might have a beer and a burger there later. Then, maybe when he'd gathered up the courage to go home, she'd be gone. She'd have seen there was no future for them, so she'd have packed her bags and left. He doubted it. Misery loves company and him and Sarah were the two most miserable fuckers in Wymere.

Sick of the thoughts circling round and round his head, mushing up what coherent thoughts he could muster into balls of useless shit, Tony turned the radio on.

Good morning, Wymere, it's 9:30 in the a.m., and we are in for another absolute scorcher.

That's right, Ken, this has to be longest running dry spell we've ever seen. A whole month without rain, and these tempera-

tures are just getting higher and higher. The government's calling for people to actually go indoors between the hours of twelve and two.

What? This is England, man, let's enjoy it whilst it's here, that's what I say. Global warming? Bring it on!

"Idiots." Tony flicked the radio over to Planet Rock. An injection of good ol' rock n' fuckin' roll would sort out the shit in his head. Just then, Axl Rose started singing about going home to a Paradise City. Tony thought Wymere couldn't be any further from being that.

He pulled over into the slanted parking spaces outside a small convenience shop to get a bottle of water. He left the windows open to keep the car from turning into an oven. Once inside, he grabbed the water and a pack of paracetamol to ward off the headache that was building up behind his eyes. *It's this damn heat,* he thought to himself, angrily.

He headed for the counter when a friendly voice called out, "Sergeant Thorne!"

Tony looked down the aisle where the voice came from and saw Alan Houghton walking toward him, a big smile spread across his face like he'd just won the lottery, the same smile he wore when he won the bottle of scotch at the fete.

"Hey, Alan, how's it going?"

Alan wiped at the sweat that had gathered on his brow, slapping the long greying curls to his forehead, and let out a long breath, as if he'd just finished a run. "It's hot as hell out there, Thorne. I just came in to get away from it."

"Sure is. The advice is to stay indoors from twelve till two."

"I just heard on the radio." He pointed up toward the ceiling as though that were where the radio was. "Say, did you have any luck finding Alfie? I helped last night, walked through those woods for a good few hours. I didn't see anything."

"Nothing as of yet, Alan. When there's news, I'm sure you'll know about it. News travels fast round here."

Alan looked solemn. "I just can't believe a thing like that happened. And Weedy? He was the softest guy, wouldn't say boo to a goose. To think he did something to his kid..." Alan trailed off, shaking his head. Tony saw it was hurting him; Alan was a big guy, but probably softer than Weedy was, in truth. He patted him on the arm twice.

"I know it's awful, but if the town pulls together, we'll make sure that Caroline is well looked after, and that justice is served."

"I know. It's just so damn sad."

Tony couldn't stand to see a man as sad as what Alan looked. "If you're not busy, they're doing another search today. They've got some drones to help map the woods out, get a bigger picture of it."

"If only they had that when Sophie went missing –"Alan stopped and cringed. "I'm sorry, Thorne, that was insensitive."

Tony raised his hand. "It's fine, Alan."

"Truth is, I'll have to go back to the woods at some point today anyway, 'cos I dropped my damn knife when I was on the search last night. If it was just my standard penknife, I'd leave it, but it was a present from my boy for Father's Day, has an inscription and everything. I'd go now, but Mrs. Coates has got a leaky kitchen sink that needs taking care of."

"Well, you take care, Alan. I hope you find your knife." Tony patted him on the shoulder again and moved on to the checkout.

"Thanks, Tony. And hey, there's a glass of the finest scotch money can buy at my house with your name on, any time you like."

Tony looked back and saw Alan's smile was back on his face and couldn't help but smile himself. "You're a good man, Alan, I might just take you up on that."

CHAPTER 17

"How are we feeling today, Mrs. Pearce?" Mahone stood in an awkward bend over a woman dressed in a hospital nightgown. Her short curly hair had turned grey some time ago, Lucy assumed.

"F-fine," Mrs Pearce answered, keeping her eyes down on the floor.

Mahone stood straight and turned to Lucy, then proceeded to talk about Mrs. Pearce as though she wasn't there at all. "Mrs. Pearce here, suffers from extreme paranoia and schizophrenia. Now, don't be fooled. She may seem like a harmless old woman, but Mrs. Pearce here, was convicted of attempted murder. Stabbed her husband in the neck with a corkscrew." Mahone chuckled and looked over at Mrs. Pearce on the bed. "Isn't that right, Mrs. Pearce?" He turned back to Lucy. "She won't talk back, and that's okay. Anything she has to say isn't worth our time."

Mrs. Pearce started shaking and looking frantically out of the open door behind Lucy. She looked like a prisoner deciding if this was their chance to escape. Bolt for the door and run.

"She came to us six years ago, and has made steady improvements. Six years ago, she'd have been restrained to the bed. You turned your back on her for a second and she'd be gone. I'll prep the syringe for administration, if you could pass me her medication." Mahone snapped his fingers and pointed to the chart Lucy was holding.

"Focus. Find Mrs. Pearce and the corresponding medications on my list."

Lucy looked up at him, down at the clipboard, then back to Mrs. Pearce, who still had the look of escape in her eye.

"Miss Swindle." Mahone snapped his fingers again. "I don't know what things were like in the last place you worked, but here, efficiency is key."

"I'm sorry?" Lucy said, not understanding what he meant. She was beginning to feel as though she didn't know what the hell she was doing with anything. Did Mrs. Pearce need the drugs she was about to get from the trolley? Or was it all part of Mahone's drug testing operation? If there was one. Her ear throbbed and pulsed where the skin had been torn. That sting would still be there when she tried to get to sleep tonight, which right now, felt like a million years away.

"When I do this" – Mahone snapped his fingers again and pointed to the chart –"that means I need you to find the medication on the chart that corresponds to the patient's name, and then get it from the medicine trolley in the hall."

"Do we need to examine Mrs. Pearce?" Lucy said, absently.

Mahone lifted his chin and ground his teeth. "I don't need a nurse to tell me my business. I need a nurse to do as they're told."

"Yes, Doctor." Lucy turned to head for the medicine trolley, when Mrs. Pearce let out a loud, sharp scream. She had jumped up from the bed, charged into Mahone, and knocked him into the wall. Lucy panicked; her feet were cemented to the ground in shock. She stood in the doorway, unable to move out of the way in that split-second moment when it all happened. Mrs. Pearce charged toward her, the look on her face one more of fear than anger. She hit Lucy with her shoulder, connecting with Lucy's chest, right between her breasts.

Lucy, in reflex action more than anything, shot out her arms and wrapped them around Mrs. Pearce so they both fell to the floor with a thump.

"Don't let him put that shit in me! Don't let him!" Mrs. Pearce screamed. She writhed and kicked, trying to force Lucy's grip off her.

Lucy held on as tightly as she could, until Mrs. Pearce slowed and their eyes met.

"Please. Don't. Let him. Hurt me," Mrs. Pearce whispered.

Lucy let go, with all the intention to just let Mrs. Pearce run away. But before Mrs. Pearce had a chance to leave, Mahone grabbed her by the shoulders and threw her backward toward the bed.

"Argh!" Mrs. Pearce screamed in a high-pitched wail as she clattered against the bed's metal frame. Mahone's face was purple; he shook with rage. He stood over the old woman, his fists clenched, and in that moment, Lucy was sure he was going to hit Mrs. Pearce, and something told her it wouldn't be the first time he'd hit a patient.

"You crazy bitch, you mad little cunt!" He lifted his hand to strike. Mrs. Pearce cowered away, her wails turning to huge sobbing cries of desperation and fear.

"Doctor, no!" Lucy stood and grabbed his arm; she felt the deceptively huge bulge of muscle under his lab coat. He looked at her and she watched as the rage began to drain from him.

"Don't hurt her," Lucy said. "She's a patient. She's scared. Look at her."

Mahone did look. He dropped his arm and shook Lucy's grasp from him.

"Give her the damn pills and we'll move on to the next. I'll come back and finish here when the sedation has kicked in." He moved toward the door, stopped, and turned to look at Mrs. Pearce. "Do that again and you'll be punished. I swear it."

He walked away and Lucy got Mrs. Pearce back up into her bed. She gave her the sedative pills and stroked her hair until she had calmed down. Once the tears had stopped, Mrs. Pearce curled into a ball and faced the wall.

CHAPTER 18

Lucy caught up with Mahone in the next room. They finished assessing and handing out medication to every patient on that wing. Lucy checked thoroughly that every drug they injected into the patients was the one written on their prescription. If he were using un-regulated drugs, surely he wouldn't leave a paper trail?

"This is as far as you go today, Lucy. You've done well, considering the rough start we got off to."

Lucy looked over Mahone's shoulder down the hall. "Isn't there another room?"

Mahone pulled a bemused expression and glanced back. At the end of the hall was a white door with a bracket and padlock on the outside. He sniggered to himself. "That's not a patient's room, Lucy. Christ, we don't put padlocks on our patients' rooms."

Lucy shook her head. "Sorry. Of course."

"That's a storage room where we keep the restraints." He smiled and stepped closer to Lucy. "Strait jackets, straps, muffs, sleeves – would you like to see our equipment, Lucy? It's quite a collection. Some of the things in there are from back in the old days, when things were done very differently around here. As you can probably imagine."

Lucy shook her head and looked away; she couldn't look at him when he had that smile on his face.

"Good. The nurse who worked here before you... well, the less said the better. She was fired for professional inadequacy. Something I hope you never suffer from."

Lucy had heard that a nurse had been fired; that was why there was a position available. A position that Lucy took.

"Shall I go back and help the other nurses with lunch?" Lucy said, her voice full of hope, desperately hoping that he would say yes.

"What I would like you to do is organise the medications for this afternoon. Take the trolley with you and fill the scripts as needed. Do you remember the code for the pharmacy door?"

Lucy's ear was throbbing like it had its own heartbeat; she thought that maybe it would get an infection if she didn't get some TCP on it soon. "Yes," she said, unsure if she did remember it or not.

"Good girl," Mahone said, with more than an air of condescension. He reached toward the trolley and took a syringe and a bottle of liquid Clonazepam. If Lucy remembered rightly, that was a high-strength sedative. "Run along now. And once again, Lucy, you did well today. Every now and then, patients like Mrs. Pearce try and escape, or lash out at you, but you did well."

"Thanks," Lucy said with a smile.

When Lucy had gone, Mahone moved on to the door at the end of the hall. He stepped inside.

CHAPTER 19

The police station's AC was kicking out a cool breeze that Tony Thorne thought felt very much like heaven. He wanted to be a part of the search team looking for Alfie Weeds. Apparently, the drones were there and the operatives were confident they could map out the whole woodland, from the town park all the way to the river Mere on the other side. Tony had every faith that if there was anything for them to see, they'd see it, it may take a while, but they'd see it. Those woods stretched all the way to Whitby on the east coast, a stretch that spanned twenty-two miles. Although, Tony knew Alfie Weeds would be nowhere near that far.

The mood in the station was low, but not without the intertwining strands of hope that everyone held onto when there was hope there to grab, even if it was just the slightest sliver. Until they found a body, until it was nailed on one hundred percent, there was always hope.

Ruth came over to Tony's desk, sat down, and put her feet up so that they landed between his phone and computer.

"Hey to you, too," Tony said.

"Hey." Ruth smiled. "So, the news on this front is nothing. Sweet F A. I've had Gareth in the interview room this morning, he gave me nothing. Just kept saying the same shit he said to you last night. He didn't do it, he doesn't remember, yadda yadda yadda. It was noted during processing that his arms were covered in small scratches. Not the kind of scratches that would come from a struggle or a fight."

"From what, then?"

Ruth shrugged. "Maybe when we find the body he'll start talking."

"If," Tony said.

"What now?"

"*If* we find the body, not *when*."

Ruth looked at Tony, pulling that face that meant she was holding back the words she really wanted to say.

"I just can't understand it," Tony said. "I've known this man nearly all my life, it just doesn't make sense."

"Not everything makes sense, Tony. That's the sad truth of it. Sometimes people just do because the mood strikes, or something inside them just snaps. Who knows, there could have been years and years of pressure building and the day at the fete" – Ruth snapped her fingers –"he breaks."

"I guess."

"I mean, you should know that as well as anyone."

Tony leaned back in his chair, puffed out his cheeks, and blew hot air up to the ceiling.

"You okay, Thorne? You don't seem yourself."

Tony wiped at his face with both hands and told Ruth what had gone on between him and Sarah that morning. How they'd argued about Sophie, how their marriage was a sexless, joyless prison both of them were stuck in with no chance of parole on the horizon.

"You really mean what you said? You never would have married Sarah if Sophie were still around?"

Tony shrugged. "I think I did. When I think about it, the

pain is just as strong now as it was back then. I kept thinking, 'I'll find her, someone will find her,' but no one did. I was at every search, day and night. I searched on my own, well after everyone else had stopped. All I know is that one night, Sophie went out into those woods with someone and never came back. Now it's happened again and something in me is telling me that they could be connected."

"How so?"

Tony shrugged again. "I don't know." He gripped the bridge of his nose. "I'm tired. I didn't really sleep. I need some coffee."

Ruth leaned back in her chair and snapped her fingers. "Hey, you!"

Westlake looked up quizzically from where he was sat at a desk rifling through paperwork. "Who, me?"

"Yes, you, Westlake, go grab two cups of coffee from the machine."

Westlake looked frustrated, like saying 'get your own fucking coffee' was on the tip of his tongue. He didn't though, he got up and grabbed two coffees.

"That's not what he's here for, Ruth."

"I know." Ruth smiled. "But you gotta keep these newbies on their toes."

Tony smiled and shook his head.

"I was a suspect, you know," he said, looking at the table where he spun a pencil round and round in a circle.

"What?" Ruth took her legs down from the desk.

"I was a suspect. When they ran out of ideas, they thought my eagerness to find her was like some kind of mega bluff."

"How far did it go?" Ruth stopped fidgeting on her chair and arched her eyebrow.

"You mean, did they caution me?"

"Yeah." Ruth nodded.

"No. They kept it low key, just a few more questions here

and there, trying to trip me up on my story. We'd been out together that night, we'd had a bite to eat and a few drinks, so we decided to walk home. Sophie lived down on Sycamore Drive, the posh end, I was in the opposite direction back then, near Main Street. She went left and I went right and that was it. I was the last person to see her alive. I offered to walk her home, that's the hardest thing, she said she didn't need a chaperone, she was a big girl and could take care of herself. I shouldn't have taken no for an answer, I should have just walked her home and then maybe she'd still be here."

"Or you'd both be dead. Whoever killed Sophie that night might have killed you too."

Tony went quiet. The mood that drenched over him was a sombre one. He felt miserable, had felt miserable for as long as he could remember. "Maybe." Tony sniffed. Westlake put two coffees down on the desk and stood there, as if awaiting more orders.

"You need something, new boy?" Ruth raised an eyebrow.

Westlake sighed. "A thank you, maybe."

Ruth pursed her lips and blew a raspberry. "Good one. Get back to work."

Westlake shot her a frown and went back to his desk.

Tony sipped his coffee. "I just wish I could have found her and brought her home to rest. Instead of being out there somewhere, alone in the cold."

They both sat there then, Tony thinking about Sophie and Alfie, and wondering if they would both suffer the same fate. The phone on Tony's desk rang, knocking both him and Ruth out of the sorrowful silence they had both slipped into.

"Hello?" Tony answered.

"Sergeant Thorne, it's PC Ferry here. We're down at the search site, the volunteers and the officers are struggling to go far into the woods because of this heat. We keep having to call them back, it's too dangerous. It's like the damn Amazon in there."

"Did you find anything?"

"Nope," Ferry said quickly. "Nothing. We can pick up the tracks of the two of them so far, but then they go into some overgrown thickets and the trail gets lost."

"What about the drones?"

"We get a real good image of the woods, but when we try and get closer to the eastern side of the trees, the image blurs and we can't make anything out. It's like something's interfering with the signal or something."

Tony frowned. Ruth mouthed: 'What? They found something?' at him, and he shook his head.

"Do you have any idea of what could be blocking the signal?"

"No idea. Listen, we're about out of ideas here. I know you're supposed to be keeping an eye on the suspect, but if he's not giving anything up still, you fancy coming down and helping?"

"He's singing the same song as last night," Tony said and thought about going back into those woods, searching all that old ground he'd searched before. He hadn't been into the woods since that night. The thought of going to that old reservoir, where all of Sophie's blood was found, gave him a chill. A stone grew in his stomach, making him feel sick and scared at the same time. "Sure. We'll come down. I think it's time we got all hands on deck."

"I couldn't agree more."

CHAPTER 20

The afternoon passed over into evening. The temperature of Wymere Town was still in the low thirties, but the relief in the ten-degree drop was felt by everyone. Whilst Tony Thorne and Ruth Lane helped with the search party, and Lucy Swindle finished the rest of her shift at Hill Top Hospital, the rest of the town were winding down business for the day, closing up shops, removing signs from the pavement, locking the shutters in place to keep the things they held dear safe.

They would go about their lives not knowing that discoveries were about to be made. Discoveries that would make them hold their families a little bit closer. Discoveries that would keep them awake at night, unsure if they had locked the back door or if that sound outside was just a stray cat knocking over one of the bins in search of food. Discoveries that would haunt them for the rest of their lives and make them worry about who looked after their children, because even those that you know and love can hurt you. Despite the red-hot sunshine and soaring temperatures, there was darkness hanging over Wymere, and soon, everyone would be cast under its shadow.

Chapter 21

Tiffany carried the basket of cookies. They were all uneven in shape, some were so thick that Jane was sure they'd be undercooked in the middle. She'd just tell whoever the neighbour was that Tiffany had cooked them by herself even though it had been mostly Jane's work. That always worked.

"Come on, Tiffany, those cookies will be cold by the time we get there if we go any slower." There was no path through the fields that separated the two houses, so they had gone through the cast iron gate in their garden's perimeter wall and walked through the grass, which was short and browning from the heat. Jane turned around and saw Tiffany stood completely still. The basket of cookies was held limply by her side as she looked into the woods, that seemed to go on for miles and miles.

"Tiffany? What is it?" Jane said, walking back to her.

"Are those the woods they're searching to find that boy?"

Jane dropped on to her knee to get on Tiffany's eye level. She put a gentle finger to her daughter's chin and turned her head so they were face to face.

"These woods are really big. They go from here, all the way into town, where we had the fete. So, yes, technically they are the same woods, but they won't be searching this far. They'd have to walk more than two miles through the trees to get to this part of the woods, and I doubt the boy would be that far." Jane hoped this more than believed it. She feared that if Tiffany saw a group of police officers searching near their home for a dead body, the girl would never get over it.

Tiffany shot her head back toward the woods and her hands gripped Jane's so tightly that Jane sucked her teeth at the pain of Tiffany's finger nails digging into the skin on the back of her hands.

"Ow, Tiff."

Tiffany looked back to her mum, her mouth curled down in a scared expression and her eyes wide and full of tears. "I don't like those woods. There's something in there."

"There's nothing in those woods, okay?" Jane stroked Tiffany's cheek and then pulled her in for a hug. She held her daughter tight. "I know what happened at the fete yesterday was awful, and it was scary, but there's nothing in there to be afraid of. What happened yesterday was a bad man did something bad, and now he's in jail."

"You promise?"

Jane smiled. "I promise."

Tiff hugged Jane once more, this time she rested her head in the hollow of her mother's shoulder.

"Come on then," Jane said, getting back to her feet. "Let's go meet the neighbours."

THE HOUSE DIDN'T LOOK like it was in a good state. Even though no one had lived in Jane's house for over a decade, hers looked to be in better shape than the neighbour's.

The cement pointing between the rough stone was crumbling out, roof tiles had slipped, the shutters on the windows were rotten, and the paint on the front door was peeling from the wood.

Hesitantly, Jane knocked on the door. She felt Tiffany move slightly behind her as they waited for an answer.

They heard nothing for a few moments, and just when it got to the point that it seemed nobody was going to answer, the door handle turned and a long creaking sound of rusty hinges squealed as the door swung open.

An old woman appeared; her hair was thin and a brilliant white. Deep wrinkles covered her face so it looked as though she was in a constant frown. As the door opened wider and more of the old woman came into view, Jane looked down and almost gasped when she saw the woman's right foot.

It was so severely dislocated that when she walked, it was the instep of her foot that touched the floor and bore all her weight; the sole of her foot was pointing outwards, touching nothing but air. Jane felt her skin crawl and her stomach flip at the sight of it. Imagining for that second how painful that must be.

"Hello," the old woman said.

"Hi," Jane said, desperately trying not to look back down. "We thought we'd come over and say hello. We've just moved into the Old Stone Cottage over the way there."

"Right," the woman replied, in a way that sounded like a question, like: *so what?*

"We brought cookies." Jane forced a big smile and tried to bring Tiffany out from behind her, but Tiffany resisted.

"We?" The old woman said, and a smile touched her old, wrinkled lips. She bent her hunched back and attempted to peer around Jane's legs at Tiffany. "I didn't realise there were two of you. Who is that, hiding back there?" The old woman laughed, although to Jane it sounded more like a cackle.

"This is Tiffany," Jane said. "Come and say hello, Tiff. Sorry, she's shy."

Tiffany stepped out from behind Jane's legs. "Hi," she said.

"Hello there, young lady, it's been a long time since we've had a new young family around here." The old woman's smile began to fade and she looked over toward the trees.

She bent down low again. "You haven't been in those woods yet, have you?"

Tiffany shook her head.

The old woman smiled, showing her deep yellow teeth. "Good girl. It's a dangerous place; when I was a girl, I was told to stay away from there and…" The old woman looked down at her ankle and shook her head. "Well, let's just say, I should have listened to my mother."

"I hope you don't mind us calling round unannounced like this?" Jane said.

"Not at all, dear. Come on in. I'll make us some tea for those cookies. They smell delicious." The old woman's small pink tongue poked out from behind her dry, cracked lips and moved from side to side.

Jane and Tiffany stepped in, following the old woman's lead. She hobbled into the living room, gestured with a thin, stiff hand for them to sit on the flower-patterned sofa that sat opposite an unlit fire, and walked through a door that Jane presumed went into the kitchen.

Jane and Tiffany sat. Considering the amount of pain that turned-in foot would cause her, the old woman moved surprisingly quickly.

The things people can get used to, Jane thought.

Tiffany slapped her hand on the arm of the sofa, causing a cloud of dust to erupt into the air. Jane looked at her in a way that warned Tiffany not to do that again.

"What? There was a bug." Tiffany said.

Jane shook her head. The dust seemed to hang in the air forever. Jane wrinkled her nose as the stale odour that filled the room didn't seem to dissipate. She struggled to keep her own house immaculate, but this was borderline neglectful. Surely this old woman had family or friends that could come round and help her? The idea that this woman sat over here in her own filth, unable to hoover, dust, and mop was heart breaking.

Behind the door that led into the kitchen, Jane heard a clattering of porcelain cups and the bubbling of a boiling kettle.

"Do you take sugar?" The old woman's voice came faintly from the kitchen.

"No, thank you," Jane replied. Then, hearing her father's voice in her head, she couldn't resist adding: "I'm sweet enough."

"PAH!" The old woman barked a laugh as she entered the living room backward, using her back to push the door open. She was old, in her nineties at least, Jane thought, but she was nimble enough to perform these tasks safely. Once through the door, she turned and walked toward Jane and Tiffany. Jane couldn't take her eyes from the old woman's foot, the instep and the side of her ankle that touched the floor with every step was rough and dark with callouses. Whatever had caused that injury had happened a long time ago. The old woman didn't even wince.

"Here we are," she said, putting the tray with a pot full of tea and three cups on the coffee table. "I can't remember the last time I made tea for three. It's nice." The old woman sat in the big red armchair and laid her head back against the head-rest and took a few big breaths. "It feels so easy when you start, then all of a sudden, all your energy, *poof,* disappears." She smiled at this admission and Jane felt guilty for not jumping up and helping her with the tray straight away.

"This is lovely. I'll pour the tea. Tiffany, can you get the cookies out and plate them up on the table for us, please?" Jane said.

She got her hands to the handle of the teapot before the old woman snapped: "Ah, ah, ah!"

Jane sat back and couldn't help but feel like a small child being told off by an adult stranger.

The old woman leaned forward, tutting and shaking her head. A long white strand of hair fell in front of her face. "You've got to let the tea brew. You can't just pour it out straight away, it'll be as weak as cat's piss."

The old woman covered her mouth with her arthritic hand and looked wide-eyed at Tiffany, who giggled at the bad word. "Oh my, what a foul tongue I have in my head today. You must forgive me, little one, I'm not used to company. I've forgotten how to act."

Jane smiled and stroked Tiffany's hair. "That's quite alright. We're coffee drinkers, really. Not used to brewing times."

"That's the problem nowadays, I suppose. Everyone wants instant gratification. When they want something, they want it now! No matter the consequences. I bet you get the coffee in those awful little pods that fill up the oceans as well, don't you?"

Jane felt her face flush. There was a short silence; the only sound between the three of them was the ticking of the clock that sat on the wall above the fireplace. It seemed to tick slowly, each second elongated. The silence was on the cusp of being unbearable when the old woman shuffled to the edge of her chair and reached for the teapot.

"I'll be mother," she said with a smile. She poured three cups of tea, and offered milk around that Jane and Tiffany both nodded for.

"I've just realised, you don't know my name, and I don't

know yours," the old woman said, almost laughing. "I'm Ida Leadley. You can call me Mrs. Leadley. Everyone else does. I don't get chance to go to town much, not with this bloody thing." She slapped her ankle. "I know it looks awful, but I barely feel it anymore. It healed that way, and by then the doctors said the only way to correct it was to snap it and force it straight again. And I wasn't bothered with that."

"How did you do it?" Jane asked. She dunked a cookie and took a bite. It was sweet and chocolatey. She'd done a good job, despite their appearance.

"I went walking through those woods when I was a little older than young Tiffany here."

"Sorry," Jane said, realising she hadn't introduced herself either, only Tiffany. "I'm Jane."

"Pleasure. So, there's a lot of old stories about those woods. Stories that involve witches and sorcery. Do you know what sorcery is, Tiffany?"

Tiffany shook her head.

"Sorcery is the use of black magic. Once upon a time, it was said that the most powerful black magic was right here in Wymere. But brave men stopped the witches from performing their sorcery, before it was too late. I've got a lot of stories to tell, some of those stories, however, are unsuitable for little girls. I was told them as soon as I was old enough to listen! Times were different back then, though, and times change. Maybe I'll tell you some, one day. If you like?"

Tiffany looked unsure.

"Maybe," Jane said.

Mrs. Leadley waved a hand to gesture that it wasn't important right now. "So, as young girls do, I went into those woods looking for this place that my mother had told me about, no, *warned* me about. There's a tree in those woods that has a dark, dark history.

"It was 1957, I was about fourteen at the time, and I

finally plucked up the courage to go in. See if the stories were true. It was a heatwave, we had nothing but solid sun for the entire month of June. It wasn't anywhere near as hot as it is today, but it was still mighty hot.

"It took me a long time; sweat was pouring out of me and I was starting to get worried that I'd lost my way. That's when I found it. I had followed the path meticulously, but at some point, the path disappeared. I think that maybe, you can only find that place when it wants you to find it. And I tell you, when I did, it didn't feel hot anymore. It felt cold, bitterly cold, like someone had just thrown me into a frozen lake. There's a wall of brambles in there, five feet high, probably higher now, and thicker than our cottage walls. I found a way through, got some scratches for my trouble, and behind there was this reservoir.

"I believe in the late eighteen hundreds, the town hoped to use it as a secondary water source, but no matter how they cleaned it, the water was absolutely foul. People got sick, some even died! You wouldn't water your plants with it." Mrs. Leadley shook her head, as if trying to force herself to stay on topic.

"So, I get through, and the water is almost all gone. There was about three feet in the bottom, and the smell, urgh, it was vile. I wanted to turn and run away, go back home and forget I'd ever seen the damned place. But I couldn't.

"Something compelled me to go closer. The sun was high above me, the trees seemed to form a giant circle around the reservoir, as if they didn't want to get too close. The only thing that grew was a single tree in the centre of the lake. It grew from a mound of black dirt, but its branches were dead. In the stories I'd heard, it was referred to as the 'Tree of Death,' because, apparently, its nutrients weren't found in water and sunlight, oh no, what gave that tree life was death. But I think a tree as evil as that, should be called 'The Devil's Tree'.

"I won't say what the stories tell of what's under there; young Tiffany wouldn't sleep for a month if I did. Full of teenage foolishness and that sense of invincibility you have when you're younger, I ignored my fears and pressed forward to the edge of the lake. The water bubbled, but there couldn't be life under there, no life grew within those brambled walls. That's when the fear I felt turned to terror.

"The water bubbled more, the air got colder, and I started to cry. I wet myself, a fourteen-year-old girl, pretty as a picture and fit as a butcher's dog, stood by the side of that water and peed in my pants, because I could feel the darkness under that water. A crow cawed so loudly above my head, I was sure it was diving down to attack me; it knocked me from my petrified stance and I lost my footing. I slipped from the edge of the embankment, my ankle caught a stone lodged in the mud, and it twisted, snapping my ankle and ripping the tendons in half. I screamed like I'd never screamed before. I almost passed out, the world was going dark, I managed to grab hold of the dirt on the rim of the lake and pulled myself up with my last ounce of strength. I laid there wishing I'd never gone to that awful place, that I had listened to my mother's warning and stayed at home to help with the house chores.

"Before my eyes closed, I saw a skeletal hand reach up from the water. The doctors told me after that I must have been hallucinating, that it wasn't possible, it was my pain-filled mind playing tricks on me, but I saw it!"

Mrs. Leadley looked at her tea as if she had no idea how it got there. "I woke up when the rain started. I managed to claw my way far enough toward home that my mother could hear my screams. My father carried me inside and the doctor came over. It wasn't clear that my tendons had ripped, so he thought it was best to leave it to heal, and here is the result."

She sipped her tea and reached for a cookie. She dunked it, then nibbled on the edge.

Jane looked down and saw that she was gripping Tiffany's hand, and Tiffany was squeezing right back. "Wow, that's quite a story."

Mrs. Leadley nodded and let out a "uh-huh," with her mouth full. Crumbs spilled down her chin and she licked her dry lips with her tongue. "If you're interested, I'll tell you the story of what's under that lake. It's an awful one."

"Maybe another day," Jane said, forcing a smile.

"These cookies are delicious; may I have another?"

Jane nodded. "Of course." She watched as Mrs. Leadley devoured three more cookies. They made small talk; Jane told her that they had moved up from London, deciding the country would be a better place to raise a family. Creepy stories aside, Mrs. Leadley seemed like a nice person, a little bit out there, but that was quite quirky.

Jane promised to come see her again, maybe bring a bottle of wine, and she'd listen to some more of her stories.

As they were leaving, Mrs. Leadley bent down as far as she could so she could look Tiffany in the eye. "I know what I sound like, a crazy old bird, but please, don't go in those woods. Even if you feel like you have to. Fight it. Fight it with all you have."

Tiffany nodded.

"Promise?" Mrs. Leadley added.

"Promise," Tiffany said and got her cheek pinched.

Later, she would break that promise.

Chapter 22

The rest of Lucy's shift went by in a haze. Her mind replayed everything that had happened from the moment she stepped into Mahone's office. Her ear was still throbbing like a sonofabitch, and her back and shoulder hurt from where Mrs. Pearce had knocked her over. Every time her ear throbbed, she thought she should report Doctor Mahone, for the way he treated his patients and the fact that he definitely had something else going on. Was it illegal drug testing like Tammy said? Lucy didn't know, but there was something about him, something bad that lurked under the surface of that smile. It was the arrogance in his eyes that almost dared whoever stood in front of him to try and call him out. It was as if he thought he was untouchable.

She'd write a complaint, but she knew he'd only intercept it. Then where would she end up? Stuck in a flat she couldn't afford with no job. And she liked her job. She was no good at anything else and, at least if she was on this side of it, she could be there to look after the patients and give them the respect they deserved, keep them safe.

Lucy remembered the look in his eyes, the fierceness that

burned in them when he threw Mrs. Pearce across the room. If Lucy hadn't been there, God knows what he might have done.

It wasn't just that, though. The other things Lucy saw that day only troubled her further.

When Mahone had told Lucy to prepare the medications for the afternoon round, they parted ways. It was only as Lucy got to the pharmacy that she realised she had forgotten the code to get in. The only time she'd been in the pharmacy to do that job was with Nurse Greta. Lucy had been told the code once and, as important things often did, instead of sticking in her mind it had dissolved away. It could be put down to the extra-long shifts, but that didn't help her now. She went back to where she and Mahone had parted. She had been twenty minutes and any hopes that he would still be there were slim.

She stopped in the corridor and saw the padlock was unlocked. He was still in the equipment cupboard. That's what he said it was anyway. What could he be doing in there for that long?

Lucy had an internal debate as to whether to knock on the door or wait until he came out. She dallied over this decision until the decision was taken out of her hands. The door opened and, for some reason, she darted around the corner into the adjoining corridor. She felt like a teenager again, trying to sneak past her parents after curfew. Her heart was beating heavily. Sweat dripped down her back. She peered round the corner and saw Mahone close the door of the equipment room behind him and snap the padlock shut. He had blood on his right hand across his knuckles. He saw this, pulled out a handkerchief, and wiped it clean. He looked down and saw the zipper of his trousers was low; he pulled it up and looked over both shoulders.

Lucy's mind started racing as fast as her heart then. What did it mean? Then she had a thought. There were always stories about doctors getting struck off for prescribing themselves medication. What if Mahone was an addict? He could be using the hospital's supply of drugs to fuel his own habit.

Why the blood? Why's he zipping up his fly?

Lucy asked herself these questions and answered them immediately with the first thing that came to mind. He was injecting. He couldn't do his arms because his arms were regularly on show. Some addicts took it in the neck, but again, he'd be discovered. Mahone must be shooting up in his crotch. Lucy had seen it enough in some of the patients that came into this place. Some could get quite messy. The puncture wound from the needle must have bled as he took it out and it got on his hand.

Was this what he was doing that the nursing staff thought was illegal drug trials?

"It could be both," Lucy said in a whisper.

She held her breath as he walked past her. Praying that he wouldn't look down the adjoining hallway and see her skulking there. God knows what he would do to her.

He didn't look. She waited until the sound of his echoing footsteps were nothing more than gentle taps in the distance, then she let out the breath she was holding. She peered in the direction he had walked to check that he was gone, then she ran down the corridor she was hiding in; that way, she could come round the other side of the hospital. Use the back exit to come out by the bins where the staff went for smoke breaks.

She'd go back in the front door and ask Helen for the passcode.

CHAPTER 23

Mahone went back to his office. Morning rounds done, all went well, aside from the mad, psycho bitch Mrs. Pearce almost making him look like a fool in front of the nursing staff. He clenched his fist at the memory and thought about how hard he'd have hit her if Lucy hadn't been there. He made an audible *oooo* sound of pleasure at the image in his head. A clean shot, a rib-breaker. He'd fill in an accident report, say she tripped and fell down a set of stairs. Nobody would bat an eye. They never did.

He opened his hand and clenched it again. He hadn't hit Mrs. Pearce, but that didn't mean he couldn't take his frustration out elsewhere. That was the beauty of being in charge of so many people, if one pissed you off you could take it out on another. It didn't do much to dampen his hatred toward Mrs. Pearce; that would only disappear once he had dished out his own punishment to her, which would come, in time. Mahone never forgot a slight against him, he remembered every face and name of anyone that ever talked down to him, tried to make him look like a fool.

He opened his desk drawer and saw he had several text

messages and seven missed calls on his phone. He frowned at it, picked it up, and opened the first text. It was one short message after another, all in capital letters.

> WE NEED TO TALK!!
>
> ANSWER YOUR PHONE!!!
>
> DON'T YOU FUCKING IGNORE ME!! WE NEED A PLAN IF SHIT HITS THE FAN!! CALL ME!

He smiled and shook his head. "Hysterical bitch," he said and laughed.

When Sarah had called him the night before, whining and panicking about what would happen when they searched those woods, he knew how irritating she'd become. Did she think he was stupid? Did she really think he didn't know how to cover his tracks? They wouldn't find a thing because he didn't *want* them to find anything.

He smiled at the thought of just simply leaving Sarah to stew in her own juices. She'd be just about ready to blow her top right now, and as amusing as it would be to see that, the idea came to him that she could inadvertently confess to her dickless husband about the whole thing and *that* would not be so amusing.

He sent her a quick text.

> If you want to talk, meet me at my office, after six.

He'd put her mind at rest then. Then maybe she'd leave him the fuck alone.

CHAPTER 24

"What you got for us, Ferry?" Tony and Ruth walked up to PC Ferry, who sat in the back of a silver police van. The back was kitted out with multiple screens and recording equipment. The van was parked on the field where the fete was held the day before. It was surrounded by more than a dozen others, a mixture of police and civilian vehicles.

Ferry looked up and waved them over. He turned one of the screens and began typing on the keyboard. The screen filled with a bird's eye view of the woods. Ferry hit play and talked them through what was happening.

"So, this is from the tree line where we're based, we move over to the west and we can drop down, zoom in, turn on the thermal imaging, we can get a really good look at everything in there."

"But you can't see everything? How is this really helping?" Ruth said, sounding sceptical.

"It's not just about the drones finding the victim, it's about seeing where he isn't. From the images we collect we're able to create a map, cut it up into grid sections, and specifically locate areas that we know he definitely isn't and places we're not sure of. Think of it as solving a puzzle, if you know from the start where half of the pieces go, you've got a much better chance of completing it.

"As I was saying, we can go anywhere in the west, to the north, back down to the southern line of the woods, but watch when we go over here to the east."

The video, which was showing pictures with such clarity and definition, started to fade like someone was messing with the contrast dials. Then static lines appeared and the image froze before turning black.

"Why this happens," Ferry shrugged, "I've no idea. It's like something's blocking the signal but, from what I can tell from the survey maps we've been given, there's nothing there. I thought you might know more, as you're far more acquainted with this town than I am."

Tony leaned in. "Show me the map and point to where the drone is when it cuts out."

Ferry quickly got the map and laid it out on the side. He pointed to the east side of the forest that reached toward the edge of town. "Here is where it cuts out, we come back over this way, or go too far east and the feed comes back. Good as new. It cuts out about two miles into the woods."

"Well, there's nothing out there that would interfere with a signal, not that I know of anyway." Tony pointed to a patch and moved his finger in a circle. "Around here is an old reservoir. I don't know exactly where because whenever a surveyor has tried to put it down on the map, they've all had a difference of opinion when it comes to nailing down a specific location."

"How's that possible?" Ferry scoffed.

Tony shrugged. "I don't know. I'm not versed in the art of map drawing, so I don't know what's getting in the way. But I know it's here, because I've searched these woods before. A long time ago now, though."

"So, nothing to block the signal then?"

Tony dragged his finger to the edge of the forest on the east side. "There's a couple of houses out that way, Old Stone Cottage and Cherry Tree Cottage, on New Road. But I don't see why that would mean anything, do you?"

Ferry shook his head. "Not unless they were actively trying to block our signal."

"One house is occupied by a new family. Been here a month or so. We don't know much about them; they've so far kept to themselves. The other belongs to Mrs. Leadley. I can drive by and check it out."

Ruth put a hand on Tony's shoulder. "Tony, I think we'd be better used helping to search the woods. Give them a few hours at least. These guys have been out here baking in the sun all day, let's give them a hand."

Tony chewed his lip and had an interior debate. "Okay," he said. "No longer than seven, though. Then we're going down to that house. If they've got nothing to say, we'll start to search the woods from that side."

Chapter 25

Lucy Swindle saw the turn of the big hand hit twelve and the little hand land on six and told herself: "You are going home on time tonight. I don't care what else is going on, after the day you've had, you are going straight home."

She headed for the exit, waving bye to the patients that were conscious enough to acknowledge her presence in the first place, then Gerald, with his big toothy grin, beckoned her over to where he sat in front of the TV in a tall-backed armchair. Lucy looked up at the clock, saw the big hand tick over, and closed her eyes. When she opened them again, she saw Gerald's smiling face and couldn't help but smile back.

"Hey, Gerald. I'm just about to finish for the day, are you okay?"

Gerald waved frantically for her to come over and sit beside him. Gerald was in his fifties. His hairline had receded to the halfway point of his head, leaving a small tuft of hair where a fringe would normally start. He suffered with schizophrenia, paranoia, and manic depression. He was never aggressive or hostile. He reacted well to the medication; he just couldn't cope with the outside world. Too many times he had been released, only to be brought straight back after having a relapse. Lucy was given a rundown by one of the other nurses when Gerald first started taking a shine to her. They told her that he loved to talk; now, Lucy knew that better than anyone.

"Hiya Lucy," he said, that smile growing ever wider. "I saw you today, in the hall."

"I saw you too. Just before I was going into Dr, Mahone's office."

Gerald's smile faded at the mention of Mahone's name and a frown creased his brow. It was the first time Lucy had seen Gerald frown like that.

"He's a bad man."

Lucy looked at him quizzically, wondering what Gerald knew. Before he told her, she realised that Gerald had been here longer than Mahone; over all those years, he must have seen something that could confirm some of Lucy's theories.

"What do you know, Gerald? Does Doctor Mahone do things he's not supposed to?"

Gerald nodded.

"Can you tell me what he does, Gerald?"

Gerald opened his mouth but stopped himself. Lucy could see he was scared; he wanted to tell her something but was afraid of what would happen to him if he did.

"You can tell me, Gerald. Does he give patients here stuff that he shouldn't?"

Gerald nodded more vigorously.

"Does he steal some of the medications for himself?" Lucy could feel her mouth going dry.

Gerald shrugged. "He hurts people. He's not nice."

"Hurts people? How does he hurt people?"

Gerald looked as though he was on the verge of tears. His big wide eyes stared back into Lucy's. "He does 'orrible things, Lucy." When he said her name, it came out *Loo-see*. "Worser things than you know." He stopped and wiped his eyes. "No one can stop him. Cos then, he'll hurt them too."

"If he's hurting people, Gerald, I need to put a stop to it."

Gerald shook his head violently, "No. He'll hurt you, Loo-see. You don't know what he's capable of. I don't want to talk about this anymore."

A horrible thought came to Lucy, making her reach out and hold Gerald's arm. "Has he hit you, Gerald?"

Gerald sat up straight and raised his chin. "No."

"That's good," Lucy sighed with relief.

"I'd knock him out if he did," Gerald said and then laughed. It was a nice sound. A happy sound.

"Gerald, I can see that this is upsetting you, but if you know something, you have to tell me. Have you seen him hit someone?"

Gerald nodded, and the smile disappeared again. "I don't want to talk about this anymore, Loo-see." Gerald started to cry; he rocked slowly in his chair. Lucy looked down and saw his hands gripping the arm rests, his knuckles white. "I don't want to talk, I don't want to talk, I don't want to talk." His voice grew louder and louder until he was nearly shouting. Lucy put a hand on his arm and stroked him.

"Okay, okay, shush now. I'm sorry, I didn't mean to upset you." Lucy wiped her face and looked up at the clock; it was quarter past six now.

"You just relax and watch TV. I'm going home now." She held his hand and squeezed. "Good night, Gerald. I'll see you tomorrow."

Gerald smiled. "Good night, Loo-see. See you tomorrow."

Lucy left, gathered her things from the locker room. She kept her hoop earrings in her bag; she'd have to let her ear heal before she tried to put them back in again. She walked briskly toward the exit, feeling a pang of excitement to get home and put an end to this day. Before she could put an end to it, she thought about writing down everything she had seen, as well as Gerald's comments. Perhaps someone would listen to her suspicions? But who, the police maybe?

"You need to be careful."

Lucy looked around and saw the only person in the reception was Helen. She was reading files, her rimless glasses perched on the end of her nose making her look like the snob she was.

"Excuse me?" Lucy asked.

Helen licked the tip of her finger and flicked through a few sheets of paper, as if she hadn't heard Lucy speak. "You need to be careful. Mahone doesn't take kindly to nurses that question him or spy on him." Helen's eyes never left the paperwork she flicked through.

Lucy's throat tightened. "I don't know what you mean."

Helen looked up at her now, her eyes big and full of pleasure over her glasses. "Is that right?" She smiled. She waved lazily with her hand for Lucy to come over to the desk. Lucy did, reluctantly. When she got there, Helen gestured with a simple twitch of her head for Lucy to lean over the desk. Behind it was an HD colour TV separated into eight different frames.

"Great little set up we've got here. State of the art CCTV in every hallway and public communion area. It doesn't pick up sound, but that's fine, we rarely need to look it over. Only if something gets reported, and it never does." That pleasurable look returned to her eye, a look dangerously similar to the arrogant look Lucy had noticed in Mahone's.

"I was skimming through the cameras today when I saw this." She clicked on a saved icon on the bottom of the screen. The image that came up was Lucy, stood with her back against the wall, peering around the edge as Dr. Mahone came out of the equipment room.

Lucy shut her eyes.

Helen hit the space bar, pausing the video. "Now listen, I don't like you. I don't like anyone much, truth be told, but I know the patients seem to like you and, despite your tardiness, you are good with them. I won't bring this to Ian's attention."

"Thank you –"

Helen held up a finger. *She was getting off on this*, Lucy thought. "But, you stop spying, or doing whatever the hell it is you're doing. You're not the first to do it, but you will be the last, unless you want to end up like Lauren Kelly."

"Who's Lauren Kelly?"

Helen took off her glasses in a display of frustrated exasperation. "The nurse whose position you filled. She was good with the patients too. Got ahead of herself, got to thinking she could take Ian down a peg or two." A smile spread across her lips. "God, what a mistake she made. She's ruined now. No job, no money. No one in town will hire her. Troublemaker and a liar. She got a lump sum from Ian because he's a reasonable man. She used the money to buy the piece of shit hovel she calls a home. There she stays, a recluse. So, take my advice, or don't take my advice. Leave shit alone."

Lucy swallowed the lump that had formed in her throat. "Night, Helen."

Helen raised an eyebrow and watched Lucy leave, then she got back to her papers.

As Lucy walked out of the automatic doors, her skin felt prickly and any appetite she had built up over the day had disappeared. Gerald's words rang in her head.

He's a bad man. He hurts people.

She wasn't sure if she could let it go. She was twenty-six years old, she needed this job, she wanted the career it promised, to help those that needed help. She didn't know what to do for the best.

Lucy, so wrapped up in her own thoughts, barely noticed the blonde woman storm past her, with a face white with fear.

CHAPTER 26

Jane picked at her dinner. She wasn't hungry. Her appetite had gone because all she could think about was Mrs. Leadley, telling her about The Devil's Tree that sat in the woods behind her house. Jane wasn't a superstitious person, not really. She wouldn't walk under a ladder and she'd salute a lone magpie, but believing in a supernatural evil that lived in the woods? That was too far.

So why the hell couldn't she stop thinking about it? And why did it worry her so?

As she sat there, she thought of Tiffany running into those woods, and the mere thought of it terrified her.

"You okay, love?" Matthew said, touching Jane's hand with his. She felt the rough calloused scratch against her soft skin and it felt nice. It felt familiar.

"Yes, I'm fine. Sorry, I was just miles away."

Matthew smiled and wiped at the tomato sauce that dribbled on his chin. He managed to get most of it, then Jane smiled and wiped the bits that had got stuck in his wiry black and grey beard.

"You guys haven't told me much about the neighbour, what's she like?"

"Scary," Tiffany said, absently pushing her spaghetti around her plate.

"Tiff," Jane tutted and shook her head. "She wasn't scary, she was just... different. She doesn't get many visitors, so she was a little... sharp."

"She says there's an evil reservoir in the woods," Tiffany added, making Matthew look at Jane with a confused frown on his face.

Jane shook her head dismissively. "She said there were some old stories about those woods, part of which is that there's a tree. I didn't get the full story, so it sounds ridiculous now, but she went when she was a girl and she thought she saw some scary stuff there. She fell and broke her ankle and now she walks with an in-turned foot."

Matthew grimaced. "Nice," he said, arching one eyebrow. "It'll be a while longer before she gets any more visitors then?"

Jane shrugged. "I might go round and see her tomorrow. I thought I might help her clean up a bit, it looks like she struggles."

"Her house a dump?"

"No."

"Yes," Tiffany butted in. "There's dust everywhere, if you hit the sofa dust clouds fill the room and you can't even breathe. Can I stay with Dad? I don't want to go back there, Mrs. Leadley gives me the creeps."

Jane looked at Matthew as he swayed his head from side to side debating the idea.

"You any good at plastering?" he said.

"No, but I'm great company and my wages are cheap."

Matthew laughed. "Go on then."

Jane cleared the pots and washed them in the sink. She was looking out at the trees through the window; the woods were so dense, she couldn't imagine there would be a way to walk through it.

"Why don't you and Tiff go for a walk? Check out the trail through the woods, see if there is a 'Death Tree' or 'Devil's Tree', whatever it's called."

Jane looked at him like he was crazy.

"What?"

"After what Mrs. Leadley told us today? No way."

Matthew laughed and put his hands on her shoulders. "Oh, come on, don't tell me you believe that rubbish? You're the least superstitious person I know. It seems crazy to me that you're going to be deprived of a lovely nature walk that's right behind our house, just because a lonely old woman told you some two-bit scary story about how she broke her ankle."

They both turned at the sound of footsteps as Tiffany ran down the hall to the living room and turned on the TV.

Matthew moved his hands up and down Jane's arms and kissed her on the cheek. She felt his arms move around her and hold her tight. She didn't feel any fear then. Only love and safety.

"Go on, go pick some flowers, they'll brighten up the place." He kissed her cheek and squeezed her tighter.

Jane laughed and turned to face him. Their fingers laced together and she kissed his mouth. Their lips lingered together for a short time before the kissing grew more passionate; an intensity filled Jane, blowing away all of her irrational fears.

They pulled apart. Jane bit her lip. Their eyes locked together.

"You go for a walk, I'll finish up for the day in the basement, and how about we have an early night?" Matthew's hand traced the curve of her hips and ended on her bum. He squeezed; Jane let out a low moan of impatience. She breathed deeply and pecked him on the lips.

"Deal," she said.

TIFFANY WAS HANGING BACK. Jane could see that she was anxious and part of her, a big part of her, wanted to cave in and take her back home. Then, she thought that if she did, Tiffany might then believe that there was some truth to Mrs. Leadley's story. Matthew was right, there was no way the story was true, just something interesting she made up to account for her dodgy foot. Jane had to prove that to Tiffany, and to herself.

"How far are we walking?" Tiffany said, a whiney sound to her voice.

"Not far, we're just going to follow the footpath, see where it takes us. The woods should be full of beautiful wild-flowers this time of year. Let's see how many pretty ones we can pick."

"I thought we weren't supposed to pick wildflowers?"

"Well, we're not, really, but just a few to make a nice bunch for on the kitchen table will help brighten the house up a bit," Jane said, and gestured with a waving hand for Tiffany to move quicker.

Tiffany did a half jog-half run until she was side by side with her mother. "It does need brightening up, the house is so old looking. Nothing like our old one."

Jane smiled. "I know, love. Once your dad's finished with the basement, he'll re-decorate the old house. Bring it into the twenty-first century."

They reached the path that started at the tree line. Jane leant on an old post that had carvings in the wood. She brushed away some of the moss that had grown in the cracks and crevices and found that the carvings had once been words. She tried, for a short time, to make out what the words had once said. She couldn't be sure, but the first word looked to be BEWARE. Jane tried to trace the letters with her fingers again, until Tiffany got bored of waiting and said, "Can we just go? I want to get back home."

Jane laughed and rolled her eyes. "Come on then. I can't make out what it says anyway."

Then they both stepped into the woods.

CHAPTER 27

Tiffany liked the woods once they were in. The birds and animals were abundant. The green trees were full of life, the sun's rays filtered through the green canopy and showered down a hot, humid glow on them as they walked. Her mum was now behind her. Tiffany had forgotten all about her fears and anxieties; now she was just full of excitement. She jumped from one fallen log to another, hurdled a bunch of nettles, and then the path opened up for her. She sprinted at full speed.

"Slow down, stay in sight!" her mum shouted, but Tiffany was gone.

She'd never felt so fast before. The path was a slight gradient, which helped her go faster, but she was going *really* fast. Maybe these woods were full of magic after all, but good magic.

She ran and ran, and the breeze she created felt blissful against her red-hot sweaty cheeks.

She heard a cry in the distance. It echoed around the trees. Tiffany came to a sudden halt, her heels digging up the mulch of half-composted pine needles and leaves that hid a thousand little insects underneath. They wriggled and squirmed to get back into hiding, away from the light and back into the dark.

"Mum?" she shouted in response to the cries.

It wasn't her mum who had cried out, she knew that really. She looked over her shoulder and saw the path that she had run down. It was wavy, and completely covered like it hadn't been walked over in years. It weaved in and out of the trees like a meandering snake.

How could that be? she asked herself. It had been straight; she ran as fast as she could because the path was as straight as an arrow.

She started to panic.

"Mum?!" she shouted again. Louder this time. "Mum, where are you?!"

She heard no reply. All the birds in the trees had stopped singing, the breeze that created a gentle ruffling of the leaves above her head had gone dead still.

Tiffany was circling, spinning round and round, desperate to see something that would ground her, explain where she was, but everything looked alien, as if she had been picked up and dropped into the middle of the woods with no concept of how far in she was or which way led home. She could run in one direction for miles, but if it were the wrong direction, God knows where she could end up.

She tried to calm herself; she was breathing heavily. The *BOOM BOOM BOOM* of her heart was thundering in her ears. It was all she could hear.

"Mummy?" She was crying now.

Her head snapped to the east when she heard the cry again. It was a wail, like that of an old woman in desperate pain. She pictured Mrs. Leadley's ankle and it made her stomach turn into knots.

"Hello? Is somebody there?" she shouted back. Her tears glistened on her cheeks. Moving toward where she thought the sound was coming from, she crept between the trees, trees that she was sure had been spacious before that were now pushed so closely together that she had to squeeze herself through sideways.

The voice cried out again, louder this time. And clearer. It wasn't a woman's voice like she had thought it was. It was more like a young boy's voice. She was heading in the right direction, she knew, because she could now make out the words.

Help me, came the first cry. Then, the closer she got, and the denser the trees became, he said more.

They're hurting me. Make it stop. Please! Make it stop! It hurts!

Tiffany was desperate to get to him now; she'd never heard someone in so much pain. The trees were so dense, so dense and spikey that they seemed more like a thicket of brambles then trees. Thorns caught and tore at her clothing, and she cried when they tore small cuts in her pale skin. Everything seemed so dark, it was like she was in a dream. Or a nightmare.

Please help!

After what felt like forever, she fell through the thicket of brambles and landed in dry mud that blew up in a cloud of thin dust. She coughed, choking on the dry earth. She spat; a glob of white spittle landed on the ground and was absorbed almost instantly.

It was hard to make her legs stand, it was as if they had turned to jelly, but she knew she had to, because a young boy was calling for her help. She looked up for the first time and saw that she stood before an empty crater. Something that looked as though it once held water, like the reservoir Mrs. Leadley had told them about.

The thought of Mrs. Leadley's story ran through her head and as it did, she looked to the centre of the empty reservoir and saw the mound of black dirt where the dead tree grew from. It was worse than what the old woman had said. Its branches were curled like skeletal fists, beckoning her to come forward, even though there was no wind to move them.

Help.

The voice was there, but it was weaker now, as if it were fading away.

Her eyes focused on the tree and the mound from which it grew. She had to get closer. It was a crazy urge, but an urge she couldn't control: she had to get closer to that tree. There was a lump on the ground in front of the mound, but it was hard to make out what it was from where she stood.

With the deftness that only a child possesses, Tiffany jumped down the dry embankment of the reservoir and ran toward the tree. The earth was scorched; cracks fractured the dry mud like black lightning bolts on a brown sky.

The closer she got to the tree, the larger it loomed. She felt her skin prickle with goosebumps and the hair on her arms stood on end. The mound was jet black, the tree roots that protruded from it as white as bone.

Then she saw what the lump was.

By the base of the mound where the tree grew from was a small boy. The same boy that had gone missing that day at the fete. He lay in a crumpled mess in the mud. She remembered the picture the police showed them, the one where he was wearing his blue t-shirt and his red shoes with the yellow emoji faces on them.

She looked closer at him and wondered how he could have been crying out for her to help him. His throat had been slit, and not in the past five minutes. The thick, deep line that ran across his neck was black.

Tiffany drew breath and was about to scream when her breath was stolen from her lungs. Two arms wrapped around her chest and squeezed as she was spun around.

"Don't you ever do that to me again! You understand

me?!" Her mum was shouting and crying at the same time. She had turned Tiffany to face her and then embraced her, squeezing her tighter than Tiffany had ever been squeezed before.

Tiffany grabbed hold of her mum and never wanted to let go. She opened her eyes; her mum's shoulder was blocking out most of Alfie Weeds' dead body. All she could see was his bright red shoes that seemed to shine against the blackness of the dirt. The big yellow smiley faces on them grinned.

CHAPTER 28

As Jane and Tiffany set out on their walk, Alan Houghton finally made it back home after spending the day trying to fix Mrs. Coates' leaky kitchen sink. What was supposed to be a quick fix turned out to be one of those nightmare jobs, where nothing went right.

"Hey honey, you're late home." Jenny, Alan's wife, stepped out of the kitchen with a hand towel thrown over one shoulder and white handprints all over her red cooking apron.

"Sorry, sweetie," Alan said. "Mrs. Coates' kitchen sink was an absolute pain in the back side. I thought it was just a busted washer, then I found a crack in the U-bend, then I saw the worktop had rot behind the tap and I couldn't leave her with it like that, so I had to go out and get a whole –"He stopped himself and raised his hands. He was tired, it wasn't just the long day, it was the heat, it was so damn hot! "Sorry, you don't want to listen to me. I'm boring myself talking about it. How was your day?"

Jenny walked over, put her hands on his shoulders, and planted a great big kiss on his mouth. She pulled away and smiled, and not just because his furry beard had tickled her lips.

"What's that for?" Alan asked, putting his hands on his wife's hips.

"For being a wonderful man. How much extra did you charge Mrs. Coates for doing all those extra hours?"

Alan frowned and recoiled a little. "I couldn't do that, Jenny. She's an old woman, she reminds me of my grandma before she passed, God rest her. And we all know that a state pension doesn't stretch very far these days. I couldn't have slept tonight if I'd have charged her any more than what I quoted her."

Jenny's smile broadened at this. "And that's why I love you, Alan Houghton. Any other man would have added more and more numbers to that invoice, but not you. You are a kind and gentle soul. If all men were like you, I think this world would be just fine."

"Jenny," Alan said, his cheeks turning a rosy red above his thick brown beard, "stop it."

Jenny planted a big wet kiss on his lips once more. "I will not stop it." She smiled and then turned back toward the kitchen. As she walked to the door, she said, "I made your favourite, steak and ale pie."

Alan's eyes sprang wide in delight and hunger. "I'm starved! Did you make it yourself?"

Jenny turned and gestured to the white hand-marks on her pinafore. "I certainly did! The flaky pastry, steak, the gravy – even got that fancy dark ale you like."

Alan licked his lips like a child in a cartoon.

Jenny smiled. "You are funny. Freddie's upstairs playing on that computer game we got him. Go up and see him, he's dying to show you it."

The pen knife Alan had dropped in the forest came back to the forefront of his mind. With the palaver at Mrs. Coates', he'd forgotten all about it. "My knife!" he said, putting his hands up to his face. He looked out the window and saw the evening had turned a blood red as the sun descended across the sky. If he was going to find it, he needed to go now, whilst there was still light outside.

"What do you mean *your knife*?" Jenny stood in the doorway with a hand on her hip.

"The penknife Freddie got me for Father's Day, with the inscription. I dropped it in the woods during the search last night. I need to go get it before the sun goes down."

"You'll never find that in those woods. They can't even –" Jenny stopped herself before she said something that was indecent and off colour. Alan knew what she was going to say, and he wouldn't judge her for it. *They can't even find a dead body in there, you're definitely not going to find your little old penknife.*

"I will, I know where I lost it, I was using it to cut through vines of ivy that blocked a path, and when I went to put it back in my pocket, it must have missed and fallen straight to the ground."

Jenny checked her wristwatch and sighed. "Go, now. Be quick; I've put a lot of effort into this pie, Alan."

Alan put his hands together like a prayer. "Thank you, sweetie, I won't be long. Twenty minutes, half an hour, tops."

"Better be." Jenny flung the dishcloth over her shoulder and went into the kitchen.

Alan grabbed the keys from the mantel and headed for the door when Freddie bounded down the stairs.

"Dad!" he shouted.

"Hey, son, I'm just –"

Freddie wore a gaming headset, his eyes wide with excitement. "Oh my God, Dad, you've got to check out what I can do on this game. C'mon, I'll show you!"

Alan grimaced. "I will, I promise, I've just got to run out

and grab something. I'll be really quick, half an hour, forty minutes, tops."

"Dad, you said."

"I know, I know. I will, I'll come home, we'll have dinner and I'll spend the whole evening playing that game with you. Okay?" Alan leaned in closer. "I'll even let you stay up past your bedtime."

Freddie's frown turned into a smile at this thought of breaking the rules. "Okay. Be quick!"

Alan gave Freddie a big hug and kissed the top of his head. "Won't be long. Love you."

"Love you too, Dad."

Alan walked out.

He walked back in over three hours later.

CHAPTER 29

Tony was feeling the heat in the woods. The muscles in his legs ached from navigating through the overgrowth, ensuring he stopped and inspected anything that might be classed as evidence. A snapped twig, a boot print – he found a bloody handprint on a tree trunk that had already been marked. The blood had turned brown and sticky; small flies that had landed on it looking for something to eat had found their death in the same place.

"Thorne! Lane!" someone shouted from the back of the woods where they had entered. Ruth and Thorne both shouted back in response.

"It's despatch, they've had a call!" The urgent tone in that voice sent a kick into Tony's heart, making it skip like he'd just touched an electric fence. He started running, forgetting his aching legs and sore back. He moved through the bushes and the trees until he got to the clearing. Then, he opened his legs and got running at almost full speed down the narrow path that weaved in and out of the trees. He could tell from the thudding footsteps that Ruth wasn't far behind him.

"What is it!?" he almost shouted at the PCSO, who stood by the side of the cop car with one hand gripping the car radio.

"It's despatch. Someone's found him!"

Tony stopped dead and looked at Ruth. She looked back at him, eyes sprung wide like she'd stood on a nail.

"They've found Alfie Weeds."

Without hesitation, Tony jumped in his car; Ruth got in the passenger seat and buckled her seat belt. The location popped up on the screen on the dash. "New Lane," he said. "At the old cottages, near where the drone's footage went out."

"Coincidence?" Ruth said, raising an eyebrow.

"C'mon Ruth, you know there's no such thing as coincidences." The car roared as Tony threw it into gear and floored the accelerator. The back tyres chewed up a section of dry grass and mud before getting out onto the road, heading east for New Lane.

The drive would normally take about fifteen minutes, having to do a loop of around eight miles of narrow country lanes, despite the fact that the old cottages were only two miles away if you walked it through the woods. Tony, however, would do it in less than ten. Having lived in Wymere his whole life, he knew the roads like the back of his hand, knew when he could floor it and get up to eighty, and knew exactly when to slow down for a sharp bend. The cars that followed him from the search site were still behind him but were no longer visible in the rear-view mirror. A voice came over the radio, updating every officer on that wavelength that the volunteers had been sent home and the original search site had been cleared.

"Should we tell the family?" the voice said.

Tony shot his hand to the radio, hit the button, and almost screamed into it. "Don't you dare notify the family. Not until we've got eyes at the scene."

"Copy."

Tony rarely ventured down New Lane; there was nothing down there, just a pair of cottages, and another entrance to the woods that was seldom used. It was a forgotten place, and Tony wondered why the hell anyone would want to live there.

"Ruth, get up what you can on Matthew and Jane Stanford."

Ruth nodded and pulled out a keyboard from the onboard computer. She typed in Matthew first. "Matthew Stanford, born in 1977."

"Not his life story Ruth, Jesus. Any priors."

Ruth frowned and scrolled down the page. "Nothing, not so much as an unpaid parking ticket."

"What's he do for a living?"

"Carpenter. Worked for a firm in London, part of a team responsible for building thousands of homes each year."

"He's not going to find much work up here. Most people do things for themselves; if not, there are a few tradesmen around that everyone knows and trusts. He'd have a job taking work off them."

"Might be why they bought Old Stone Cottage?"

Tony nodded. "They knew they would struggle for money, so bought the cheapest house they could to keep money in the bank, until they found something stable. Why move all the way out here though?" Tony chewed his lip.

"The wife's an artist. And not a famous one, not from what I can see here. No priors, before you ask. They've been married eleven years." Ruth took a deep breath. "You're not thinking they're involved in this, are you?"

Tony shook his head. "I doubt it, but it feels odd that they've been here two minutes and something like this happens."

"You said before that you thought the Weeds kid and Sophie might be linked; that wouldn't be possible if they're involved," Ruth interrupted.

"I know. We've got to keep every avenue open until we know for certain. The area near their house can't be filmed by the high-tech drones that cost the government thousands of pounds. Something's wrong, and I'm going to find out what it is."

"Maybe it's not the people living there, but more to do with the area itself? Maybe we should be researching more about the history of these woods?"

Tony shook his head. "I heard some stories when I was growing up. It made the allure of drinking and smoking pot in the woods as teenagers all the more enticing. But those stories are nothing but tall tales, myths."

"You talking about something supernatural?" Ruth asked, her head bent quizzically to one side.

"Apparently. But I don't buy into that."

Ruth smirked.

"What?"

"Maybe we should keep every avenue open until we know for certain."

Tony turned sharply to the left onto a narrow country lane; dry stone walls flanked his car on either side. The two small cottages looked dark, despite the brightness of the falling sun. The sky was still a crisp blue overhead.

Tony pulled the car next to Stanford's and got out. He didn't need to knock on the door; Jane came running out to meet him.

CHAPTER 30

Mahone was sat at his desk when his office door swung open, rattling on its hinges as it hit the back wall. He looked up incredulously. In the doorway stood Sarah. Her eyes were wide, her hair was a mess; the rough ponytail she'd done held half of what she had wanted it to by the looks of it. Mahone's eyes met hers, and he saw fear in them. Fear, anger, and what he saw most of in those big wet eyes was desperation. It made him want to smile, but he held it back.

"How dare you storm in here!" he shouted as he got to his feet. He moved toward her, taking giant strides. He gripped her forearm, his fingers able to curl all the way around it like he was holding a small stick. He pulled her inside the office roughly. She made a short cry and when he released his grip, she put her hand there to rub where his fingers had been. Mahone looked down the hall to see who was watching and only saw Helen's chubby little face peering around the corner from her desk at the end of the hall. When she saw him, her face disappeared. Mahone shut the door and turned to face Sarah.

He moved toward her and placed his hands on her upper arms and squeezed.

"What in hell's name are you doing? Storming in here like this?"

Sarah started crying. "I don't know what to do," she said through the tears. "It's over. They're going to find her and we'll be done."

Mahone winced at the use of the word *we* but moved past it. "You have to keep your head. What did I tell you? *They* won't find anything. The only thing that will give you away is you not keeping your cool."

Mahone stepped back and looked her up and down. "I mean, look at you, for God's sake. You're a mess. You couldn't look more guilty if you tried. Would it have hurt you to put some make-up on this morning?" He grabbed a piece of her hair between his fingers then wiped his hand on her jacket. "Run a brush through your hair maybe? Jesus, Sarah, you worry about getting caught and then run around looking like a complete disaster."

Sarah began to sob and tried to fall into his chest for comfort. Mahone pushed her away and recoiled, pulling a face of disgust. "Get off me," he spat. He moved toward his desk and grabbed a bottle of scotch from the drawer. He poured a glass, picked it up, and perched on the corner of his desk. He lifted the glass and offered it to her.

Sarah stared at it. Her heavy breathing filled the office. Finally, she shook her head.

"Take the fucking drink. You obviously need it."

Sarah's lip quivered. She took the scotch and drank it in one swallow.

"Good," Mahone said. "Now, tell me what has you so... rattled."

"They're searching the woods."

"I'm aware," Mahone said, rolling his eyes.

"Tony told me they have drones, drones with heat sensors."

"Well, that's dumb. You won't find any dead bodies with a heat sensor. They're cold, dead cold."

"I googled it and, apparently, there are drones fitted with cameras that can tell where the earth has been disturbed in places, even detect where bones might be if they're not that deep. What if you didn't bury her deep enough?"

Mahone smiled thinly, then the smile grew, showing his brilliantly white teeth. "You think I'm stupid? You think I don't know how deep to bury a body?"

Mahone stood from his desk and moved his face toward Sarah's. In a deep, cold voice, he continued. "What makes you think I buried her, for that matter? I might have burnt her. Chopped her up into little pieces and fed her to the pigs on Webster's farm on Old Road. I might have just thrown her in the old reservoir, for all it matters to you."

Mahone saw Sarah's face curdle in horror. Frown lines creased her face and the sobbing began again.

"I can't take it," Sarah said. "I can't take it anymore. I need to come clean; I need to tell Tony what we did."

Mahone stepped toward her suddenly, so that they almost bumped heads. "You'll do no such thing!" he snarled at her. "After all, it was *you* who wanted poor, beautiful Sophie Rose dead. It was you who begged me to take care of her because she was hogging the hero of the hour, Tony Thorne."

Mahone chewed his lip and shook his head, looking thoughtful. "What she saw in him I'll never know. He never was the sharpest tool in the box. I did what I did so you could have the life you wanted, and you got it! He married you, didn't he?"

"He doesn't love me," Sarah said through desperate, heartbreaking sobs.

Mahone stepped back and pinched the bridge of his nose.

"Pull yourself together, woman! What's done is done. We can't change it. I did what *you* wanted, now we have to live with the consequences."

Sarah shook her head. "I can't. I just can't do it anymore."

Mahone moved closer now, so close he could smell her sweat, feel the warm breath come out from her trembling lips.

"You tell anyone what we did and I will turn all of this around on you. You think I killed her and got rid of her body without the thought crossing my mind that you'd suddenly grow a conscience? I have everything I need to make sure that this all falls back on you. And *solely* you. You were the one mad with jealousy, full of hate and contempt for the town's sweetheart, Sophie Rose. You were the witness that saw her going into the woods with an 'unknown' companion. You are the one who had something to gain by her dying, and by the grace of God, you got it."

Mahone spread his hands. A thin smile crept along his lips, then his face darkened. "That's the best-case scenario for you. I could, of course, decide on another course of action to keep my reputation unsullied."

"What do you mean?" Sarah hugged herself, subconsciously protecting her body.

"Let's not forget, I have experience in getting rid of people without leaving a trace." Mahone reached out a hand and stroked Sarah's cheek with his knuckles, removing a tear that had rolled over her skin. He spoke softly, almost sweetly. "I could kill you, wrap a rope around your neck and hang you from the River Mere bridge. Nobody would question it. Everyone can see the state you're in; the whole town knows you're a drunk, a tiresome old slut whose marriage is on the rocks. The love in your marriage has disappeared as fast as those good looks you once had."

Mahone laughed as he said this. "To think, all you had to do for me to kill someone for you was spread those long legs of yours. I was a fool. But you once had something that was quite appealing." His hand dropped and he took a step back, looking her up and down and pulling a face of indifference.

"Now you have nothing. You are nothing. Just a trouble-some, unlovable bitch who has ended up with nothing but a life of lies and mediocrity," he finished in a whisper.

Sarah's sad, tear-streaked face turned into a snarl. "Fuck you, you son of a bitch! It wasn't hard to convince you to kill her. All the times she knocked you back. I bet every time she said no to you it was like a slap in the face. Humiliating, wasn't it? You weren't used to not getting what you wanted. Even now, you get what you want by blackmail or bribery, and if that doesn't work? You turn to violence. I have –"

"You have nothing! Get the fuck out of my office and don't bother me with this again or else I will dispose of you like the rubbish you are. Nobody will mourn you, Sarah. Not even your husband."

Sarah opened her mouth to say something; nothing came out. She turned and left, slamming the door behind her. Mahone caught the glimpse of Helen's red hair peering around the corner again before the door closed.

Mahone poured himself a glass of scotch. He nursed it in his hand, letting the liquid grow warm in the glass. Thirty minutes after Sarah had left, Mahone drank it in one swallow, grabbed his coat, and headed for the exit.

"Night, Helen."

"Good night, Doctor," Helen said in a soft tone.

The doors spread wide and the fresh evening air filled his nostrils, bringing the scent of the pine woods on the gentle breeze. It did nothing to soothe the anger and frustration that burned in him after Sarah's visit. He thought of how satisfying it would be to crush her, squeeze the life out of her, shut her up for good.

He descended the steps and found his car. The paint work

gleamed in the dying light of the sun, the wheel rims sparkled, and the interior looked as fresh as the day he drove it off the forecourt. Mahone leaned over the bonnet, inspecting the area that had been damaged by that foul stray earlier that morning, and saw that Ben had managed to buff it out. Mahone would give him a tip, but that was his job and if he couldn't do it right, he shouldn't be getting paid in the first place.

The yellow indicator lights flashed as the doors unlocked. Mahone opened the door and put his briefcase on the passenger seat. He walked around and was about to climb in when he heard the softest cry come from the side of the hospital. He waited, and when he heard it the second time, he shut the car door and walked round to investigate.

The industrial bins were lined up along the wall next to the stairs that led up to the staff exit. Trees lined the perimeter; the ground was covered in an overgrowth of long grass and untrimmed bushes. He waited, his ears readied for the slightest sound.

There.

His eyes darted to the long blades of grass that started quivering without the aid of the soft breeze. The gentle cry grew louder and more frantic. From out of the grass emerged a small kitten. Despite the even surface of the tarmac, it struggled to walk without stumbling. It was so thin he could count every rib; its eyes were crusted with infection.

Mahone half smiled, remembering the stray bitch that scratched his car. He remembered how her teats hung like udders full of milk. He assumed she must have not long since birthed a litter and here it was.

It was an inquisitive little thing. It had come right up to him. Its mother had obviously not taught it the dangers of predators. It sniffed and meowed by his feet, then began licking the black leather of his shoes. He lifted his foot, making it stumble and fall on its side. When he put his foot back down, he did it gently, placing the heel of his shoe on the kitten's head. Now the meowing became the panicked cries of an animal in danger.

Mahone at first thought he heard the kitten's cries echoed, only to then realise the rest of the litter was coming out of the grass. Two more emerged, far healthier and stronger looking. They saw him and stepped back; these had been taught to watch for predators, it seemed. Their mother, the tatty old bitch that scratched his car, appeared from behind them and hissed at him, her claws out and ready to attack.

Mahone smiled. "Try it," he whispered.

The cat hissed once more, moving closer by one measured step.

Mahone let out a low laugh filled with pleasure. "Do not fuck with me." He pictured Sarah in his head, how she tried to stand up to him, turn it around on him, remind him of how Sophie had made a fool out of him.

His smile turned into a lip-curling snarl. In a quick, sudden movement, he pushed all of his weight down into the heel of his foot. The cat under his shoe cried wildly until it was silenced forever. The crunch it made sounded like the snapping of dry twigs. The mother hissed and retreated, the strong kittens following her back into the long grass.

Mahone lifted his foot, took a few steps to the side, and scraped the bits of skull and cat brains from the bottom of his shoe onto the asphalt. He slapped his hands together, to free his skin from any spots of dirt, and returned to his car.

CHAPTER 31

J ane walked with the officers to where she and Tiffany had found the body.

"This was the first time we've explored these woods," she said to Sergeant Thorne. "We thought it'd be a nice walk; we were going to pick wildflowers." Jane covered her lips with her hands to try and keep them from trembling.

"It's okay, go on." Thorne put a hand on her shoulder.

"She ran ahead, I shouted after her, told her to slow down but the next thing I knew, she was gone. I ran after her. She could only have been twenty metres ahead, it should have been easy to catch up with her, but it was like she just disappeared." Jane put her face into her hands. "Then I saw it, and I knew she had gone in there."

"Saw what, Mrs. Stanford?" Sergeant Thorne and the woman officer he was with were talking nice, but Jane could see in their eyes that they were desperate to see the body.

The blue flashing lights of the arriving police cars were only just visible through the rows of trees. Matthew was back at home looking after Tiffany, he hadn't wanted Jane to go back into the woods, but he didn't know where it was to take the officers in there himself. He'd have to talk to the other police and tell them where they were. Thorne didn't want to hang around for them, Jane sensed.

"Here, it's easier to show you."

Jane took them down the dry dirt path. It meandered through the trees; bunches of hostile nettles and thorny brambles sprouted around them. Jane wanted to point out to the officers how the number of hostile plants increased the closer they got to the old reservoir, like it was nature's warning.

"Mrs. Stanford, we're going off path here," the woman officer said – Ruth Langford, if Jane had remembered that right.

"Yes, the path is swallowed by the overgrowth, but I knew that Tiffany had come this way because of that." Jane pointed into the woods where they were walking.

A wall of intertwining thorn bushes, thistles, bracken, briar, and brambles stood more than six feet tall. The wall seemed to go on for miles before curling round.

"The trees get really dense the closer you get to it, it's not easy," Jane said, weaving between two trees.

Thorne and Langford followed behind her. Jane heard grunts of effort from Sergeant Thorne, though not much from Ruth, whose slim figure seemed to be able to move through the trees with ease. There was something in Thorne's face that Jane couldn't quite put her finger on. Was he scared?

"Are you okay, Sergeant Thorne?" Jane asked. Officer Langford turned back to look at him, and Jane could see concern on her face as well.

"Fine, let's just keep moving," Thorne replied, waving a hand for them to push on.

Officer Langford looked at Jane and flashed her a smile.

"How did you get through? It looks to be completely overgrown," Sergeant Thorne asked.

"There's a gap, it looks to have been hacked at by something. Birds maybe, at first, and then people." Jane reached the wall of thorns and moved round until she got to the hole. "Here," she said, and moved through it, all the time mentally preparing herself for what she knew she was going to see on the other side.

They all got through, though Sergeant Thorne had to smash a few branches here and there to allow room for his broad frame, and once they were all in, Jane pointed to where Alfie Weeds lay.

Even stood far enough away that she couldn't make out the look on the young boy's mangled face, she could see it in her mind's eye, and that was enough to set her off crying again. All Jane wanted to do was be at home with her husband and daughter. Curled up on the sofa watching Tom and Jerry cartoons and drinking hot chocolate, without a care in the world, enjoying each other and talking about what the future held for them. She started sobbing, and almost screamed when Sergeant Thorne grabbed her by the hands.

"Mrs. Standford, thank you for bringing us here. I know how hard it was for you. I'm going to ask Officer Langford here to take you back home, okay? She'll take a statement from you and Tiffany."

Jane couldn't believe how much her hand was shaking, and when she looked down, she realised it wasn't her, it was Thorne. "I don't think Tiffany will be up to it," Jane said.

"I know, but if she could try her best, I know it's difficult, I do. But it would really help us out a lot if we got statements from the both of you."

Jane nodded. "Okay. Thank you." She paused and then said, "Have you been here before, Sergeant Thorne?"

His hand moved from hers. His eyes fell to the ground at his feet. She didn't think he was going to reply; she looked at

Ruth, who kept her face still. Jane had started to turn to leave, when Officer Thorne said: "Once. A long time ago."

The way he said it did not fill her with confidence.

CHAPTER 32

The back-up officers had arrived and were running yellow tape all the way around the suspected murder site. Tony watched as Ruth took Jane Stanford back home and felt relieved it wasn't up to him to do that.

He looked down at his hand and saw it shaking. He gripped it with his other and rubbed it. It had been so long since he had last seen this place. The police officers, the yellow crime scene tape; it brought it all back. All of a sudden, he was eighteen years old again, back when they were looking for Sophie Rose and all they found were pools of her blood. He wanted to throw up. His stomach twisted into knots and he was sure he was going to pass out or have a fucking heart attack.

He closed his eyes and took three deep breaths until his head stopped swimming. His heartbeat slowed and the feeling that he was going into cardiac arrest passed. The nausea went with it.

He opened his eyes and focused on the job at hand. He wanted to find out what had happened to Alfie Weeds and put the town's mind at rest. The thought of something like this happening would shatter a small town like Wymere; at least if they could close this case, let everyone grieve, there would be chance for everyone to move on. Accept it as just one of those awful things that happens in any place every once in a while, no matter how small the town. They could learn from it, then move on.

Tony walked down into the crater. The mud at the bottom was dry and cracked.

He took in the surroundings. The reservoir was big, but not huge. He remembered the old story he'd been told as a kid, that this was once considered a gateway to hell, where all of the world's evil came from. Whoever lived in Wymere hundreds of years ago must have really believed that was true; toward the back of the crater was where they dug a channel that connected this crater to the Merc River, so it filled with water, creating the reservoir that had sat in these woods for centuries.

The earth surrounding the crater was desolate; no life grew within the wall of thorns. The sky was clear and open above him. Tony thought about how in the middle of the day the sun would sit above it, drying up all the water that had lain there for hundreds of years.

The tree that grew from the mound where the forensic team had started work looked bone white. How it was still standing was a mystery. It looked as though it had died many years ago. It had looked that way eighteen years ago when Tony was last here, only, it hadn't looked quite so... *menacing* was the word Tony thought of then, but he didn't know why.

Tony got to the officers clad in white overalls crouched down by the boy.

"Is it him?" Tony said. He couldn't see the boy, only his shoes. The red shoes with big yellow smiley faces stuck on the sides. The faces were smiling, but drops of dried blood spotted them.

One of the forensic officers stood, giving Tony his first

glance of the boy's face. His first reaction was to hurl. Acidic vomit shot up his throat and filled his mouth. A hot flush rose to his cheeks, and for a second the world went dark and flashes of white sparkles filled his vision like sparklers on Bonfire night.

"You okay, Tony?" Officer Bailey said. "You don't look so good."

"What... what the fuck happened to him?" Tony covered his mouth with his forearm and forced out the words. They sounded husky and raw.

"We don't know. Not without further examination. It looks like his throat was cut, that much is obvious from the great big gaping slit in his neck."

"Easy," Tony said.

"Sorry, I remove myself from the emotional side of things, I have to, otherwise I wouldn't be able to get through the day. I forget that other people don't have the same cut off switch in their heads," Bailey chortled.

Tony twirled his finger around, gesturing for the officer to get on with it.

"Sure, as for what has caused the shrinking and creasing of his skin, I have no idea. It's like every ounce of moisture has been sucked out of him. I'll be honest, I've been doing this work for over twenty years and I've never seen anything like it. He kinda looks like, you know when you're in the bath too long and your hands go all wrinkly, like that, but bone dry."

Tony raised a hand and closed his eyes in a grimace.

"Sorry, that switch again. Take a look, see what you think."

Tony took a deep breath. The initial shock had passed and, although it was awful, he felt he could get closer and inspect the boy. He couldn't call him Alfie yet, not until he was sure. He crouched down. It was Alfie's clothes, the red trainers, the shorts, and the blue polo shirt. Although, it looked more of a reddish-brown than blue now. His skin had turned a dark grey, almost black in the wrinkles that were more like grooves, they were that deep. The boy's eyes were still in their sockets, looking up blankly. Tony looked up as if there was something up there the boy had noticed that he hadn't. All he could see was that dead tree looming over them, its dead branches reaching out like the hands of a corpse.

"Is it normal for the skin to blacken this quick?" Tony asked, getting back to his feet.

Bailey shook his head. "Nope, there are a lot of different contributing factors when it comes to the decay of a body, temperature is one of them. With this heat, it would have sped up the decaying process, as well as all of the bugs that are around here." As he spoke, a fly crawled out of Alfie's mouth and went back in through his nostril. "But to this extent, I don't think so."

"Getting a positive ID is going to be difficult," Tony said.

Officer Bailey looked at him with a raised eyebrow. "Know of any other kids this age going missing lately?"

Tony nodded, conceding that this was of course Alfie Weeds, but he had to do things by the book. "How long until we can get him back to the mortuary for examination?"

"We want as much time as we can have with the scene whilst there's a bit of daylight left. Make sure we get every piece of evidence. Last thing we want is for the case to crumble because we weren't thorough enough on the scene. And in a place like this, evidence can be easily missed."

Tony looked around. "I don't think it'll be filling with water again anytime soon."

Bailey weighed his head from side to side. "I dunno. A little bit of rain is all it takes. If that river starts to swell and the water comes gushing through that channel at the back there, this place will fill up pretty damn quick."

"Well, you better crack on then."

Bailey crouched back down and started placing yellow

cards with numbers in different areas; the accompanying officer took photos of every area from every angle.

"Thanks. Let me know when you're done. We need to get this boy IDed ASAP. There's a grieving mother that needs to be told that we found her boy."

CHAPTER 33

As Alan walked around the empty woods, the day was still light, but the sky was turning a deep blue as night drew near. If he had arrived fifteen minutes earlier, he would have seen Tony and Ruth jumping into their car and flooring it out of the park, heading east toward the two cottages on New Road.

When he got there, he walked through dry patches of grass where all the cars had been parked, the cars owned by those out in the woods searching for little Alfie Weeds. The cars were gone but their tyre tracks were scored in the earth; the litter from their lunches blew across the ground in the soft breeze. Alan bent to pick one up, but when he grabbed it and stood up, it was as if the sandwich and sweet wrappers had multiplied. He dropped the scrap of plastic wrap he had in his hand to the ground, not seeing the point in the little act of environmentalism he had attempted.

Once he got deep in the woods, the shade cast down from the trees meant it was harder to find the knife than Alan had expected, but still he laboured on, spreading wide overgrown weeds and lifting rotten logs and tree branches that had snapped off one winter in a wild wind. Sweat poured down his face; a bead reached the end of his nose and dropped down on the ground. He watched it fall, and, as if it were pointing it out to him, it landed on the engraved handle of his wooden penknife.

To the greatest dad in the world. Love Freddie x

"Yes!" Alan almost shouted it. "Got you, you sono-fabitch!" He laughed and kissed the penknife. Then wiped it to get off the dry bits of leaf, twigs and whatever the hell else was on it. He put the knife into his pocket, double, then triple checked it had gone in this time and not fallen back into the overgrowth.

He started walking away when a whisper tickled the hairs in his ears. He didn't know what it said, but it spoke to him and only him.

"Hello?" he said to no one.

The whisper came back, and now his arms broke out into gooseflesh. His bottom lip quivered and suddenly he felt that he wasn't alone. It filled him with a fear so deep and pure that his bowels turned to water; his stomach sloshed and twisted around itself. He needed to puke, cry, shit; he needed to run and get away from this place.

The sweat that had been pouring out of him continued to come but he felt a coldness, a coldness he hadn't felt before and would never feel again.

"Who are you?" he said to the voice that whispered noth-ings in his ear that were far from sweet. The voice had a malig-nancy that burrowed into his mind, then further, into his soul.

"I'll do what you want," he began to sob. "Please don't hurt me."

He was stood in a half run, his front leg bent at the knee in an awkward lunge, for a time, hours in fact, but he wasn't aware. It was a stress position that could have been used for torture; however, Alan stood like that without feeling a single pull of a muscle, a creak of a tendon or an ache in his knees. All he felt was an engulfing chill, and the sensation of a cold, dead hand gripping his mind from the inside. He looked like a sprinter on the blocks waiting for the pistol. But Alan Houghton wouldn't be running anywhere, not of his own free will. Not tonight. Tonight, he was someone else's plaything, a puppet with a new master. And he would be made to do terrible things.

The last whisper came; the words made no sense, but the laughter was unmistakable. Alan's tears stopped and he stood up straight, his face blank and free from emotion. Inside his head was only black.

CHAPTER 34

Jenny sat at the kitchen table. She looked up at the clock on the wall above the back door, acknowledged that it read 10:30 p.m., then looked down at her watch to double check. She glanced over to the kitchen side where the pie she had spent all day making sat with one slice taken out of it. She hadn't eaten any, but Freddie had to eat, and he was starved. She made him wait until nine but, any longer than that and he was apt to call child line. She made him a promise that he could stay up playing that damned video game until his father came home, seeing as how Alan had promised he would play it with him. Looking at the time now, she wished she hadn't made that deal.

"At least it's the summer holidays," she said out loud, surprising herself at the sound of her own voice. "No school to get up for in the morning."

She stood and put the pie back in the oven with the temperature on low in a feeble attempt to keep it warm. Not that it would be good now, a pie was best when it was piping hot and fresh from the oven, not cooked, then left on the side, cut open so all the juices ran out of it, then put back in to keep warmish. The gravy congealed and you got that awful skin on top. Jenny shuddered at the thought of it; her own appetite had faded away like an old thing long forgotten.

She removed the pinafore and pinched her blouse with two fingers. She wafted it and felt the blessed relief of cool air over her breasts. It was hot as hell outside, and had been for the entire twenty-four hours of the day, and she'd spent most of it in the pokey kitchen with the oven going full blast. And for what? Alan was a good man but sometimes his simple mind ran away with him and he forgot what the hell he was doing.

Just then Jenny saw the flash of headlights come down the street. She waited; her jaw jutted to one side in growing frustration. The head lights entered the driveway.

Knowing that he was home released something inside of her, and for the first time that night she realised what it was. She had grown nervous; that was why her appetite had disappeared, that was why she had sat at the kitchen table for hours watching the clock go by instead of sticking on the TV and finishing off that half a bottle of white wine that was in the fridge. With what had happened to that poor Weeds boy, she had been hit with the strangest feeling that something bad was going to happen. Alan might be half simple, but he was very rarely this late home without letting her know.

She went back into the kitchen and got two plates out, then pumped the temperature of the oven up to get the insides of the pie steaming hot. She'd spent a lot of time making that damn thing, so she was going to make damn sure that Alan enjoyed it.

The front door opened and closed.

"What the hell sort of time do you call this?" Jenny walked to the door that joined the kitchen and the living room, put her hands on her hips and looked at him with an eyebrow raised in a teacherly 'you're in trouble' fashion.

Alan just stood in the room, the pen knife in his hand.

"Oh good, you found it then." She walked toward him and, when she got close, she could feel the coldness coming from him. "Alan?" she said and put her hands on his shoulders. "You feel cold, what's happened?" She began to feel him up and down; his arms and chest were stone cold. She hugged him and squeezed tight.

"Alan," she said, her voice sounding frantic now, "talk to me."

Alan's eyes met hers, but she felt as though he were looking straight through her, like she was a stranger to him.

"I don't know what's gone on, but you come in and sit down. I'll get you a piece of this hot pie; that will warm you up." Jenny took Alan to the sofa and gestured for him to sit. She ran back into the kitchen, not noticing that Alan hadn't sat, he only stood there, fidgeting with the penknife in his hand.

Jenny got the pie out of the oven. She sucked her teeth in pain; in her haste to get the dish from the oven, she'd not folded the kitchen towel enough, burning her fingers on the dish. She grabbed the big knife from the wooden block by the sink and cut a big piece. Steam rose from the pastry crust, filling her nose with the rich smell of gravy and beef.

"Dad!" She heard Freddie's faint shout from upstairs. "Come up and watch me on this game, you've been gone ages."

Jenny doubted her husband would be running upstairs to play video games. She felt panicked and if she was honest with herself, downright frightened. She'd never seen her husband like this, never in their twenty-two years together.

She plated up the pie and grabbed a knife and fork from the drawer, knocking it shut with her hip.

145

When she got to the living room door, she stood still, frozen to the spot. Her mind muddled in a daze of confusion. Alan wasn't there, but he was in no fit state to –

Jenny's thoughts were cut off dead at the sound of a screech, screaming bloody murder from upstairs. Many years ago, when Freddie was just six years old, he caught his fingers in the boot of the car. Jenny hadn't seen him creep up beside her and she had slammed it down with all her might because of the rusty hinges. He was lucky to keep those fingers, the doctor said. The scream he had emitted then was the same scream she was hearing now.

The plate full of pie and steaming gravy tumbled from her hand, spilling to the floor. She bolted toward the stairs before a single dot of gravy managed to spray her.

She took the steps two at a time, her heart thundering along with every step.

When she reached Freddie's bedroom door, she gasped and flung a hand up to cover her mouth, stifling the immediate scream that flew up her throat.

The sound of shooting guns and army tanks came from the TV, the game playing along idly now no one was controlling the character on screen. Her son's lifeless body was strewn across Alan's lap. His eyes had come back to him now. They weren't dazed anymore, they were confused. Blood was everywhere, streaked across Freddie's gaming chair, spattered on the TV. Alan's face was smeared with red.

"I don't know what I did." Alan began sobbing. "I don't know what I did!" he screamed.

Jenny dropped to her knees, both hands clasped at either side of her face. She looked at Freddie, his mouth agape, full of blood, his hands covered in cuts. The pool of blood on the carpet kept growing. Something twirled from Freddie's throat that looked like a wisp of green smoke. It twirled up in the air and drifted out the open window.

She looked back at Alan and saw the pen knife trembling in his hand. The words *To the greatest dad in the world, love Freddie x* were crusted in blood.

CHAPTER 35

Tony felt the first chill in the air that night at 11:00 p.m. It wasn't the temperature, even though the sun had long since gone down and the mercury in the thermometer had dropped by half. He didn't know where the chill came from, but when he rubbed his hand along his forearm, he could feel the bumps of gooseflesh through his thin shirt sleeve. He had a horrible feeling that something bad had happened, but he didn't believe in superstitious bullshit like that, so shook it off and drank a mouthful of the barely-warm coffee Ruth had brought over in her flask.

He was resting against a tree, watching as the forensic team finished up their night's work. They had brought out some site lights when the sun went down, and now worked under a bright white glow beneath that horrific tree that Tony could not take his eyes off. What sort of tree was that, willow? Birch? It could have been birch; the roots that protruded from the mound of earth looked white, and he was sure he'd seen that birch wood was whiter than any other. Though he could just be making that shit up. It'd been a long day and he felt his mind had taken too much crap for one day. Seeing that boy like that, all wrinkled and dried out like he'd had the life sucked out of him. It was a lot to take in.

He sipped the coffee again and winced. "Fuck this," he said and threw the contents of his cup to the ground.

"Sorry it's not a Starbucks." Ruth appeared from the tree line to his right.

"Any news?" Tony said, putting the cup down on the ground. His back ached from being stood for so long.

Ruth shook her head slowly. "Not really. They're just about done now; the body will be moved and taken to the hospital. They'll tent the area overnight to keep some of the elements out of it, then a team will come back at first light to finish off."

"We ready to tell Caroline Weeds?"

"The lab will have a definite answer in the morning, but we can safely assume the boy is Alfie Weeds. Do you think we should go now, or wait till morning?"

Tony took a deep breath. "Now. If I know Caroline as well as I think I do, she ain't sleeping tonight. She's sat by the phone waiting for it to ring. Waiting for news on her boy."

Ruth put her hands to her hips. "You don't have to do this, you know; we can send someone else to talk to her."

"No," Tony said, cutting Ruth off. "People know me in this town. I grew up with most of 'em. It's only right I do it. I just can't believe it's something I've got to do." He shook his head as if still struggling to believe all that had happened.

"Come on, let's go. I'll come as well. It looks to me like you might need someone to support *you* whilst you're supporting others."

"You're a good friend, Ruth."

"You know it," Ruth said with a wink.

As they began to walk back, Tony's walkie burst into life.

149

The voice on the other end sounded calm, but with a hint of a panic bubbling underneath.

"Sergeant Thorne, copy?"

"Copy, this is Sergeant Thorne." Tony and Ruth made eyes at each other. He felt his skin prickle again and knew this was not going to be good.

"We've had a call from Jenny Houghton, it's her husband."

Shit, Tony thought, *something's happened to Alan.* What sick fucker would hurt Alan?

"What's wrong with him, is he okay?" Tony said into the walkie. He walked faster now, desperate to get back to the car.

The radio crackled, muffling the response.

"What's happened, do you copy?" Tony shouted into the walkie; the car was in sight now.

"He's stabbed his son."

———

As TONY's car came to a skidding halt on the quiet street where Alan and Jenny Houghton's modest semi-detached house sat, the armed police had already stormed the house.

"Killed his son?" Ruth had said when they were halfway there.

Tony shook his head. He began talking fast, trying to piece it all together like it was a solvable puzzle, he just needed to lay all the pieces out. "How can this happen?" he said. "First Gareth Weeds, the weakest, most timid man I've ever known murders his son, leaves him to rot in the summer heat in a dried-up old reservoir, and now Alan Houghton, a family man who has never so much as raised his voice, stabs his son whilst he's playing video games? It doesn't fit. These people aren't capable of this, something's going on."

"Let's deal with what we've got first. Work it out later." Ruth said.

They jumped out of the car and waited outside until an armed officer shouted *clear*. Tony felt a knot in his stomach, a knot formed of anxiety and desperation to get in there. He had to see it with his own eyes; only then could he believe it.

An officer came out of the house, pushing a screaming woman out against her will. It took a moment for Tony to realise it was Jenny. She looked like someone ten years older; her face was drenched in heartache. It made a pain stab in Tony's chest and a lump formed in his throat.

"Clear!" came the shout. As soon as it was uttered, Tony was in the house, running toward the sound of an officer screaming orders of, "Lay down on the ground, hands over your head."

Tony got to the upstairs bedroom. An officer stood outside, his gun strapped to his chest and a hand held over his face in shock. Tony pushed past him and stood in the threshold.

He saw the boy, young Freddie Houghton, on the floor in a puddle of blood. His throat had been slit from ear to ear. The amount of blood was shocking; a smell of copper filled the air and reminded Tony of the town's abattoir. On the floor, laid face-down, crying into the blood-soaked carpet, was Alan Houghton.

"It wasn't me, I don't remember," he sobbed. An officer lifted him up. He got to his feet and looked at Tony, half of his face red with his son's blood. "I don't remember. I didn't do it."

Tony had nothing to say. He saw the knife on the floor, the knife Alan had lost in the woods. Like Gareth Weeds, his cries of confusion and declarations of innocence seemed sincere, almost believable, were it not for the evidence. Even so, Tony's brain racked itself looking for an answer that would explain all of this.

Tony watched as Alan looked down at the lifeless body of his son. As he was hauled away, he screamed, "Noooooo!" at the top of his lungs. "Freddieeee! Noooooo!"

CHAPTER 36

They weren't going to get anything out of Alan that night. If he wasn't screaming, he was sat sobbing, muttering confused words to himself. Tony looked through the peephole of the cell Alan was kept in and watched as the big man curled up onto the holding cell bed; he made it look even smaller than it was with his big frame. His incoherent muttering made Tony shudder.

"Jenny is ready to talk, Tony," Ruth said from behind him.

"Good. Let's find out what the hell happened tonight."

Tony and Ruth sat opposite Jenny at the interview table. She had stopped crying, but now there was a vacant look on her face, void of expression or feeling.

"How you doing, Jenny?" Ruth asked.

Jenny said nothing. She was fiddling with a plastic cup full of water in front of her, twirling it round and round; wet rings of condensation covered the tabletop.

"Tell us what happened, Jenny," Tony said. "As best you can. You have any idea –"

"Do I have any idea why my husband, my soft, warm, lovable husband, would come home and murder our son? Is that what you're going to ask me, Sergeant Thorne?" The words came out in a monotonous drone. Jenny's eyes never left the plastic cup as it twirled round and round on the desk.

Tony straightened his shirt collar, felt a sudden choking sensation clawing at his throat. His head was cloudy with emotion, tiredness, confusion. It was the confusion that was the worst.

"I know it's hard, but can you tell us what happened?"

Jenny's face didn't change, Tony was about to repeat himself, thinking that she hadn't heard. Then she nodded and started talking.

"He went back to the woods. He'd been out looking for Alfie Weeds the night before with all the other volunteers, because that's the kind of guy Alan is. He wanted to help whenever he could, and most of the time he did. He'd lost his pen knife. He loved going fishing in the river Mere, he liked to camp and always moaned he didn't have a good enough knife for what he needed. Freddie saved up his pocket money and got that one. It was special; Alan loved that knife more than anything else he owned. He said he'd be half an hour, he wasn't going to spend all night, but he knew it would upset Freddie if he'd lost it, so he went. It was over three hours before he came back."

"Three hours, that's a long time. What was he doing?"

Jenny gave Tony a sharp look. "I don't know; plotting on how to kill my boy, it looks like. I hate those damn woods, there's something wrong with them, something that's just plain bad. When he came back, he was cold."

"Cold? How so? He say something?"

"Not his demeanour, his touch. His skin was as cold as ice. I spoke to him and he wouldn't respond; I nearly phoned an ambulance right then because I could see something was wrong in his eyes. It wasn't Alan behind them eyes. They were like dark pits; the longer I looked, the deeper they went, and it scared me to death."

It wasn't Alan behind them eyes. Tony thought on that; it was the first thing that made sense. But what was this, a case of the body snatchers? Aliens from outer space taking over people's body's and killing their kids? It didn't make sense and yet, someone or *something* else controlling Alan seemed like the only logical explanation.

"I went to go get him some hot pie, hoping to warm him up and bring him round. It took me a while to plate it up, get it right for him. As I was walking through the door to bring it to him, I heard Freddie screaming. by the time I got upstairs, it was too late. I found Alan on the floor with Freddie in his arms. Blood was pouring from his neck and his mouth." Jenny put a hand over her mouth and began to cry.

"Anything else you can think of that we should know?"

Jenny shrugged. "That's about it, Sergeant. That was the end of my boy's life. I did see something come out of his mouth."

She said that last part as though she were talking to herself.

"What did you see?" Tony said, leaning in.

Jenny sniffed and wiped her nose with her sleeve. She stared blankly into space, looking at nothing in particular. A thin smile spread across her face. "I go to church every Sunday. Father Thomas talks about how when we die, our soul goes up into heaven, to be received and welcomed by God. I'm not sure what it was, but I like to believe that the wisp of green smoke I saw coming out of my boy's mouth was his soul, on its way to heaven."

CHAPTER 37

By the time Tony got into his car heading for home, it was gone three a.m. Another officer had gone to tell Caroline about the discovery in the woods. She had taken it as expected. Lots of tears, lots of questions. She, too, couldn't understand why Gareth would hurt their son. To slit his throat as if he were slaughtering a pig.

Tony wished he were there to tell her, although he supposed it was more for his sake than for hers. When someone lost a loved one, he liked to be there to give them support, to help give them closure, no matter how awful the scenario, because it was something he never got. He had to live knowing that Sophie Rose was buried somewhere in those woods; he may have even stepped over her grave last night whilst looking for Alfie. The thought was a disturbing one.

He pulled up outside his house, the grass was still dying despite the watering he had given it. There had been a letter from the local council, telling residents that a hosepipe ban was in place due to the lack of rainwater; the reservoirs were drying up and the rivers were running low. Now he'd seen it for himself, he wouldn't use the hosepipe again. Instead, he'd just watch the grass burn.

He walked across his garden to the front steps. The big moon in the sky helped light the way; it also helped illuminate the giant dog turd in the middle of the lawn, sparing him from having to pick dog shit out from the tread of shoes at three a.m.

When he walked through the front door, he saw the living room light was on. The TV glowed in the far corner; the sound was muted and an old re-run of Stephen King's *Salem's Lot* played, showing vampires lurking in the shadows of a small unsuspecting town.

He smelt the alcohol before he saw it. Sarah was passed out on the sofa; a bottle of wine and an empty bottle of Gin laid on the table like fallen soldiers. The glass was still in Sarah's hand. He bent down low and took it from her. He was surprised, and saddened, by how tight her grip was on the glass. He placed it down and Sarah stirred.

"Sarah," he said, shaking her gently, "you need to get into bed."

Sarah flung a hand at him, no anger or malice in it, just a drunk wanting to be left alone.

"Come on, let's get you up." Tony put his hands under her arm pits and raised her to her feet. Her head lolled before she finally woke and realised what was happening.

"Tony? Isss that you?" She was slurring. Her eyes were half open and her legs didn't seem to be able to co-operate with her thoughts.

"Yes, it's me. I'm taking you to bed."

"Mahone's a fu-fucking bastard."

Tony screwed up his face and almost laughed. She was right, Mahone was a bastard, but why Sarah thought so, he didn't know. He put it down to a drunken dream. "I know darling, I know he is."

Sarah, her legs now managing to bear most of her wait and propel her toward the stairs, kept on muttering quietly, "Bastard. Bastard. Bastard." Like it was some mantra. "His a pig!"

Tony said nothing, only guided Sarah until they reached the bed. He stripped off her trousers and t-shirt, was going to put her in her PJs, but decided against it. The bedroom was hot as hell, it would only dehydrate her more and make the hangover tomorrow more severe.

He watched as she flopped into bed, her head hitting the pillow, drool dripping from her lips. She belched from one end and then farted from the other. Tony thought she only needed to piss herself now for the final indignity.

The worst part of it was that *he* had done this to her. He had married her because he'd fallen into a place where he thought it was the best thing to do. It was a small town and she was nice and she loved him. When someone loves you, it's hard to ignore it, especially when you're so alone. He had been sure that he was going to marry Sophie, and when she was taken, his whole future had died with her.

None of it was fair on Sarah, she was a good woman whose only aspirations in life were to get married and have a family. She didn't need a fancy job, a flashy car and big house; she just wanted a family that she could love. Tony had taken that chance away from her and now they were stuck in a loveless marriage. Tony knew that Sarah still loved him. Why? He didn't know, and didn't think he ever would. He hoped that she would leave him, kick him out, tell him where to go, because he sure as shit didn't have the guts to break it off. It was easier to get dumped than do the dumping.

The mention of Mahone made Tony think of the day of the fete, the little interaction he'd had with him and the mayor. Smug sonofabitch brought up the fact that Tony had been a suspect in Sophie's murder. Tony thought Mahone should have been on that list too, Mahone was always watching them when they were together. He was more than ten years older and yet, it was clear he was in love with Sophie Rose. The fact that Sophie barely knew who he was probably infuriated the arrogant bastard. Then, seeing her all over Tony, madly in love, that could have tipped him over the edge, made him mad with jealousy.

"To-neee," Sarah moaned from the bed.

Tony removed his shirt and trousers, grabbed two glasses of water, and placed one beside Sarah. He got in bed and kissed her forehead.

"I'm sorry," he said. "I'm sorry for everything."

Sarah squirmed for a moment, as if she had laid on something uncomfortable. "I love you," she said when she settled. "I did it because I love you."

Tony watched Sarah sleep, the deep, comatose sleep of an alcoholic. He moved onto his back, stared at the ceiling, and thought of how two families had been destroyed, people who had made their homes and their lives together, brought a child into the world just to have it torn apart, their lives to be changed forever.

Then he thought of Sophie Rose, pictured how she would have looked if she were here now, what their kids would have looked like, and how different life would have been. He let himself cry for a moment; it felt alien because he never cried. Couldn't remember the last time he had. He wasn't sure whether it was because of everything he had seen in the past two days or whether it was because he was realising just how unhappy he really was and had no one to tell. How his unhappiness had ruined someone else's chance of being happy, a disease that spread like a black shadow. Maybe it was because of everything.

When the bad thoughts eased, he was left with the images of Alfie Weeds in that dry reservoir, beneath that dead tree that looked as if it were made of bone instead of wood. He reached out and held Sarah in a reflex action of fear.

She murmured at his touch but didn't wake.

He laid there with an unshakable sense of dread that stuck in his gut and made acid rise up his throat. He laid like that for a long time.

Chapter 38

Despite the heaviness in her eyes and the dullness in her brain that came from working twelve-hour shifts for a boss that, quite frankly, scared the life out of her, Lucy got up an extra hour early the next day. She was due at work for eight, so she got up at six, made a coffee (with an extra spoonful of coffee), and opened her laptop. The business card she was given whilst searching for Alfie Weeds was on the table, with the contact details for the officer in charge of the investigation.

You don't want to end up like Laura Kelly.

It was the warning Helen had given her when she played the CCTV footage of Lucy spying on Mahone. Helen obviously took no notice of him coming out of that equipment storage room. Maybe she knew what he got up to in there and was more than happy to turn a blind eye? Well, Lucy wasn't.

She searched the name *Laura Kelly*. A few hits came up on Facebook and Instagram, but none seemed to match up. She clicked away from the social media hits and scrolled down the search results.

Nothing.

She deleted *Laura Kelly* and instead typed *Wymere, Hill Top Psychiatric Hospital.* Lucy scrolled past the links that led to the facility's websites and several newspaper headings of how Dr. Mahone had transformed a rundown, underfunded facility into a haven for those with severe mental disabilities and those that suffered from psychological conditions that could make them a danger to society (there was no mention of the convicted criminals in there). The results went on to explain how the hospital had been known in the past for performing methods and procedures from the dark ages, all hidden from public knowledge behind their tightly closed doors.

There were plaudits laid bare for all to see. Mahone was a God amongst men, his work for the community kept him in high regard, and his contribution to those less fortunate was worthy of nothing less than a knighthood and a Nobel prize. The last statement was a direct quote from the editor of the Wymere Gazette.

"Why not throw in a pride of Britain while we're at it?" Lucy said to herself.

She sipped her coffee and began mindlessly scrolling down when she saw, buried away farther down than anyone else would ever bother to go, an article of a court case that was brought against a "Doctor," no name mentioned – at Hill Top Psychiatric Hospital.

Lucy put the coffee down and sat upright, uncrossed her legs, and let her bare feet touch down on the worn-out pile of the carpet. She clicked the link. The article told briefly about the case, then stated that the case was thrown out before it began. The accuser who had taken the hospital and its doctor to court failed to show. As the accuser was standing alone in their accusation, the case was thrown out and the details kept hidden under a cloak of non-disclosure agreements. The reporter hinted that the case would possibly have been settled out of court, in private, to save any doctors, or the facility itself, any further embarrassment.

It mentioned no names, but Lucy didn't need many guesses to figure out who those involved were.

She looked at the card with the police officer's details. "Sergeant Thorne," Lucy read aloud. She wondered if he could be trusted. If Mahone was running an illegal drug scandal, and had a lot of the town's authorities in his pocket like Tammy suggested, then who was to say Thorne wasn't one of them? Lucy took a deep breath, closed her eyes, and listened to what her heart said. It said *call*.

The phone rang several times before it was answered.

"Hello, Wymere Police Station," a female officer said, quite perkily for so early in the morning, Lucy thought.

"Oh, hi," Lucy said, caught off guard that a woman answered. "I was trying to reach Sergeant Thorne?"

"This is his office but he's not in until later today. Is it anything I can help you with?"

Lucy paused, wondering how much to give this officer. "Do you work closely with Sergeant Thorne?"

"Every day."

That was good enough for Lucy. "Okay. I work at Hilltop Psychiatric Hospital. I'm calling about suspicious activity regarding one of the doctors there. I believe they are involved in some sort of illegal drug activity? I believe the patients are being abused, treated like guinea pigs."

There was silence on the other end. Then finally: "Let me take some details, I'll pass it on to Sergeant Thorne when he gets in and he'll be in touch."

Lucy gave the officer all the details she had, including all of her suspicions and reasoning. After, the officer thanked her for her call and told her they'd get back to her.

"Thank you, Officer."

"No problem."

Lucy drank her coffee and got ready for work.

CHAPTER 39

J ane had barely slept. The digital clock on her bedside
table flashed 07:03 and she knew she had to get up. Last
night, she had watched that clock until it turned to 03:00
a.m., then at some point, a few minutes after, she fell asleep.

She dreamt of that place, that awful reservoir with the
dead tree. She saw Alfie's face, dried out and wrinkled – bugs
crawling up his nose and coming out of his mouth. Maggots
writhing with pleasure in his half-eaten eyeballs. In the dream,
she hadn't been able to look away; she was staring down at
him, looking at his decomposing body through tear-filled eyes
that blurred her vision, and for a moment, it made it look as
though he was moving.

There were no noises in her dream; no birds sang and no
wind blew. It was a dead place. This was a place where the
dead ruled. She looked up at the tree and felt her knees tremble
at the sight of it. It looked so much bigger than it did in real
life; it was daunting, hanging over her like a dark cloud, blot-
ting out the sun.

Her heart almost stopped when she looked back and saw

Alfie's head had turned to look back at her. She cried out and stepped back.

Help me, he said. *They're hurting me.* He got onto his front, his movements sharp and disjointed, like an old stop-motion film. His arms cracked as he forced them to the floor and dragged himself toward her. His head flopped and she heard the audible *pop* his vertebrae made as they snapped.

Jane staggered backward, desperate to get away, but no matter how far she went, he only crawled closer. Worms and maggots fell from his mouth as he spoke; bugs crawled from the holes in his skin and scurried through his hair. He was crying, taking in dry rasping breaths that sounded like choking. He reached for her with his clawed hands, stiff and cold from rigor mortis, after every movement he reached for her, always reaching.

Help me, please.

"No!" she screamed. "I can't, it's too late."

They won't stop.

"It's too late! You're dead!"

She's coming. They're all coming. When they come, you're all dead.

Alfie stood. Jane had frozen to the spot; she was sobbing so hard that snot hung from her nose and covered her top lip. Her heart turned cold, sure that she was about to die.

She watched Alfie stumble toward her with stiff legs unable to bend, his arms outstretched and his eyeless face drawn down in a look of deep desolation. His hand was inches from her face when she started screaming.

The clock was flashing 03:36 when she woke, and she watched it until it was time to get up.

JANE SPENT the morning in a foggy daze. She made breakfast for Matthew and Tiffany; they chose pancakes, so Jane whipped up a batch. Her mind was stuck on her dream and that poor boy's face. The way he looked at her through half-eaten eyeballs, the insects dropping from his mouth as if his insides were bursting with them. She burnt the first two pancakes before Matthew made a comment about her needing to get some sleep on a night.

Tiffany was quiet. She would normally be so full of joy on a morning, laughing and joking with Matthew, but that morning, she was just quiet. Jane wondered how much sleep she got. She'd talk to her, she'd decided, but first, she needed to speak to Mrs. Leadley.

After breakfast, she washed the dishes and Matthew took Tiffany into town for a few bags of plaster. He wanted to get all of the basement plastered in one day, one hell of an achievement if he did. She bet that he would do it, though; he was pretty determined when he put his mind to something.

Jane made the walk over to Mrs. Leadley's just after ten. She knocked on the door and expected to have to wait a few minutes to give Mrs. Leadley the time to waddle over to the door on that dislocated ankle, but the door opened only a matter of seconds after she knocked.

"Come in, dear," Mrs. Leadley said. Her face was dark, no sign of a smile on those dry, cracked lips.

Jane stepped in and the door closed behind her.

"I need to know," Jane said. "I need to know what the hell is going on in this town."

Mrs. Leadley jutted her jaw sideways, her teeth cracked together, or it could have been her mandible clicking out of joint. "You better come sit down then. This story isn't pretty."

CHAPTER 40

I t was seven a.m.; Tony was desperate to get to work to help try and find some answers to this completely fucked up situation. He had one hand on the front doorknob when he heard Sarah's laboured footsteps descending the stairs. He winced as if he'd stepped on a pin with no shoes on. Part of him wanted to just continue with what he was doing, open the door, jump in the car, and get to work. He didn't have the energy or the mental head space to have more arguments with Sarah. Not right now. Perhaps, not ever again. For her sake as much as his own.

He loosened his grip on the doorknob and turned to see her as she stepped into the kitchen.

"Morning," he said. "How's the head?"

Sarah grunted in response. Her hair was a shaggy mess; she scratched at the side of her head making it worse. The brief moment she actually looked toward him showed the features of her face all screwed up. Deep frown lines covered her forehead. Those lines were growing deeper lately, Tony had noticed. He put it down to the abundance of alcohol she'd been consuming.

"I'm heading out to work. We found the boy, Alfie Weeds."

Sarah stopped. She had run the tap and filled a glass with cool water and now just stood motionless over the sink. "Where was he?"

"In the lake."

Sarah took a sip, then, before she moved it away from her lips, she put it back and took a bigger, longer gulp. "Did you have to send in divers?"

Tony frowned for a second, then shook his head as realisation dawned on him. "No, because of the soaring temperatures and the nationwide drought, the reservoir's completely dry."

Sarah turned and looked at him, and those frown lines deepened once more. "Dry?"

"Evaporated, gone, empty. We found the boy laid on the bed of the reservoir beside a tree. They're confirming today, but we're pretty sure it's him. And..."

Sarah stepped forward rapidly, as if lunging toward him. "And what? What is it? What else did you find?"

Tony could see her hands were physically shaking but put it down to the alcohol leaving her blood stream. "Nothing. I probably shouldn't say, but people are going to find out soon. It'll be all over town by this afternoon." Tony took a breath. "There was another murder last night, another young boy. The Houghton boy, to be precise."

Sarah looked surprisingly relieved, Tony thought, then her face turned to horror, the horror that came across the face of any person when they found out a neighbour or friendly acquaintance had died. "That's awful, who on earth would hurt that poor boy? Do you think the incident with Gareth Weeds gave someone the idea?"

Tony shook his head. "It was Alan."

Now there was real, utter shock on Sarah's face. "What the fuck, Tony? This can't be happening."

"No hunt for the body this time though, he did it in the boy's room. I'm heading to the station now to interview him and get to the bottom of this because, Sarah, I got a funny feeling that something's not right. I don't know if it's the fucking heat or if someone's put something in the water, but something is driving people crazy out here. And I need to find out what it is."

Sarah nodded, drank the rest of her water, and went back to the sink to refill it. She looked out of the window and anger seemed to flash across her face.

"That bitch," Sarah snapped. She dropped the glass into the sink and marched over toward the front door. Tony touched a hand to her shoulder as she barged past him and swung the front door wide open.

"Maggie Colter! You get that damn dog off my lawn or I swear to God, I'll be stuffing rat poison into steaks and posting them through your letter box. If I step in one more giant dog shit, I'll do it," Sarah shouted.

Tony peered round the door frame and saw old Maggie Colter, struggling to pull her big chocolate Labrador from his front lawn. The Labrador, Dexter, Tony now remembered, was squatting over Tony's lawn with a long brown log hanging out of his arse.

"Mrs. Colter, we talked about this," Tony added, stepping outside.

"I know, Sergeant Thorne; I just can't control him. He's a big bugger y'know. I'll clean it up. I always do."

The tread on my shoes might not agree with you there, Tony thought but didn't say. He turned back to Sarah. "I'm heading off to work. They'll be finishing at the reservoir soon and I want to see what they've found."

Sarah had that look on her face again, that look of fear and anxiety.

"Okay," she said. She scowled toward Maggie Colter before stepping back inside.

CHAPTER 41

Lucy got to work fifteen minutes early. Her sore ears, that she had bathed in warm water last night and this morning, were a painful reminder not to be late again. After what her search had yielded that morning, she was desperate to find out more. She just hoped the police would do the same.

She'd looked for contact details in the local directory for Laura Kelly and found nothing. There was no Facebook page, Twitter, Instagram – who in this day and age didn't have some form of social media?! It was a red flag to Lucy, and made finding Laura Kelly all the more important. Lucy figured that Laura Kelly must know something, or had some sort of concrete evidence on Mahone. Only, for some reason, she'd lost her nerve at the last minute.

Lucy wasn't working with Doctor Mahone today, and that was a relief.

After helping with breakfast and clearing the pots, Lucy talked to some of the patients. Some of them had so many stories to tell, and told them so quickly, it was as if they were running out of time to tell them! Lucy found Gerald, her favourite person in Hill Top (although she'd never say something quite so unprofessional out loud), and sat with him in front of the TV. He was watching a re-run of Wheel of Fortune, and by the look of Bruce Forsyth's smooth face and brown hair, it looked to be an episode from the eighties.

"Hey, Gerald."

"Heya, Loo-see," Gerald said, smiling.

"Can I ask you something, Gerald?"

Gerald nodded enthusiastically, keeping his eyes on the TV.

"Can you remember, and it's okay if you don't, but can you remember a nurse called Laura Kelly? She left a while ago, six months or so, I think."

Gerald grabbed the remote from the arm of the chair, lifted it to the TV and hit pause. His head turned to look at Lucy, he looked her dead in the eye, and the smile that so often graced his face was gone.

"Stop," he said.

Lucy showed him a confused smile. "What do you mean?"

"Stop what you're doing. I like you, Lucy. I don't want you to go."

"Hey, I'm not going anywhere," Lucy reassured him and put a hand on his shoulder. He was tense, the muscles under his shirt tight.

"That's what Laura said, she was kind, like you. Then she –"

Gerald stopped talking, his eyes darted over Lucy's shoulder, and his brow creased in an expression of anger Lucy had never seen from him before.

Lucy turned to look at what he had seen and saw Mahone coming toward them.

"Gerald, so nice to see you. How are you doing today?" Mahone stood directly behind Gerald and placed both hands on his shoulders. Gerald slumped his head down and looked as if he was shaking with fear.

"Don't feel like talking today, huh?" Mahone laughed. "Used to be we couldn't shut you up." Mahone patted Gerald's head, ruffled his hair like one might do to a child, and moved away. "Lucy, my office, ten minutes."

"But I'm on the rota to help in here today –"Lucy started talking, then when she saw Mahone giving her a look that said *he wasn't asking, he was telling*, she shut her mouth. "Yes, doctor."

Mahone nodded and left.

Gerald started breathing heavily. "Laura told me she would help get *him* out of here. She saw what he was doing to those people back there, she said she had evidence, and she would use it. But she didn't! She just disappeared and left me here!"

Lucy put her hand on Gerald's hand and squeezed. "Calm down, Gerald. Don't work yourself up."

"He's a monster, Lucy. A monster you can't fight, cos he always wins."

CHAPTER 42

Mahone sat at his desk. A small stack of papers sat by his right hand. He picked up a pen, found the dotted line on the bottom of each page, and signed his name, a signature of excellent penmanship.

He checked his watch. It had been five minutes since he had given Lucy a ten-minute deadline to be in his office, and he was eager to see how she reacted after yesterday's incident.

There was a knock at the door. A knock that sounded soft and timid. A smile crossed his face as he said: "Come in."

The door opened and Lucy stepped in. He hadn't noticed yesterday how pretty she was. Her creamy brown skin looked flawless. She had a skinny waist and firm breasts that sat nicely in her blue nurse's uniform. How hadn't he noticed before? He put it down to stress; when he got stressed, all he saw were the things that annoyed him, the people that annoyed him, and the only way to see anything good again was to release that anger.

"Doctor, you wanted to see me?" Lucy walked up to his desk and stood.

"Take a seat," Mahone said, gesturing to a small leather chair.

Lucy looked at it, then sat. The leather squeaked against the skin of her toned thighs. She shuffled her bum back trying to get comfy, but she wouldn't be able to get comfy; Mahone knew that, and this made his smile broaden.

"Thank you for coming, and thank you for being punctual. You're learning, that's what I like to see from promising new nurses such as yourself. You've got potential, Lucy, I can see that."

Mahone clicked about on his computer, read something on there, then turned back to Lucy. He rested his elbows on the desk and steepled his fingers together. "I see from your job application that you view caring and nursing work as more of a vocation; it's something you actively enjoy doing."

"Yes, sir." Lucy shifted in her chair.

"That's good. I see you having a long career with us here at Hill Top Hospital. We've not had a manager for the nursing staff for most of this year. The last nurse manager left. It was a shame because she was good, she loved her job and was great with the patients. But, she had problems of her own, which I won't go into. I wasn't sure we'd find a suitable replacement, but I think that person could be you." He looked at Lucy. "Is that something that would interest you?"

Lucy nodded. "Yes, it would."

Mahone clapped his hands together. The sound was loud in the office; he saw Lucy jump at the suddenness of it. "Excellent. Keep working hard, putting in the effort, being punctual, and you'll get there. You could even go on to bigger hospitals and bigger jobs in the city."

"Really?" Lucy said, her eyes glistening.

Mahone nodded. "I believe in you, Lucy, and I want you to be the best, and have the best. We look after each other here,

I look after you... you look after me." Mahone raised an eyebrow.

Lucy shifted again and her smile faded.

Mahone pursed his lips and made a clicking sound with his tongue. "There is another reason I called you in here."

Lucy cleared her throat. "What is it?"

Mahone shifted in his chair, making out that what he was about to say made him uncomfortable. "I need you to sign off on a piece of paperwork I have here." he tapped the pile of papers by his right hand.

"What are they?"

"They are regarding Mrs. Pearce. After yesterday's... incident, I've decided that going forward, it would be in the best interests of Mrs. Pearce for her to be restrained for the majority of the day. Especially during rounds."

"Restrained?" Lucy sounded horrified.

Mahone continued quickly. "Yes. It is for her own benefit. She attacked us yesterday; if she had inflicted a severe injury to either you or myself, the ramifications would have been far worse. If we can keep her in restraints, then that would mean we were saving her from herself."

Lucy shook her head. "I don't like that, Doctor. It doesn't sit right with me."

Mahone frowned deeply; his head shook slowly from side to side. "That is regrettable. For I had such high hopes for you, Lucy. If a nurse can't see that sometimes, making tough decisions is what's best for the patients we dedicate ourselves to helping, then well..." He lifted his hands and shrugged.

"But..." Lucy stammered, "she's an old woman. Surely her mental health will only deteriorate if she's confined to her room, restrained to her bed."

Mahone sighed and looked around his desk as if he had grown weary of Lucy. "If you can't see the good in these difficult choices then maybe I was wrong about you." He stood and gestured toward the door. "I may have to reconsider your position here with us at this hospital."

"No, wait," Lucy cried, sounding desperate. "I'm sorry, I wasn't thinking. Maybe it's just something I have to learn. After all, they do say that sometimes you have to be cruel to be kind."

Mahone smiled and re-seated himself. "I thought you'd see things my way, Lucy. I need you to sign these documents as a witness to the incident." He pushed the papers toward Lucy. She picked up the pen and scanned the pages for where to sign.

"What is this?" Lucy asked.

"It's nothing really, just boring red tape stuff. I've written an incident report. It basically states that Mrs. Pearce tried to attack us, and *together* we apprehended her, safely, and put her back to bed before giving her a sedative. What I need from you, Lucy, is to sign at the bottom of the page, next to mine."

"But," Lucy shifted in the chair, sweat beading down her face, rounding the smooth curve of her jaw, "but that's not what happened. I don't want to tell a lie, Doctor Mahone."

Mahone wiped his face. He was getting frustrated. He was getting mad. "Lucy, I don't have time for this. That is what happened, and that is what you're going to sign."

Lucy put the pen to the paper, then lifted it again. She wavered, and for a second, he thought she was actually going to refuse. That would have pissed him off and he would have had to use a different method to get her to sign, but she'd sign it, alright. She'd sign that fucking paper in blood if he wanted her to. Then, Lucy scrawled her name on the two pieces of paper. As soon as it was done, Mahone took the paper away and began folding it.

"You made the right decision, Miss Swindle. I'll file this." Mahone stood, opened the top drawer of the filing cabinet, and flicked through some files before slotting in the folded report.

"Will a file be kept on record on the server?" Lucy asked and pointed to the computer.

Mahone smiled. "Yes, it will, but I'm a little old school, I like to keep paper files of everything for a time."

Mahone closed the cabinet, turned the key to lock the drawers shut, and put the key in the top drawer of his desk. "You can leave now, Miss Swindle."

Mahone enjoyed the view as Lucy pulled down her uniform where it had ridden high enough to show off the very tops of her thighs, only an inch away from revealing her panties. He bit his lip as he watched her leave.

CHAPTER 43

There was an audible buzz in the police station. In a country where hot weather isn't around long enough to cause a problem, air conditioners were not a luxury that could be squeezed into an already anorexic law enforcement budget, so desk fans would have to do. Every officer on a desk had their own personal fan that sat ten inches from their face, blowing mildly cool air over them to keep the heat exhaustion at bay for that little bit longer. Located in strategically placed positions around the room were bigger, taller fans that rotated from side to side, trying to cool the room off.

Tony had the top three buttons of his uniform unbuttoned, revealing a hairy chest that glistened with small beads of sweat. Instead of coffee, he held a plastic cup of water in his hand. He downed one full cup of cold water from the cooler and immediately filled up another. The water felt smooth on his dry throat, soothing some of the rawness he felt in his windpipe.

He stepped over to Ruth, who sat at a desk, eyes closed, her face an inch away from one of the fans, her mouth gaped open as if letting the air cool her down from the inside out.

"They done at the site?" Tony asked, awaking Ruth from her cooling-down trance.

"Not yet, I spoke to Officer Bailey, who started back on the scene at first light. He says he'll be there another two hours. They don't want to miss anything. It's a strange case, and with another murder of the same type happening the day after, they want to be sure they've got everything. I still say it's the heat. It's enough to drive anyone crazy. Sally Hartfield, the owner at Sally's Café, made me a full-fat latte instead of skinny and I bit her fucking head off."

"Snapping and sniping at someone isn't quite murder, Ruth," Tony said.

Ruth shrugged. "You wanting to get down to the site before they close it off?"

"I'd like to, yeah." Truth was, Tony felt like he needed to; he wanted to get a look at the place in the full light of day, try and make sense of it all in his own head. There had to be something that connected the two, and if there was, could it happen again?

The thought was a sickening one, because for some reason, it felt logical. Crazy, but logical. If there was something out there causing all of this, maybe it was linked to Sophie's death, too. He had to know.

"In fact, yeah, I definitely do. We need to talk to Alan first. I want to hear everything he has to say so we can analyse it next to Gareth Weeds' interview. Something's going on here, Ruth, and it's starting to scare the fuck out of me."

"Sergeant Thorne, Alan Houghton has been briefed by his lawyer, he's ready to be questioned," Officer Westfield shouted over. His voice was whinier than the fans that buzzed in the office. He had a look about him Tony couldn't stand. Like a weasel or a rat. Something rodent-esque anyway.

"Ready, Ruth?"

"As I'll ever be."

Tony and Ruth each grabbed another cup of cold water, when another officer came over.

"Sergeant Thorne, sorry to bother you, can I have a minute?"

Tony looked up and saw it was Angela, the new constable who spent her days answering phones and taking messages. "What is it, Angela? We're about to interview a murder suspect here."

"Sorry, I've had a call from a woman about a potential drug scandal up at the psychiatric hospital –"

Tony raised a hand that told her to stop. "We haven't got time for that right now. Just put whatever information you've got into a file and we'll look at it when this is all over."

Angela shifted from one foot to the other as if flustered. "Right, yeah, sorry. I'll do that, sorry." She turned on her heels and walked back to the front desk.

Tony looked at Ruth, who smiled and sipped her water.

Tony opened the door and they both stepped into the interview room.

Alan sat across the table from them. His eyes were swollen and red, and he had that same look of confusion and utter heartbreak that Gareth Weeds had when he sat in the same seat. His lawyer whispered something in his ear; Alan barely seemed to take it in.

After making a short statement for the benefit of the tape, Tony asked his first question.

"What happened, Alan?"

Alan shook his head; his eyes were wide, his lips cracked and white-looking. "I don't know."

Tony sat back in his chair and took a long breath. The man opposite him looked like the man Tony had always known, the man Tony liked and considered a friend, more than just a neighbourly acquaintance. "You went back to the woods to collect your knife, you told me you'd lost it in there, is that right?"

Alan nodded.

"Speak up for the tape please, Alan."

"Yes, that's right. I was searching in the woods, I knew where abouts it would be, so I didn't expect it to take me long. And, well, I did find it, not as quick as I expected, but pretty quickly." Alan wiped a bead of snot that fell from his nose with the back of his hand.

"Then what, Alan?" Tony looked through some notes he laid out in front of him. "Jenny tells us you were gone over three hours? What were you doing in that time?"

Alan's brow furrowed; he clenched his eyes shut tight and grimaced. "I don't know," he said, releasing his facial features. The white frown lines on his forehead showed up distinctly against the redness of his face.

"Come on Alan, think. Did you see anyone, anything? Do you remember driving home at least?"

Alan dropped his head low, brought up his cuffed hands and scratched at his hair manically. "I don't know!" he shouted in frustration.

"I don't know. I was walking around the woods, looking for my knife, I found it, it was easy, it was right where I thought it was, in amongst the briars and long grass. This time of year, the forest floor isn't covered in dead leaves and such, there's a bit of bad overgrowth here and there, fallen pine needles, but it's mostly fine. I bent down to pick up my knife, read the inscription from my... from my boy..." He began sobbing.

Tony looked at Ruth and then to Alan's lawyer.

"You don't have to say anything else," his lawyer said to him.

"That's handy, cos I've got nothing else left to say. I don't remember. It's the dumbest fucking thing I've ever heard of. I killed the most precious thing in my life, and I don't even know how I did it. It was like I was blind, like I couldn't see what my actions were doing until it was too late. It was as if I was staggering around in darkness and then BOOM! the lights were turned on and my boy was dead." Alan raised his hands up over the table. "I held him in my arms."

Tony sighed with pity for the man he had promised to share a glass of scotch with. That felt like a million years ago now. He didn't know anything, hadn't said much about how he felt in the woods or –

Alan's eyes shot open. "I do remember something."

Tony sat up straight. "What?"

Ruth leant forward; her elbows left sweaty prints on the tabletop.

"It was so hot, sweat was pouring down my face as I was bent over searching through the long grass for my knife, but then I remember being cold, and I mean *really* fucking cold. Like it was Christmas morning and there was three feet of snow outside. But, the coldness was inside of me, like my organs had frozen, my heart, my blood; the air pushed out of me and I think I heard a voice, in my head."

"Did this voice tell you to kill your son, Alan?" Ruth said. Tony noticed the tone.

Alan shook his head definitively. "No, it didn't. I don't know what it said, it wasn't like it was saying words, it was more like a feeling, I don't know what that feeling was, but I know it was bad."

"Then what, Alan? Help me out. We've had two fathers murder their sons in the past three days; this shit doesn't happen in Wymere."

Alan shook his head, clenched his eyes shut again as if trying to force a memory up. He let out a sharp breath that stank of bleeding gums and dehydration. "Shit! Fuck! I don't remember, it all just goes blank. After that, it's like I just open my eyes and I'm on the floor of my son's room, holding him as blood poured out of his throat." Alan started sobbing again. "His lips were moving as he died, he wasn't making a noise because my knife had gone so deep, but his lips were moving, they were saying 'Why daddy, why?'" Alan broke into full sobs; his head dropped to the table.

Tony looked at Ruth and then back to Alan.

"I think we're done for the day; my client is clearly too overwhelmed to answer any more questions."

"Yeah, killing your kid is quite overwhelming, I imagine," Ruth snapped.

"Ruth," Tony scolded. "Interview terminated at twelve hundred hours." He clicked the stop button on the recorder and stood.

"I'm sorry this happened, Alan, I don't know why you did what you did, but I'm going to do my best to find out."

Tony was about to leave when Alan raised his head from the table. "Because I'm a fucking monster, that's why, Tony! I'm a monster!"

In one sudden movement, he smashed his head down on the table. The lawyer pushed himself away and fell to the floor in a heap, his hands raised to cover his face, his knees drawn up to his chest to protect himself.

Tony, momentarily stunned, could only watch as Alan raised his head and smashed it down again, harder this time. He raised it and slammed it down three times before Tony managed to get an arm around Alan's neck and hold him back. Ruth shouted for help and more officers came running in. Alan was a big man, big and strong. It took three to hold him down, it wasn't until a fourth came in that they were able to drag him off to his cell.

"Someone call Doctor Mahone, we need a doctor to sedate this mad fucker!" Westlake shouted into the office.

Tony wanted to object, but that was probably just what Alan needed.

CHAPTER 44

Lucy spent the rest of the day in a hate fugue. Mahone had tried to manipulate her, and he thought he had done it successfully. Did he think she was that easy? That gullible to fall for his tactic of bringing her up with compliments and then shoving an apparent wrecking ball into her face, making out as though the only way she could carry on was with his help? Then what? She was supposed to be eternally grateful for his kindness? What an arsehole.

If only he knew that she was planning to bring him down! If she was feeling nervous and anxious about doing more digging and finding out the truth about him and Laura Kelly before, she wasn't now. Now she was propelled by a rage born from his own smug arrogance.

He was on the psychiatric ward now, examining the patients, filling out their prescriptions and signing them onto the necessary plans to help heal their conditions and work through the traumas that had turned them into the people they were. Lucy was supposed to be in the rec room, but instead, she was making her way to Mahone's office.

He had said he liked to keep paper copies; he was old-fashioned like that. That didn't surprise Lucy much; he seemed old-fashioned in lots of things, like medical practices and attitudes toward women. She had to fill out a paper application form, and she would put money on it that Laura Kelly had to do the same.

Lucy crept down the carpeted hallway, glad for the silence the carpet gave. Helen was on a late lunch, so sneaking past the front desk wasn't an issue, and the cameras wouldn't be monitored as they were before, but she had to be quick. She got to Mahone's office, put her hand on the doorknob and turned, praying to God that he hadn't locked it.

It was open.

His own arrogance was his downfall, once more. No one would dare break into the great Doctor Mahone's office. Lucy smiled and closed the door gently behind her.

The office had an air of old potpourri and a musty smell, like that of an old library.

She moved around the desk and opened the top drawer. For a second, she thought she couldn't find the key for the filing cabinet; the plan would fall to pieces and she'd be stuck not knowing where to start in trying to find Laura. She found the key jammed in the corner of the drawer and breathed a sigh of relief.

At the filing cabinet, she started methodically from the top. The top drawer was full of patient files, accident reports – of which there seemed to be more than what should be acceptable. The second drawer... bingo. It was the staff files. She rifled through, and the heat of the day mixed with the excitement she felt beating in her chest and made her fingers slippery with sweat.

Chapter 45

"Just lay still and it'll all be over soon. You know the benefits this brings." Mahone held up a syringe and showed it to his patient, who cowered against the wall on her bed. Her long, untamed hair covered her face. Her eyes looked as if they were sat in dark hollows. She wore a strait jacket, something rarely used in modern medicine, but Mahone thought there was something about them that really hammered home the difference between him and his subject.

"Come on now, how long have we been doing this? I stick this needle in, you feel nothing." He whispered the last part. "It's nothing to you but a bad dream, a hazy memory that will simply evaporate the more you try and remember it. I don't want to hurt you; I don't want to hurt any one of my patients." The thin smile he wore disappeared and his face hardened. "But I will. You fucking bet I will. You've got the scars to prove it."

Mahone moved forward. The needle point shimmered as droplets of liquid gently ran out of the pin point and glimmered in the whiteness of the strip light. The patient moved away, backing herself into the corner, shaking her head and scowling at him. Drool spilled from her mouth as she tried to talk past the gag Mahone had fastened in there.

Mahone took a frustrated breath and ground his teeth. "You are trying my patience. Why must you insist on fighting me? It's not as if you have a fight to win. No one cares about you. You've been a patient here for years, and not one person has come to visit, you don't even have a fucking name. No one is going to see the bruises, the scars, the chipped teeth... you are mine!"

Mahone lunged forward, put one hand on her face, and gripped, digging his fingernails into her cheeks. He pulled her over; without her hands there to protect herself, she fell face-first onto the hard plastic-covered mattress. Mahone moved on top of her, straddling her back, putting all his weight down on her spine. He could hear the air being pushed out of her, her back cracking.

She writhed and kicked in pain. "You're like a bucking bronco," he laughed. He grabbed her left arm by her bicep, put the needle into the back of her arm and depressed the plunger. When it was half empty, he stopped. "No," he said softly. "You're going to feel some of this. Maybe then you'll obey a little easier." He took the needle out of her arm and threw it into the yellow hazard bin by the toilet. He rode her attempts to knock him off until the sedative worked its way through her system and she slowed her kicking and bucking and laid still. He wiped his face; it got hot in those rooms and sweat was beginning to bead on his forehead. He stood from her, recoiling as his elbow grazed the wall beside her bed, that was streaked in lines of old blood and faeces.

He poured a generous amount of hand sanitizer into his hand and rubbed the gel in.

"You're going to get it now, bitch." He laughed again. The sound was low and harrowing. He loosened his tie, lifted it up over his head and laid it on the end of the bed. He kicked off his shoes and placed them neatly by the door. His hand touched his belt; he pulled the leather and removed the metal fastener from its hole.

He could see the blankness in her eyes as she looked up at him from the mattress. Hard to imagine she was once pretty. Now, she was nothing but a used-up whore. He pulled his belt from the loop and began unfastening his trousers, the front of which bulged from the excitement. His heart was pumping, his muscles shaking, his cock throbbing with anticipation – all was cut short when someone began pounding on the outside of the door. The handle flapped wildly, someone trying to get in.

Mahone buttoned his trousers and fed his belt through the loops hastily.

"What is it?!" he shouted. "I'm working with a patient, God damn it!"

"Doctor, it's the police." it was Helen's voice, shaky and panicked.

"What do they want?"

"They've got a situation at the station. A prisoner has gone mad, they've got him under restraints, but he won't stop screaming and fighting. They need him sedated."

Mahone gripped his nose and swore furiously under his breath.

"Doctor?"

"Alright, Helen!" he shouted. "I'm coming. Give me a minute."

"They were really insistent that –"

"Go back to your desk, Helen, I'm coming now." Mahone looked down at his patient, laid on her front, motionless. He grabbed her and rolled her into the recovery position. "I'll get you next time." He slapped her face with an open hand twice, hard enough to make a sharp sound. "Until then, get some rest."

Mahone left the room in a hurry and walked down the corridor toward the main wing of the hospital. He saw the door at the end of the hall closing, and then saw the flash of Helen's skirt as she ran away from it. That woman infuriated him sometimes, but she did as she was told, and that meant she was worth keeping around.

Once in the main hall, the feel of soft carpet under his feet, he shouted to Helen, who was nearing the reception area next to the hospital entrance. "I need a prescription pad from my office. I'll take two shots of sedative, and if the police want us to have him over night, he's going to need a room. You can sort that."

"Yes, Doctor."

Mahone marched toward his office and looked inquisitively at the door. It seemed to be open, just a sliver, but enough to show a line of bright light coming from his office windows. He reached the door and pushed.

CHAPTER 46

Lucy sifted through the files. She found her own and resisted the urge to look through what he had on her. The more she looked at the people's files he had, the more she saw that he had done his own digging into their lives. A lot of the files were handwritten notes of things he had observed, pictures taken from social media, personality assessments from the photos he'd seen.

Drinks too much, can't control their behaviour in public, susceptible to peer pressure and easily led. Well kept, trim figure, low aspirations, confidence issues, past trauma?

Assumptions and character assassinations based on things he found online, a rating system with the heading **Potential.** Potential for what it didn't say, but Lucy could guess. She had a 9 for her potential. It made her skin crawl. There was a photo of Lucy with her grandma. Lucy was fifteen, her grandma was in a hospital gown, laid in bed with tubes coming from her nose and arms. The photo was taken only a day before she died. Mahone had printed it off and written ***useful?*** in black marker in the margin.

Lucy closed her eyes and swallowed her rage. She sifted

through the papers until she found Laura Kelly. She almost yelped in celebration when she found it. The file was thin; any photos he had of her had been thrown out or destroyed, Lucy guessed. She found Laura's information sheet though, and right at the top was her address.

"Yes!" Lucy said and pumped her clenched fist. She folded the paper and put it in her front pocket. She began gathering the papers up into a neat pile, but edges of photos and note paper stuck out of the sides, making it infuriatingly time-consuming to put them back. Her mother always said that Lucy rushed in without thinking about the consequences; she could almost hear her mother's voice now, full of the tones of 'I told you so.'

"You should have gone through those files carefully, putting each one down neatly before moving onto the next, then you wouldn't have found yourself in this mess, would you?"

"Not now, Mother," Lucy said in response to the voice in her head, but couldn't help but smile. She had all the files in a neat pile ready for the cabinet when she heard Mahone shout from the hall.

"I need a prescription pad from my office. I'll take two shots of sedative and if the police want us to have him over night, he's going to need a room. You can sort that."

Lucy's heart stopped. She put the files in the drawer and closed it. Desperate, she looked around the room for a place to hide. There was nowhere. A chest of drawers, his desk, and row of bookshelves. She looked at the door. she thought she could hear his footsteps, but that was impossible because the carpet swallowed all the sound in that hallway; she realised then it was her own heart thudding in her ears.

The desk, she decided, was the only possible place she could hide. She knelt and crawled under the desk and began pulling the chair closer to cover her. The desk was deep, that was good, it meant she could get her legs in far enough without them being stuck out in the open.

Then she saw it: the key was still in the filing cabinet. If he saw it, he would know that someone had been in there because he had taken the key and put it back in the drawer. She went to push the chair to get out, when she heard the office door click shut.

LUCY SAT BACK in the darkness under the desk. She was sure her breathing was too loud; her chest rose and fell rapidly, sweat trickled down her back and followed the curve until it ended at the waist band of her trousers. She said a prayer in her head; she wasn't a God-fearing woman like her mother was, but it couldn't hurt.

She could hear his footsteps now; they were slow and it was difficult to decipher exactly where in the office he was. The sunlight that flooded in from the window seemed to light the spot of carpet right in front of where she hid.

She's here, Doc, right here, come and get her!

The footsteps grew louder; so did the drumming of her heart. Then, the light from the window turned to black, and she knew where he was. He was to her left by the window. His breathing was heavy, too, as if he had been running. The light came back strong, then his feet appeared in front of her face. She stifled a gasp and covered her mouth with her hand.

He's gonna find me, he's gonna find me and when he does, he's gonna fire me.

Then she thought that, maybe, it would be worse than that.

He's gonna hurt you.

It was her mother's voice she heard now.

You didn't think about the consequences, did you? Once

again, you've gone jumping in feet-first without thinking of an end game; what you're trying to do is good, but the way you're going about it is reckless, Lucy. You gotta be smarter.

Lucy promised her mother that if she got out of this unscathed, she would plan ahead, think of every possible outcome and how to deal with those outcomes should they arise. She wouldn't get caught like this again.

Mahone stepped around the desk, stopped, then moved back again. He opened his drawer, seemed to stare into it for a long time. Lucy tasted the saltiness of the sweat that covered her lips. Mahone slammed the drawer shut, then thundered his way toward the office door. There was a space of about five, maybe even ten seconds when there was complete and total silence. Then the door slammed shut.

Lucy didn't step out from under the desk right away; she was planning ahead. It could have been a trick, he could have seen the key in the filing cabinet, he could have noticed the sweaty handprints on his mahogany desktop, and he could be waiting there with his office door locked and no one around but him and her.

She gave it five minutes, although it felt more like an hour. Then she got up. The office was empty. She quickly grabbed the key from the filing cabinet and put it back in the drawer, laid it flat in the corner so it was difficult to spot, exactly where she had found it.

Chapter 47

The living room in Mrs. Leadley's house was dark. The sun rays filtered through the holes in the curtains, but the main source of light came from the lamp in the corner of the room, although it did little to alter the dimness. Jane wondered if the darkness was just following her; after what she had seen yesterday and the nightmares she'd had, everything she thought about was tinged with darkness.

Mrs. Leadley sat in her armchair; her elbows used her knees for support as she leaned forward and poured two cups of tea. She overstretched at one point and Jane saw her foot bend so far out it was a wonder the old woman didn't scream out in agony. She barely seemed to notice it.

"Tell me," Mrs. Leadley said. Her voice was hoarse and dry. "Tell me what you saw?"

Jane picked up her tea and held it in both hands to try and stop them from shaking. She was terrified. Of what she wasn't sure, but she was sure that this old woman would be able to tell her. She sipped her tea; it was hot and stung her lips. Jane winced and put the tea back down, wiped her mouth, and then proceeded to tell Mrs. Leadley what she had seen. From running after Tiffany in the woods, as if she'd just disappeared into thin air, up to when she found Tiffany stood over Alfie Weeds by the tree.

She left out the dream.

"The boy," Mrs Leadley said after Jane had finished, without an ounce of shock in her tone, Jane noticed (Though she did detect worry in the old woman's voice.). "The boy was wrinkled, you say?"

"Yes, I don't know why or how, but it was as if all the moisture had been sucked out of him."

Mrs. Leadley drank her tea in gulps now that it had cooled. Then she looked off into space; her eyes were wide, they seemed to dart from side to side as if she were reading an invisible book.

"What is it?" Jane asked.

Mrs. Leadley looked at Jane. "The time has come. For centuries they have lain in those woods, waiting until they had their chance to walk among us. Those vile, evil things were merely trapped all them years. Dark magic never dies, it only gets buried."

Jane shifted in her seat and grabbed her tea. She gulped hers down too, desperate for the warm liquid to soothe the dryness of her throat. "What is? What's buried out there?"

"Evil!" Mrs Leadley snapped. "Pure. Evil."

CHAPTER 48

Tony watched Alan kick and scream in his cell. Three officers were holding him down, and even with the handcuffs on him, he still managed to thrash and kick a few of them. Tears streamed down his swollen red face.

"If Doctor Mahone doesn't get here quick," Ruth said, nudging Tony in his ribs, "we might have to knock him out the old-fashioned way."

Tony watched as Ruth made a fist and smacked it into the palm of her hand. He knew she was joking, but he couldn't laugh, or even force a smile. What they were watching was a man ripped apart by grief, torn into pieces by what he had done. Tony couldn't bear to watch.

"I'm here, where is he?" Mahone charged through, his face as red as Alan's. Tony couldn't remember a time when he had seen Mahone so flustered.

"You're looking a bit flushed there, Doc. You alright?" Tony said.

Mahone shot him a contemptuous look. "I was in the middle of some very important work before I was called out to do *your* job for you. I must say, Sergeant Thorne, if you can't keep control of your own prisoners, I doubt the day will ever come when you make police superintendent."

Tony and Mahone stood staring at one another, Tony blocking the doctor's path through. Part of Tony wanted to stop Mahone from going in. It didn't seem right for Alan to be pumped full of drugs and then sent to that psych ward to be under the care of this arsehole.

"What you waiting for?! Let the doctor through!" a voice shouted from behind him.

Mahone smiled and made a gesture with his hand for Tony to move aside.

Tony ground his teeth and slid to the left, allowing Mahone safe passage through to the holding cells.

"I hate that sonofabitch," Tony growled.

Ruth put a hand on his shoulder. "Let's leave these guys to handle this. You still want to catch up at the crime scene before they close it off?"

Tony's eyes spread wide; he checked his watch. "Shit, can we still make it?"

"Maybe, but we gotta go now. And if we are too late, I think a drive around with AC blasting might do both of us a world of good."

Chapter 49

Before Mahone set off from the hospital, he paid a visit to Helen on the reception desk. She was tapping away on the computer, making it look like she was busy, because she knew how he hated idle workers.

"Helen, I've just been in my office and I'm sure that something in there had been moved," he said. He had seen the key in the filing cabinet, the one he had put in the drawer earlier. He also saw, in the highly polished surface of the wooden cabinet behind his desk, the reflection of Lucy Swindle cowering behind his chair. His first thought was to call her out, but he stopped that thought as soon as it arose. She was up to something. If he were to call her out, she was more than likely to lie, or refuse to answer his questions. He'd dealt with nurses who had a need to impose their strict moral compass on to him, and he promised himself to be more careful in future. Hence the camera he had installed in the top corner of his office, the one so small it couldn't be seen unless you knew it was there.

"I could check the CCTV for you if you'd like, Doctor?

But I didn't see anyone go in there," Helen said, and began clicking for the correct files on her computer.

"Please do, Helen. But do it quickly, I'm in a rush."

Helen shuffled in her seat and leant forward toward the screen. Within five clicks, she had the video playback of Mahone's office for that day. She used the mouse to move the video forward to the right time. Helen gasped when Lucy appeared on screen, running across Mahone's office toward the desk. Mahone watched intently, his eyes narrowed as he concentrated, almost recording the images as they appeared into his internal memory log.

"Doctor Mahone, I'm so sorry. I had no idea she was in there."

"That's alright, Helen, she's a slippery one."

They watched as Lucy found the key and worked her way through the files. Scattered them around on the desk like the unorganised sloth that she was.

"Why would she be going through my files, Helen?" Mahone asked.

Helen shook her head. "I have no idea."

"The files in that drawer are reserved for staff details. Which member of staff is she wanting to get hold of?"

"I don't know. I did give her a warning yesterday, though."

Mahone put a hand, firm but gentle, on Helen's shoulder and spun her round to face him. "What cause did you have to warn her?"

"She was spying." Helen gave the information up immediately. Mahone knew Helen would never lie to him if he asked her a straight question.

"On what?"

"You, sir. She was spying on you when you were in the equipment storage room. I warned her, told her not to put her nose where it wasn't welcome or else she'd end up like Laura Kelly."

The mention of that vile, troublesome bitch sent Mahone's face burning with rage. He stood and put a hand over his mouth to keep from screaming into the ceiling like a comic book villain.

"She's trying to drag me down, just like Laura. That fucking bitch!" He paced the reception; Helen kept her eyes on him as he walked back and forth. Then it clicked. If Lucy was wanting to talk to Laura, Lucy had ambitions of reporting him to the police. She was a resourceful young woman and had a certain tenacity about her that Mahone had almost admired. Mahone would have to get ahead of it, stop it before it went too far. He had his friends, those that sat in high places, the ones that orchestrated the grunts below them. But he had his fair share of enemies.

"I'm heading to the police station now. Don't mention this to Lucy please, Helen. This is our secret."

"But, sir?"

"But, nothing. This is between us and no one else. Understood?"

Helen nodded.

After Mahone had arrived at the police station and sorted out the buffoon who insisted on kicking and screaming bloody murder, he took a moment to accept the thanks and gratitude from the officers who were there.

"That was really something, you did great!" an officer said, with an excitement and a demeanour that would place him at least ten years younger than the age he looked.

"What's your name?" Mahone asked, wiping Alan Houghton's sweat from his hands with a white handkerchief.

"Westlake, sir. Constable Jamie Westlake." Westlake held out a hand that Mahone desperately wanted to avoid. After a brief consideration, he stuck his own hand into Westlake's and shook, then wiped it once more with the handkerchief.

"Are you new here, Jamie?"

"Yes, sir. Been here six months."

"I bet Tony gives you the run-around. Makes you get coffees, do the endless paperwork, dot the I's and cross the T's?"

Westlake made a scowl and kicked the ground lazily like a sulking teen. "Yeah. He's a..." Westlake stopped and looked up at Mahone, who nodded and smiled, letting Westlake know it was okay to continue. "He's a dickhead," Westlake whispered. "And his partner, Ruth, she's a bossy little bitch. Always ordering me around. The other week, before everyone in the town started growing crazy, she had me handing out lost kitten flyers on Main Street."

"I sympathise. That must be frustrating."

"Yeah, it is. They get to do all the good stuff. I don't get to do nothing. I want to arrest someone, shove them in the back of a van, give them a dig in the ribs, something to show them we ain't messing around. That's why I became a cop."

"Were you bullied as child?"

Westlake blinked in confusion at the change of subject. "Sorry?"

"At school. Were you bullied? Forgive me for saying, but I'm a pretty good judge of character." Mahone put a finger to his lips and narrowed his eyes as if reading Westlake like a book. He watched Westlake fidget awkwardly. "You were small in school, smaller than you are now. You were bullied, not a lot, but when you were it was bad. They overpowered you, made you do things perhaps? Humiliated you in front of other pupils?"

Westlake opened his mouth and shut it; he had the look of someone that had been read his fortune. "That's... about right."

"I know how you feel. I was the same. The only way to get your own back on these people, Jamie, is to use the strengths we forge for ourselves. Look at me, I'm not a big, muscley oaf of a man like Tony Thorne, but people respect and fear me. Why is that?"

"Because you're... because you're you!"

"No." Mahone raised a finger. "It's because I made myself this way. I did what I had to do to climb the ladder, I stepped on those who stood in my way to get there. I earned my power, my respect, by *not* taking orders from those who thought they were better than me."

"I wish I had you as a boss." Westlake was looking up at Mahone, in more ways than one.

"You've got a good head on your shoulders, I can see that. You're destined for higher things than this." Mahone looked round, screwing up his face as if everything that surrounded him disgusted him.

"There's nothing else I can do; I trained to be an officer, it took me years."

"What would you say if I told you I could fast track you up the chain of command? I'm personal friends with both the mayor and the current police superintendent."

"You could do that?"

Mahone nodded. "However, something you'll learn, and it is a lesson best learnt quickly, is that everything has its price."

Westlake nodded. "What do you want me to do?"

Mahone put a hand on to Westlake's shoulder and pulled him closer. Then they took a walk, and Mahone told Westlake everything he wanted him to do.

CHAPTER 50

Tony parked his car in the gravel driveway of The Old Stone Cottage. He didn't stop and say hello to the Stanfords, although he did wave at the little girl who waved hello to him out of the living room window.

He wanted to run when he got to the woods, but the heat of the day wouldn't let him. How long could the people cope with this relentless heat before the government had to step in and do something? What exactly, he wasn't sure. Hand out bottles of water for a start; the town reservoir was as dry as the old reservoir where they'd found Alfie Weeds. A hosepipe ban was in place and if the weather didn't turn soon, there'd be a cap on how much water any household could use each day. It wasn't just the heat, it was the humidity, it was how Tony imagined trying to breath in Hell's waiting room.

"The tent's gone," Ruth said from behind him. She was panting; Tony was glad the heat was affecting her as bad as it was him.

"Shit," Tony said. "I hope we've not missed them."

They walked through the gap in the border hedge of thorn bushes. The gap had been made a lot bigger, so it was easier for equipment to be taken to and from the site. They reached the edge of the empty reservoir. The vast brown mud hole laid out before them, the mound of dirt in the centre where the dead tree grew, it all looked like the scene from an old horror movie. The silence didn't help. Tony looked back then and frowned. He had heard birds, crickets, all kinds of different sounds from the animals in the woods on the walk here, but now that he was stood near that empty hole, it was dead quiet.

"Officer Bailey's still in there, he's digging for something." Ruth tapped Tony's back and they both descended the bank of the lake into the mud.

"Bailey, I'm glad we caught you before you left," Tony said, then he stopped, ten feet short of Bailey, who was hunched over on the ground. At the sound of Tony's voice, Bailey looked up over his shoulder toward Tony. His eyes were wide.

"I think we need the forensic team back again," Bailey said. His voice seemed to quiver.

"What do you mean?"

Bailey stood; his finger pointed down toward the ground where he had been digging with his trowel. "A body. There's another body in here."

CHAPTER 51

It was turning from evening to night; the worst of the day's heat was gone, but the lingering thirty degree Celsius was close to debilitating. Mayor Rose looked out from his window, over the browning grass of the town park toward the woods where his daughter had been lost all those years ago. He dabbed at his sweaty face with a handkerchief; his white shirt was transparent, soaking with sweat. A fan sat on his desk whirring loudly, doing little but pushing hot air around his office.

"Eighteen years," he said out loud into the empty room.

He rarely thought about Sophie in great detail; it was just too painful. Although she was never far from his mind, he was sad to admit that the image of her face had faded over the years. Pictures were great reminders, but they weren't the same. He tried his best to hold on to the memories of her being a baby, how he had read her bedtime stories, watched Disney films with her. The memories he had built thinking that he could reminisce with her about them when she was an adult. Now those memories had begun to deteriorate.

Everything had started coming back, forcing the memories

forward, since Alfie Weeds had gone missing in those woods. The search parties, the media coverage, the interviews, the arrests, the suspicion on everyone's face. It had brought it all back and now he found himself thinking of her constantly.

So, when the phone that sat on his desk in between his computer and an empty pack of sugar ring donuts started to ring, his heart jumped, and the first thing that popped into his mind was Sophie.

He picked up the phone and answered. The *hello* he gave sounded like a stranger's voice.

"Mayor Rose, it's Tony Thorne." The mayor noted how Tony's voice was an octave higher and talking at a much faster pace than normal.

"Good evening, Tony, what can I do for you?"

"They've found a body, sir, at the reservoir where Alfie Weeds was discovered. The forensic team were finishing up, and they found a body buried in the dirt. They think it could have been dumped in the lake, a weight or a stone could have made it sink to the bottom and over the years it became buried under the sediment and dirt."

The mayor coughed; he grabbed at his windpipe, which seemed to be closing in like he was having an allergic reaction. "What are you saying, Thorne?"

"Sir, they're taking the body to the hospital, but it could be her. It could be Sophie!"

Chapter 52

The hospital lights were harsh and bright in the long hallway. Their intensity was exacerbated by the white walls, ceiling, and floor tiles. Tony was sat on one of the chairs by the coffee machine, long since off duty but still in his uniform. He cradled a cup of coffee in his hands; he'd lost count on how many he'd had. It was getting late but he wouldn't be able to sleep even if he went home and crawled into bed next to the woman he no longer loved.

Could it really be Sophie in that room? Being tested and probed, having bits of her bone chipped off for analysis, any remaining tissue sent for DNA testing. It all seemed too ludicrous, too obscene.

The doctor, a nice old man who had been doing this work for as long as Tony had been alive and then some, had been working hard on the body all night. He promised to push through all results that could give some indication as to the identity of the person that had been found. After all, this could be the mayor's missing child. Tony drank down his mildly warm coffee and tossed the plastic cup in the bin.

"Where is she!" The doors down the hall swung open and

the mayor, dressed in a sweat-soaked white shirt that had untucked itself from his trousers, marched toward Tony.

"Mayor Rose, thank you for coming."

"I couldn't get here any earlier. I've been talking to the police officer that found her; Bailey, is it?"

"That's right."

"He said he found her in the bottom of the reservoir? How is that possible? Didn't we dredge all of the lakes and reservoirs?"

"I don't know, sir, but we have to remain calm here, we don't know it's Sophie yet, or that it's even a woman," Tony said, holding up both hands.

The mayor scowled at this. "Oh, come on, Tony, who the hell else could it be? I've been doing my research, when a body's been submerged in water for years, it can mess with the decomposition time. You said the body you found had..." The mayor stopped himself for a moment, needing to gather his thoughts. "Had bits of flesh still on the bone?"

Tony grimaced. "That's right, sir, but they can't say with any definitive answer when the body was from."

The mayor looked upward and flapped his hands in despair. He sat down on one of the chairs and put his face into his hands. "I don't know if I can bear it, Tony. To think that she had been out there in that dirty, God-forsaken water all these years whilst we just got on with our lives."

The mayor was echoing Tony's own thoughts. Tony had been wracked with guilt for years, never knowing where Sophie was or if she was even dead. The thought of finding out definitively gave him a strange sense of relief, yet the guilt was still there. He felt guilty for getting married, for being with another woman; he knew it was stupid and that Sophie would have wanted him to move on, but it didn't feel right when he hadn't had chance to really say goodbye to Sophie.

"I know, sir, I really do."

The mayor put a hand on Tony's knee and squeezed. He cleared his throat with a loud scratchy cough, then said: "So what's happening? What *do* they know?"

"They're rushing tests through, trying to get a match on DNA. They are trying to find a cause of death, too."

The mayor looked at Tony quizzically. "They can do that?"

"It's difficult, but they can sometimes come up with a pretty clear picture."

"Which doctor is it?" the mayor asked. The look on his face was almost amazement.

"It's not the doctor that determines that, it'll be an anthropologist. But the doctor who's in there performing the autopsy and running the tests is Doctor Francis Moss."

The mayor started to laugh. "Jesus, is he still going? That guy's a dinosaur."

"He's good though, sir."

The mayor nodded in agreement.

"If you'll excuse me, sir, I better go phone Sarah. Let her know what's going on and that I won't be home tonight."

"That's fine, son, I'll be here waiting."

THE PHONE RANG ENDLESSLY, to the point that Tony didn't think Sarah would be answering. Probably laid up on the sofa, halfway to wasted, not knowing what time of day it was. He had a moment to feel guilty for the anger he felt toward her, then the ringing stopped.

"Hello?" Her voice was dull and sloppy. She had been drinking.

"Sarah, it's Tony."

"You phoning to tell me you're not coming home?"

Tony could hear the hurt and pain in her voice and felt the

added weight of yet even more guilt laid upon his shoulders. Guilt over Sophie, guilt over Sarah, guilt that he hadn't been able to do anything to save two young boys being killed by their fathers, and guilt that he couldn't figure out why two good people had been driven to commit such atrocious murders.

"No, it's not that," he said, shaking away the overwhelming weight of it all before it swallowed him whole. He had to focus on what was happening if he was ever going to make sense of it all. "I was ringing to tell you I won't be home tonight. But not because I'm *not* coming home, it's because they found a body."

"You said that already, the little boy in the reservoir," Sarah said tiredly.

"No, when they were searching the site, they found a body under the dirt. They think it could have been dumped in the lake and covered over with sediment and muck over the years, they're not sure yet, but I need to be here while they run tests, Sarah."

"You think it's her." It wasn't a question. Her voice was alert now, snappy and clear.

"It could be, yeah. If it is, then maybe I can put it all to bed, maybe I can finally say goodbye to her and we can start afresh."

"Don't do that, Tony. Don't give me false hope." She was snapping at him, she'd gone from sounding docile to angry and worked up in a second, and could Tony blame her?

He opened his mouth to say he wasn't, but he couldn't in good conscience promise her something that he didn't know for sure was true. His head was a mess; he didn't know what tonight held, let alone tomorrow or years ahead from now. "I'll let you know if there's any news."

"Please do," Sarah said, and hung up.

Chapter 53

"Bye, Helen. See you tomorrow." Lucy waved at Helen as she walked out of the doors and noticed that Helen only smiled at her. There was something sinister behind that smile, but Lucy had more important things to think about. The address she'd found for Laura was on the outside of town, to the west side. It would take half an hour if Lucy were to go right now. She wanted to go home, grab a shower, maybe a bite to eat, but she decided against it; the lure of finding out more about Mahone and what Laura knew was too strong. She got in her car and hit the road, putting the windows down so the air could blow the sweat from the back of her neck.

Lucy pulled up to a small bungalow on a quiet street that looked like a community care estate for the elderly, the ones that have a red pull string in their house that alerts a warden who checks up on them. Every garden looked the same; a square patch of grass bordered with bright roses, most of which had wilted in the heat.

Lucy checked the address against the piece of paper she had scrawled it on from memory. Number 22, it checked out. Lucy took a deep breath. She had no idea what she was going to say; she had been practicing the entire drive over but now her mind seemed to have gone blank. She decided she was going to play it like she always had, by jumping in with both feet.

The doorbell was one of those with a camera that sends the feed to the homeowner's phone. Lucy pressed the ringer; a chime sounded and then after a few seconds a voice came through the speakers: "No."

Lucy stammered, then said, "Excuse me?"

"Whatever you're selling, preaching – I don't give a shit."

Lucy cleared her throat. She didn't expect to be welcomed with open arms, but this level of hostility took her by surprise. "I'm not selling or preaching anything. Are you Laura Kelly?"

"Who's asking?"

"My name is Lucy Swindle, I'm a nurse at Hill Top Psychiatric Hospital. I was wondering if I could talk to you about your time there?"

There was a silence.

"I think you better leave."

"Please, Miss Kelly, I really need to speak to you."

"Get the fuck off my front step, and don't come back here."

Lucy felt a rage building inside her. Her whole life no one had listened to her. She'd always been kind little Lucy, wouldn't say boo to a goose, wouldn't ever stand up and be heard, happy to get brushed off like the rest of the dirt. Well, not today.

"Laura, you need to talk to me. I have seen and heard some awful things in that hospital, stuff that makes my skin crawl, and I think you might know something too. Even better, I think you've got evidence. Only for some reason, you backed out of doing anything about it. Well, now it's time for you to help me do something, because you're a good person who nearly put a stop to the suffering those patients are going through."

Silence.

"Or maybe I'm wrong, maybe you're just a coward." Lucy waited, and when no response came, she turned and walked back to her car, her head hung low, dejected.

"Lucy," a voice called from behind her. Lucy turned and saw a woman stood in the doorway. She looked middle-aged with wiry, untamed hair in a messy bun, a big woollen cardigan wrapped around her.

"You better come in," Laura Kelly said.

THE LIVING ROOM WAS BARE, a sofa with red wine stains and cigarette burns in the arms sat across from a TV hung on the wall. Laura came in from the kitchen with two cups of coffee. She handed one to Lucy. Lucy took it and felt the heat of it burn her hands. She quickly put it down on the floor and spilled some on the carpet.

"Oh my god, I'm so sorry!" She jumped up to start dabbing at it with a tissue from her pocket.

"Hey, don't worry about it," Laura said and gestured with her hand for Lucy to get up and sit. Laura grabbed a pack of Marlboro Reds from the coffee table on her side of the sofa and sparked one up. Lucy wrinkled her nose at the smoke that drifted into her face, but said nothing.

"So, you work for Doctor Mahone."

"That's right."

"And you've seen how he treats the patients, seen how he talks to the nurses."

Laura nodded to Lucy as she blew a thin stream of smoke

out of one side of her mouth. "He have anything to do with that?"

Lucy realized that Laura was referring to her ear; she put a hand to it and felt the warmth it was still radiating, and the sensitive pain that shot through her when she touched it. She nodded.

"He's a piece of work, alright."

Lucy sipped her coffee, it was sweet, like it'd been loaded with five sugars. "He almost beat an old woman who suffers with paranoid schizophrenia. I stopped him just in time, but another patient, Gerald Thomas –"

"Ahh, Gerald," Laura interrupted. "I love that guy. How is he, still telling his stories?"

Lucy smiled. "He really is a lovely man. I love his stories, almost as much as he loves telling them."

"Sorry, I interrupted, continue."

"Gerald told me, or insinuated is probably more accurate, that Mahone has been hurting patients for years. Gerald is scared of him, he told me Mahone was a monster, and nobody can stand up to him. I don't know if what you know is the same as the rumours that go around between the nursing staff, but they say he's running some sort of illegal drug testing operation? Using the patients as guinea pigs for the pharmaceutical companies."

Laura dragged deep on her cigarette; the ash on the end was so long, it was agonisingly close to falling.

"I've heard those rumours. Whether that is what he's up to, I don't know for sure. But what I do know, is that he *is* up to something. I was gathering up evidence to make a case against him. The police wouldn't listen to me at first. It's hard to get anyone in authority to believe you when the person you're accusing is one of the top figures in town."

Lucy rubbed her forehead despairingly. "What were you trying to prove?"

Laura stubbed the cigarette out in an ashtray she kept on the floor.

"That he's abusing those patients. I can't say for certain that he's using them as human testing for unlicensed drugs, but with the stuff I found..." Laura shrugged. "It could be connected."

Laura pulled out another cigarette and lit the tip. Lucy was going to say something, but she could see Laura had only paused, and wasn't done talking.

"I knew I couldn't nail him by taking him to court, I didn't have enough to get a criminal conviction and he knew that. Which is why he wasn't concerned at first. All I wanted to do was make headlines, get the ball moving. If I could create enough of a case that it ended with an independent study of everything that goes in and out of that hospital, I knew that they'd find something.

"That day in court was to demand an independent welfare investigation into Hill Top Psychiatric Hospital's practices. It looks clean to everyone who doesn't know, but when you scratch the surface, it's dirty as dog shit. I took him to court and I would have got what I wanted. That's what got him worrying, got his little arsehole doing this." Laura made a hole with her fingers and pulsated it rapidly; she laughed.

CHAPTER 54

"It's over."

"What are you talking about?"

"It's over. I've just got off the phone with Tony. They've found a body in the woods. In the bottom of the reservoir buried in years of sediment and shit! You couldn't even be bothered burying her, you just dumped her body in the water. What did you do? Weigh her down with rocks? Tie her feet to a stone? How could you do that?"

"What I did with Sophie's body is nothing to do with you! You wanted her gone, I did it. How I disposed of her is of no concern of yours. Don't bother me again, and keep that drunk mouth of yours shut. You go to the police, and you're dead."

"It doesn't matter. They'll figure it out and they'll come for you. And me." Sarah laughed.

"No one's going to be coming for me, Sarah, of that I can assure you."

"Mahone, you are a filthy piece of shit and one day, you're going to get what's coming to you."

"You're as guilty as me in this, Sarah, don't you forget that."

"Yeah? Only it seems to me that I'm the only one that feels guilty because of what we did. It seems to me that you can just take murder in your stride. Like it's as simple as taking out the bins."

"Goodbye, Sarah."

"Sometimes, I think it might just be easier if I were to end it all now. My husband is going to leave me, I've made that easy for him. I have no family, no children of my own, my work is remedial at best... I took a life that should have been someone else's and I've paid the price for it. I am miserable, Mahone. Miserable and alone."

Sarah could hear Mahone breathing on the other end; it sounded like stifled laughter.

"I think that's best."

"What is?"

"That you should end it all. What you have is a pathetic excuse for a life, Sarah. No one will miss you. Your husband won't mourn you; he'll only hate himself for not seeing you for the person you always were. A selfish, backstabbing whore who would do anything, even conspire to commit murder. Maybe you are better off dead." Mahone paused for a moment, but Sarah said nothing to fill the silence. "Goodbye, Sarah, see you in hell."

Mahone hung up. Sarah dropped the phone to the floor and finished the bottle of gin she had started only two hours earlier.

CHAPTER 55

I t was another two hours before Tony and the mayor heard anything from the doctor working on the body. When he came out of the green door opposite where they sat, both Tony and Mayor Rose jumped up from their seats.

"Any results, Doctor?" Tony asked.

The mayor didn't say anything. Tony looked over at him and didn't think he *could* say anything. His face was white and sweat still poured down his cheeks despite the AC working in the hospital corridor.

"No results, but I've had a chance to give the body a thorough examination." Doctor Francis Moss looked surprisingly sprightly for his age, and more awake than both Tony and the Mayor, Tony noticed. "The body is that of a female, of that we can be certain."

"How?" Tony asked.

"The pelvis of a female is wider, slightly, plus there are identifications in the skull, which suggests that of a female. And the elbow, strange as that may be, but we find that the shape of the distal humerus differs between males and females."

"I didn't know you were an anthropologist," Mayor Rose said.

"I'm not, but you pick up a lot in this type of work. All of those can be debated, however, I have just found the defining item that can confirm it. The tail bone is broken, and this happens when the baby moves through the birth canal quickly, and –"

"Whoa, whoa, whoa." Tony stepped up to the doctor and put a hand on his chest. The doctor looked down at it, then back up to Tony. "What are you talking about?"

"The body in there is that of a woman who had given birth. Did Sophie Rose not have a child?"

"No, she didn't."

Doctor Moss frowned. "Was there any chance she was pregnant when she went missing?"

Tony shared a look with the mayor, one that was awkward and confused. The mayor looked as though he'd lost the ability to speak once more. "I don't think so, she didn't say..."

Tony dropped the hand from Doctor Moss's chest and stood looking into space. A hundred thoughts whipped through his mind, trying to recall every image he had of Sophie leading up to her disappearance, every snippet of conversation for something she might have said, a hint or a clue. Maybe she couldn't come right out and say it, 'I'm pregnant.' Maybe she dropped subtle hints, too subtle for him to be able to pick them up because he was too busy thinking of how beautiful she looked, and how lucky he was to be with her, daydreaming about the touch of her skin on his, the way her breath tickled his neck when they made love, how she whispered *I love you* into his ear when they held each other. Had he been walking around daydreaming while she tried to tell him the biggest news of his life? Had he lost a child, as well as the love of his life?

"I don't know," Tony said eventually.

"What?" the mayor said, finding his voice, although it was shaky and weak.

"This might be hard for you to hear, but I have a theory. Just because Sophie went missing on that day, doesn't mean she was *killed* on that day. What if she was kidnapped? The perpetrator could have waited until the police gave up on searching the woods, then killed her and buried her in the woods, or, as the case may be, disposed of her body in the old reservoir. The child may very well be alive, if it is her body."

"When will we get the DNA results back?" The mayor was doing all the talking now, Tony was shell shocked, all of a sudden; his whole idea of how Sophie died had been turned around, why hadn't he thought of this as a possibility? She could have been pregnant, and that child could still be alive, being raised by the person who kidnapped her. How long did he keep her alive? The thought was heart-wrenchingly hard to process but he had to work through it. Was she tortured? Raped? For days, weeks, months? He couldn't bear it; his face was tingling like needles of ice were trying to break out from under his skin, his mouth filled with fluid and vomit, rose up his throat.

"It'll be a while yet," the doctor said, carrying on as Tony choked back the sick. "Getting DNA from a body that's been under water for this length of time is extremely difficult. I'm surprised she was found in as good a condition as she is, if I'm honest. The number of bacteria and bugs that can eat away at a deceased body, they don't often leave much. It's almost as if the tissue left on the bones has regenerated, like it's never been touched."

"What?" The mayor shook his head and looked at the doctor through narrowed eyes.

"Sorry." Doctor Moss held up his hands. "It's been a long

night. You two are better off going home. I'm going to be here until midnight, finishing and logging my findings, but there won't be any more news until tomorrow."

"Okay, Doctor," Tony said, wiping at his mouth with the back of his hand. "We'll be back first thing."

Chapter 56

Maggie was tired. The TV was playing nothing but old game shows and late-night news reports, full of bad news and miserable shit that she was too old to pay attention to. There came a time in life when you just had to ignore the bad stuff that happened; bad things happened every day, just like Alfie Weeds being killed by his dad, and now that Houghton boy. It was the same when Sophie Rose went missing, although Maggie was younger then, and helped out with the search parties for weeks.

Bad shit happened and there wasn't anything anyone could do to stop it. Nothing any normal people like Maggie could do, anyway.

Maggie stretched her old bones until she heard her elbows crack and felt her leg muscles stretch out that tight feeling that seemed to grow tighter every day.

"Right then, you," she said, stroking the head of her chocolate Labrador, Dexter, who lay beside her arm chair. "We best take you for one last wee before bed."

She stood; her knees popped audibly as she did, and Dexter ran straight for the door.

"Alright, alright, hold your horses," Maggie laughed. She opened the door and Dexter ran straight over into Sergeant Thorne's front garden.

"Dexter! You're going to upset the neighbours... again!" Maggie called after him, but Dexter wouldn't come. She took the steps down from the porch steadily, she was nearly eighty and lived alone, after all; a trip down a flight of stairs might break a hip, and that would just about finish her off.

She tried to speed up when Dexter began barking like a damn maniac. He howled and barked like a werewolf on a full moon. Maggie looked up into the sky at that thought, and saw how big the moon was. It illuminated what should have been a black night sky, and turned it a dark red, casting enough light that she was able to see everything as if it were approaching dawn. It looked like a planet that had got lost in space. It was the strangest moon she had ever seen, and then she wondered if it had something to do with the heat they'd been having. Maybe it wasn't just the planet that was changing, but the whole universe.

More questions that really, she didn't give a shit about. She was too old to care about things that concerned the future, she was bothered about the here and now. She needed the Sunday crossword and her Dexter, and she would be just fine.

Dexter howled louder and barked fiercely at Thorne's house.

"Dexter, you get back here this instant!"

Maggie made her way over to Thorne's front garden, grabbed Dexter by the collar, looping her frail fingers underneath it and using what little strength she had left to try to drag him away.

Dexter was big and strong, but usually when she started pulling, he would come without too much fuss. Now, though, he pulled back and nearly threw Maggie to the ground. She managed to regain her balance, and when she did, she managed to catch a glimpse through Thorne's front window.

Maggie gasped, taking in a sharp blast of warm evening air that seemed to kick-start her heart into thumping a million miles an hour. Dexter stood beside her and howled louder than she had ever heard him howl.

In the window, she saw Sarah, her young neighbour, who had a lot of problems in her life. Maggie knew this because of the fights she overheard and the recycling boxes full of wine and gin bottles. Now Sarah looked to have rid herself of those problems. She was hanging from the oak beams that ran across the living room ceiling, her legs suspended above an over-turned dining chair, gently swinging from side to side.

Maggie screamed.

CHAPTER 57

Jane was ready to hear what Mrs. Leadley had to say. The room had grown hot and yet goosebumps still covered her arms. She couldn't drink her tea; the lump in her throat wouldn't allow it. She sat on the edge of the old sofa.

"Mrs. Leadley, what is in those woods?"

"Witches," Mrs Leadley said, without skipping a beat.

Jane smiled. "Witches?" she repeated, as if she had misheard.

Mrs. Leadley smacked the arm of her chair so a cloud of dust erupted into the air. "Do not laugh! The threat is real and it is here! You think everything that's been happening is normal? This is a small town where nothing much happens, but there's an evil here. A darkness. That pit in those woods is a graveyard for the witches that were slain!"

Jane felt her face flush. She could see Mrs. Leadley meant every word she said. "Go on then. Tell me, I'm listening."

"In 1656, witch trials and executions were at their most intense after the English Civil war. The typical witch condemned to death was nothing more than a poor old woman, accused of sorcery when injury or death came to their neighbour's livestock, or the crops didn't grow as fruitfully. There were over five hundred women executed for witchcraft in England during that time. The ones that were recorded, that is.

"Wymere was believed to have been rife with witchcraft activity. The witch epidemic in Eastern Europe was even worse than England's. People believed they were coming over on boats, landing secretly on the shore of Whitby and scurrying inland to perform their dark arts. The people of Wymere were worried; they blamed everything on the curse of witches.

"It was in that pit in the woods where they held the trials. Why they chose there to kill those witches, I have no idea. All I know is that pit was said to have been the thinnest point between Hell and Earth. They said evil oozes from it like puss oozes from an infected wound. If they truly believed these women were witches, maybe they thought that was the best place to send them back. The trials went on for days. The bodies piled so high that eventually the grave became a mound."

"Oh my God," Jane cried. "The mound that the tree grows from."

Mrs. Leadley nodded. "Yessss." She hissed the word like a snake. "They murdered dozens of women in that pit. Hung each one on inverted crucifixes, so when their throats were slit, their souls would be sent straight back down to hell. The whole town gathered to watch. It was a slaughter. Women were accused simply because the crops hadn't grown, because the summer was hot and caused a drought."

Mrs. Leadley barked a laugh. "Witchcraft, they called it. I call it madness. Many of the women confessed. And believe me, you'd confess too if you went through what they had to. Thumb screws pressed into their eyes, metal braces put on their legs and held over a brazier. Lashes to their backs, bones broken, kneecaps smashed to pieces with stone hammers.

They confessed to put an end to it. The whole town watched as every single woman was tortured, maimed, and crucified. To then have their throats slit like pigs in an abattoir.

"The last woman they brought out for trial was a woman named Ragan Read. A young woman, widowed in the Civil War. She was dragged into the pit screaming, begging for them to listen to her, telling them they had made a mistake. She was no witch; she was a mother who lived a peaceful life, but she had angered the town council. Years before, she had been raped by five men. She accused the men responsible and, despite many threats and public humiliations, she had refused to back down.

"As many evil men do, they used any opportunity to rid themselves of their inconveniences. She withstood torture for as long as she could before confessing. But before she was killed and buried in the dirt, they brought her daughter out to stand before her. A girl no older than nine. They made Ragan confess that she was a witch to her daughter. Then, they condemned the daughter for sharing the Devil's blood with her witch mother. They slit the child's throat.

"Some of the townspeople who witnessed it said her screams echoed around those woods for days after. The judge ordered the little girl to be taken away and said: 'We'll take her and bury her far away from you, maybe the Lord will take pity on one so young.'

"Before they slit Ragan's throat, she prayed to Satan; she screamed her prayers. Maybe she thought he had more chance of hearing her if she did, maybe it was just the pain and the heartbreak. Whatever it was, He heard her. She begged him to give her the power to get her revenge, to grant her the power to bring her daughter back from the dead. She promised to raise every woman that had been killed, and together they would gather souls for him. The ground shook, flocks of crows filled the sky, flying in circles, cawing and swooping down to the ground, attacking the witnesses. Some said Ragan's eyes turned as red as the fires of Hell.

"Those women may not have been evil in life, but they were evil in death. Ragan began chanting, and the sound of screaming could be heard from the mound of buried witches. The judge yelled the order before the executioner lost his mettle and ran away with the frightened crowds. They slit Ragan's throat, but the words and screams kept coming from her open mouth. A voice full of evil promised to return and kill every living soul. She was buried in the dirt.

"The town knew what they had unleashed. The evil would come back if they didn't do something to stop it. They dug a channel that led from the River Were all the way to the devil's pit. Upon the last burial, they lifted the dam and the water gushed into the crater, covering the witch's graves. Once the reservoir was full, the holy men blessed the water so as long as water remained in that pit, the evil would be kept at bay."

"Now that it's empty, they're free to escape? But how can that be?"

"I believe that since the sun dried up all of that blessed holy water, those evil creatures buried under that soil have been free to commit their evil doings by corrupting the innocent. They were once innocent women, but not anymore. I believe they are back for revenge, for justice. They are harvesting souls to give them the power they need to return from the grave. Gareth Weeds and Alan Houghton were not responsible for what they did; they were puppets, guided by an evil master. The children got their throats slit to send a message. To let us know that they're returning. And Jane, if they come back, we're all doomed."

JANE DIDN'T KNOW how to process everything Mrs. Leadley had told her. It seemed like something straight out of a Stephen King novel. Evil, the likes of which Mrs. Leadley had just told her of, was a thing of myths and fiction, not small country towns in the north of England.

"Where did they bury the girl?" Jane asked.

Mrs. Leadley shrugged. "Nobody in the town wanted her to be buried in the church yard like everyone else, in case she was like what her mother was accused of being. The mayor of the town took the body away. Only he knows what he did with her."

"If what you've told me is true, then why hasn't something like this happened before?" Jane sounded almost on the verge of panic.

"It's always been there, my sweet girl." Mrs. Leadley smiled, as if Jane were nothing but a naïve child. "It infects people, makes them do its bidding. Wymere doesn't have a big crime rate, people don't feel the need to lock their doors every night out of fear that they will be robbed, but when something does happen, which it does more often than what gets reported in the papers and on the news, it's bad. Ask Anna Willow, who now lives by the sea with her maimed son, she'll tell you exactly what evil lurks in this place. How it infects those around us."

"I don't know what you mean."

Mrs. Leadley waved a dismissive hand through the air. "If you haven't heard, it'll have to be a story for another day. Sophie Rose going missing is another example; she was a good girl and whatever happened to her... well, it won't have been nice. She could be buried out there with that evil, doing God-knows-what to her soul. The fact of the matter is this: bad things happen in this town, things that can't be explained, things that are either too difficult, or just simply don't make sense. So, they push those things to one side until everyone's forgotten."

Mrs. Leadley shook her head and ground her yellow teeth together until they creaked in her mouth. "They won't be able to push this one aside, because it's too late!" She slammed her fist against her knee as she shouted. "The evil is here, and it's come for us all."

Jane spent the rest of the afternoon discussing all the avenues they could take to stop anyone else getting killed. When she checked her watch and realised the whole day had gone, she left for home, with the story Mrs. Leadley had just told her still playing over and over in her mind. She was on the edge of believing, despite the rational part of her brain screaming at her to wake up, that she was obviously caught in another vivid dream.

But when she looked up at the black night sky and saw the blood red super moon sitting up there, like an evil eye keeping watch over Wymere, her blood ran cold, and she knew it was true.

CHAPTER 58

The ticking clock in the autopsy room finally reached midnight. Doctor Francis Moss was writing up his notes and taking accompanying photographs of the bodily remains that lay on the steel table. The radio played low in the background. Creedence Clearwater Revival were singing a song warning about a rising moon, the doctor hummed along merrily. The sounds of his pencil skittering across the page seemed to compete with the song, then seemed to fall into its rhythm.

The old doctor didn't notice this; he was too busy trying to relay his findings into words that made sense. But his findings didn't really make sense to him, so relaying them was proving more than difficult. He'd tried two drafts before this one, and still the words didn't do justice to it; neither did the photos he'd taken from every possible angle.

What he said to the mayor a couple of hours earlier wasn't exactly a humorous exaggeration, even as irrational as it sounded. *'It's almost as if the tissue on the bones has regenerated.'*

Doctor Francis Moss had been a fully qualified doctor for

fifty years. He would have retired, but the ever-growing development of modern medicine intrigued him so greatly, he couldn't pull himself away. As long as he was of sound mind and able-bodied enough to work, that's what he wanted to do; he would work until his dying breath if it helped ease the workload that crippled the glorious NHS. There seemed to be new medicines and new treatments being discovered every day, as well as new diseases and viruses that needed cures to be found for them. It was fascinating to him, if he wasn't working, he was at home reading about it, learning the new ways as best he could. You can't teach an old dog new tricks, as the saying goes, but Doctor Moss said bullshit to that. He could learn just as much as the next guy.

When he started working on this body, this body that had clearly been buried for a long, long time, he struggled to understand why flesh and muscle tissue were still attached to the bone. The skeleton itself looked strong; flesh clung to the jawbone and the teeth were tight in the mouth. The eyes were nonexistent, but the black holes that were left seemed to put an uneasiness into him. He couldn't look into them for long; his whole body would shiver and the room seemed to drop by ten degrees. Maybe he was more tired than he thought.

When he inspected the tissue, he expected bugs to come crawling out, or for the flesh to simply peel away from the bones in strips, like beef jerky. But what he found was that the muscle fibres and fatty tissue that covered it were almost that of someone that had died hours ago, not years ago. But some of the bones were so bare, it was as if they had been buried decades ago. So, his crazy hypothesis that the flesh had started to grow back, to regenerate onto the bones, seemed to be a viable conclusion.

But that was crazy. Wasn't it?

It had to be, he was wrong, mistaken; he'd made a huge error and couldn't possibly send it off in his report because they would strike his practicing license from him for being of unsound mind. They could even lock him away at Hill Top, his findings were so hysterically mad. He'd rather die by torture than under the care of that evil bastard, Mahone.

Doctor Moss went over his findings again, examined the tissue and muscle fibres again, and came back to the same ludicrous conclusion. He went over it so many times that in the end, he had to write it into his findings.

He didn't look in those dark eyes again though; he felt afraid to. Then he did start to feel like he was losing it. What was he afraid of? A dead body, laid on his table? He laughed out loud and the sound made him jump. His heart raced and he was sweating, although the room was chilly, kept at a low temperature to help preserve the bodies whilst he worked on them. Still, he sweated and the collar of his shirt felt as if it tightened around his neck.

Creedence sang louder, as if someone had turned the radio up, the warning of this bad moon rising becoming more severe, a greater threat, and Doctor Moss had to get out. He felt the anxiety in his chest. He looked around the room, he felt eyes on him, as if he were being watched.

"Hello?" he said. Now he *was* crazy. "Is someone there?"

He looked around the room, saw the line of steel tables against the wall, a sink, cupboards full of medical equipment and PPE, drop lights that looked like the strip bulbs were imprisoned in steel cages... and the table where the body laid. A sheet was over it; only the feet stuck out of the end.

Moss watched the body. He gulped down a lump that had lodged in his throat, felt the hairs on the back of his neck tingle and stand on end. Was it the body he felt watching him?

You're crazy.

Am I?

YES!

He stood. He dabbed at the sweat that made his lips taste

of salt and put a finger under his collar, then tried to loosen it by undoing the top button. His fingers wouldn't work and a sense of panic came over him. His eyes stayed on the body, watching it as if it were a threat to him.

When he was unable to catch his breath, he looked down at his chest and used both hands to get that bastard top button undone so he could get some air into his lungs, so he could release the belt that seemed to be tightening around his chest!

He got the button out of the hole and the cool air rushed down his throat, giving him relief in the last moment before he passed out. He closed his eyes and chuckled to himself.

"You stupid old fool," he laughed.

He opened his eyes then. His throat closed as if he was gripped by a hand of ice. His heart stopped; he was sure it had. The white blanket that covered the body was now in a rumpled heap on the floor, the body was sat upright, those dark, empty eye sockets were looking at him, looking *in* him. They seemed to be looking at his soul the way a predator's eyes lock onto its next meal.

A voice spoke in his head, a voice that made no sense and yet he knew exactly what it wanted. His legs moved against his will and he began to cry. Through tear-filled eyes he saw the thing on the table grow closer and closer with every step he took; its hideous black eyes bore into him and its yellow teeth clenched together in a lipless grin. Clean, new tissue spotted in clumps on its jaw like in a grotesque fantasy of a corrupted mind.

"Please don't," he said.

The voice spoke again, and he knew it was all over. It wanted his soul. It was hungry. It told him so and he was defenceless against it.

Face to face with this thing, this demon of the undead, he sobbed like a lost boy, wanting to get home to his mother. Lost and afraid and alone, so alone with no one there to help him. The voice that infiltrated his head told him to be calm, that it would be over soon. The thing gripped his neck with its skeletal hand and pulled him so close that their mouths almost touched.

He could smell it now; he didn't before, and in the moments before he died, he was surprised that this was his last thought. It stank of wet rot and stagnant water. He wanted to puke, and did, but it wasn't the contents of his stomach that poured out of his mouth.

The thing breathed in what came from him, his essence, his soul. As it did, Doctor Moss's face began to shrink, his skin became creased and bone dry, as if all the moisture were being sucked out of him. When the thing let go of him, he dropped to the floor and hardly made a sound, weighing only a fraction of what he weighed seconds before. All he was now was skin and bone and dried up organs. Just like Alfie Weeds.

The thing stood from the table and stepped over the doctor, the same doctor who had once said he would have worked until his dying breath, and as it made its way toward the door, more jet-black hair began to sprout from its scalp. Flesh, muscle, and tendons grew over its bones, one eye grew in one of the black sockets, and the face that had been nothing but a skull, was now showing signs of fresh life. It was feeding, growing stronger with every soul it consumed, and it wanted more, it wanted more pain, more misery, more suffering. It wanted more souls.

It wanted them all.

CHAPTER 59

L ucy got home from Laura Kelly's and did her best to sleep, after pouring herself a stiff drink. She rarely drank, especially the hard stuff, but she needed one after everything Laura had told her.

Laura agreed that Lucy could be right, that Doctor Mahone was doing drug tests on the patients, recording a back-handed second income by performing these tests for pharmaceutical companies, privately owned ones that had the money to keep it all hush-hush. Mahone would have no problem doing it.

"It's like a power thing," Laura said. "He gets off on feeling in complete control, dominance over another living thing is his drug of choice, and he's in the perfect place to get it."

"I saw him buckling up his trousers when he was coming out of a storage room. I thought that maybe he was addicted to something? He had blood on his hands, so I thought he could have been injecting?"

Laura shook her head. "I don't think so. Mahone is many

things, but a junkie? Nope. Abusing his patients is his only drug."

"And you didn't stop him when you had the chance?" Lucy stood.

"It wasn't as simple as that."

"You took his money though, bought this house and what? Just leave the rest in the bank so you don't have to go out and face the world again? I see you've got nothing in here, you must have saved every penny. Is that your penance for your guilt? Huh?"

"I never spent the money! I live off the system, it doesn't pay a lot but it's enough to get me by. And no, I couldn't face the world, that's why I lock myself in here. I couldn't even go out now if I wanted to. I'm a prisoner, just like the patients at the damned hospital."

"Bullshit. If you didn't spend the money, why did you let him get away with it?"

Laura looked at Lucy as if she were a petulant child in the middle of a hissy fit. "You have no idea who he is, do you? He knows everybody; if he wants, he could stop you getting a job anywhere in a hundred-mile radius, he could have the police put a flag on your car so you get pulled over every time they run it through the scanner."

"But you could have had him sent to prison, surely then he wouldn't have been able to do anything to you?"

"It became clear to me that it would never have made it to trial. He would have made sure of it. I didn't sign that non-disclosure for the money, I did it because if I didn't, I wouldn't be here."

"You think he's capable of murder?"

"You don't? He told me he would kill me; that he'd dispose of my body in pieces, bury me all over the county. He's a psychopath."

Lucy ran her fingers through her hair. She thought she was going to be sick. "I have to go; I have to think of how I'm going to relay this to the police. Do you have any evidence at all?"

Laura thought about it; Lucy could see the fear as it grew inside her. "No, but I know where it'll be. There's a room in the psychiatric wing, it's the only room I never went in. It was off limits, strictly out of bounds. He padlocks it. If he's doing anything illegal, I'd bet my last pound that's where you'll find the truth. Get in there, and you'll have everything you need."

That last part ran on a loop through Lucy's mind. She tossed and turned in bed. The bright red moon shining through her window might have been the most ominous thing she'd ever seen. The street outside was lit up in a red glow.

It could be a sign, a sign that she had to do something, and it had to be now.

She kicked her sheets off and pulled on her trousers. Found a black top and black trainers, and ran out to the car. Her phone linked to the in-car stereo system; she dialled the number on the card she had been given on the first day of the search for Alfie Weeds. It was the direct line for Tony Thorne's office.

"Sergeant Thorne, I can't wait any longer for you to get back to me, so I'm going to do your job for you. My name is Lucy Swindle. I work for Doctor Mahone at Hill Top Psychiatric Hospital. I have reason to believe that he is abusing patients, running some sort of a drug testing scam on vulnerable patients, and getting paid a lot of money for the privilege. I don't have the evidence right now, but I'm going to get it. I'll prove that sonofabitch has been abusing his patients. He's a power tripping bastard. If you care at all about doing what's right, call me as soon as you get this. I need you to help me take him down."

By the time Lucy hung up, she was halfway there. Her hands gripped the steering wheel until her knuckles turned white.

CHAPTER 60

Tony used the drive home to try and piece all of this shit together. Everything seemed to focus around the woods; was there something in there that was sending people crazy? The signal for the drone was interrupted by something in there; maybe it was the same thing? Some sort of radioactive beam that turned the victim's brains into scrambled eggs, rewired their brains for long enough that they killed their children? None of it made sense. Did the same thing happen to Sophie? Had it been in there all along but nobody realised?

Try to patch it up as he might, none of it made sense. Not one bit. All he knew was that he didn't want to go into those woods. To that dried up old reservoir where the dead tree sprouted from the mound of black dirt. He thought of how nothing grew in the surrounding soil, as if it had been tainted, poisoned with something that destroyed all life. That, he thought, was probably the closest he'd come to hitting the nail on the head as to what was actually going on in Wymere.

He pulled onto his street, dreading seeing Sarah, not knowing how drunk she was going to be and not knowing what he was going to say to her, when he saw the flashing lights from an ambulance and a police car, lighting up every house on the street. He pressed harder on the accelerator, and as he rounded the corner, he saw that the cars were outside his house. He pulled onto the side and jumped out of the car before it came to a full stop. He ran toward two paramedics who were wheeling someone out of the house on a gurney.

"Sarah!" Tony shouted.

An officer appeared in front of him and tried to get him to stop so they could talk, but Tony pushed past him and got to the paramedics. He caught a glimpse of Maggie Colter giving a statement to another officer; her big chocolate Labrador that stood by her side looked straight at him.

Tony looked down at the gurney and saw Sarah laid there, her eyes were closed and for one horrifying second, he thought she might be dead. "What happened?" Tony asked.

The paramedics looked at each other.

"Come on, I'm her husband and a police officer, for God's sake!"

The male paramedic cleared his throat and carried on pushing the gurney; he was about to speak when Tony saw the rope burns deep into her neck. The oxygen mask over her mouth steamed and he felt a huge wave of relief when he realised she was breathing on her own.

"Your wife's lucky the neighbour found her when she did. Apparently her dog ran into your garden and saw Sarah through the window. Alerted them, and one of the other neighbours managed to run in and get her neck out of the rope. Your wife is lucky to be alive."

They loaded Sarah into the back of the ambulance and Tony got in beside her; he gripped her hand and kissed it. His lips were dry and tears fell down his cheeks.

"I'm so sorry, Sarah," he cried. "I love you. I really do, you deserved so much better than this, than me."

Sarah opened her eyes. They were terribly bloodshot; red

vein lines covered the whites of her eyes like a hundred spiders' legs. She lifted her hand to the mask and tried to take it off.

"No," Tony said, holding her hand again. "Leave it on. It'll help."

"Sir, we're going to have to give her some strong medications now, she's going to be extremely sedated, she caused quite a lot of damage to the tendons in her neck and every movement she makes is putting them under more strain."

Tony nodded.

Sarah freed her hand with a last show of strength and tried to move the mask down.

"Mahone..." she said.

"What?" Tony looked at her through tear filled eyes.

"Mahone... did it."

"Did what?" Tony said, unable to mask the confusion.

Then the drugs were injected into Sarah's arm, and she was unable to speak anymore.

CHAPTER 61

The sign for Hill Top Psychiatric Hospital glowed brightly against the backdrop of darkness that was the night sky. A red moon sat over it, making it look like the poster of some 80s horror film. Lucy parked down the road; without any streetlights, her car blended in with the shadows.

Lucy was one to jump in with both feet, her mum had always said it, and ever since she was nearly caught in Mahone's office, she was beginning to realise it more and more. This could be classed as one of those moments, because she knew she should really spend a day, maybe two, planning out exactly how she was going to do this. Work out an escape strategy if she got caught, liaise with an officer she could trust.

It was no secret that Mahone had half of the elected town officials in his pocket thanks to his wealth; could that filter down into some of the police on the ground? She would be naïve to think it didn't. People round town seemed to respect Tony Thorne; he had been raised in Wymere, and had always been a good guy. Lucy had never met him, but if the stories of him were true, then she thought that she could trust him.

Her mother had told her about when a young Tony

Thorne had searched the woods for months on end for his girlfriend, Sophie Rose; in fact, he had continued to search long after the police had given up. It would be romantic if it weren't so tragic. Lucy thought her mum told her that story as a warning for her to stay away from those woods, but that wasn't what Lucy had taken away from it.

Though, she thought that after recent events, maybe she should have.

Lucy grabbed a pair of bolt cutters from the boot of her car and made her way up the road, using the trees that flanked either side as cover. She emerged at the side of the hospital, where the orderlies and catering staff went to smoke and throw out the rubbish. She stepped out of the long grass and saw a big cat with ragged fur and big sagging teats, meowing over a small lump on the ground. Flies buzzed audibly in the air when the cat bent low to nudge the thing with its paws. When it saw Lucy, it hissed, its ears laid back against its head, before it skittered back into the long grass.

Lucy was about to check out what it was that the cat was looking at, when the back door of the hospital swung open. She ran behind the concrete steps and hid out of sight.

An orderly propped the door open with a stone and descended the stairs. Lucy peered round and saw him pull out a cigarette and light it up. He leaned his face back and blew a cloud of smoke into the air.

"I fucking hate this place," he said to himself. He set off walking toward the car park.

Lucy knew he would only walk so far, and then turn back. They all did it, they walked backward and forward until their cigarette was done, and then they went back inside. Her pulse raced; the adrenaline that surged through her was more electrifying than she had ever experienced before.

This is it, she told herself. *Time to jump in with both feet.*

Keeping low, she ran round to the front of the steps,

keeping her eyes on the orderly, who still walked in the opposite direction with his cigarette in his mouth. She grabbed the handrail, spinning herself onto the stairs that she took two at a time, and ran through the open door. She was in.

Lucy put a hand on her chest and tried her best to control her breathing, but she was out of breath, panting like a dog trapped in a hot car, although it was down to the fear of getting caught more than the physical exertion.

She wanted to sit and take a minute to gather herself, but there wasn't time. She had to get in and get out quickly. Get to that room at the end of the corridor and see what was inside.

A few deep breaths, and Lucy made her way through the labyrinth of corridors.

It was easier to avoid people than she thought it would be. The night shift was always quiet. Most of the hospital was full of easy patients that slept well; the other patients, the ones who were the most challenging, were kept on a lot of drugs, which helped to keep them spaced out for most of the night. The staff were mainly there on a "just in case" basis.

This didn't stop Lucy from walking down each corridor with her back pressed tightly against the wall, and peering around every corner she came to. From the back entrance, it was a surprisingly long way to the psychiatric wing, where the higher care patients were kept. Lucy thought she'd lost her way for one moment, and then saw the sign pointing her in the right direction.

Once in the right wing, she stepped quietly, for the night seemed to amplify every step she took on the hard floor. She wished it was carpeted like the hallway leading to Mahone's office, then she could run all the way to the end to the last room.

There were noises from the rooms of patients, murmuring, moans and groans. One patient was sobbing loudly and shouting incoherent words full of despair. Lucy wished she could help them all.

Focus, she thought, not letting herself be distracted. The door of the last room was in sight. She checked over her shoulder and saw a long empty corridor behind her. No one had seen her, no one was coming. She stopped outside the door and took a few extra breaths. She lifted the bolt cutters to the padlock. They were heavy, and as she squeezed them together her arms began to shake. For a second, she didn't think she had the power to cut through the lock, then *snap,* the blades cut through the thick metal, sending the padlock clattering to the floor. She looked around to ensure the coast was still clear.

It was.

She twisted the handle, and pushed the door open.

Chapter 62

The day had been long and Mahone was ready to grab a shower and sleep it all away. Lucy was going to be a problem. A problem that could wait until morning, however. It was Laura Kelly all over again. Only, Mahone had spent a day with Lucy, and he didn't think that she would be as easily warned off. Laura had a backbone, stood up to him for a time until he got serious. Told her in great detail how he would get rid of her, should the need arise for him to make her disappear for good. He suspected Lucy had a bit more fight in her; she was one of those idealists that thought good always triumphed over evil in the end. So naïve he almost felt sorry for her.

He had his shirt unbuttoned and the belt buckle of his trousers undone when his phone lit up on his bedside table. He frowned, and walked over to pick it up. It vibrated until it almost crept its way over the edge when he picked it up.

"Hello?"

"Hello, Mr. Mahone?"

"Doctor Mahone," he corrected. "Who is this?" Mahone was sharp, he was tired and after the day he'd had, he wanted nothing more than the feel of his bed underneath him.

"Sorry, Doctor. It's Constable Westlake, we spoke earlier?"

Mahone sighed tiredly. "Yes? I assume there's a reason you're calling me this late?"

"Yes, there is, sir."

"Well, go on then, spit it out boy." Mahone's patience was nil.

"Sorry, so I did what you said, I've kept my ears open, so to speak, to see if anyone rang concerning you. I was about to clock off when I heard Tony Thorne's phone ringing in his office. I didn't answer it, but I waited for it to go to voicemail. It was a woman called Lucy Swindle? She says she's got reason to believe you're abusing patients, possibly running illegal drug tests on them?"

Mahone ground his teeth; his brow creased in frustration as well as anger. "Did she say she had evidence of this?"

There was a pause from Westlake. "No, just a testimony from a former employee, as well as her own account of things she has witnessed. It sounds crazy, but I think Tony will follow this up, sir."

Now Mahone was silent. He ground his teeth until they squeaked.

"Thank you for notifying me. I will deal with it."

"Okay, I did good though, right?"

"Yes."

"So, will you put in a word to the mayor about –"

Mahone hung up the phone and threw it on the bed. He paced the room; his hands rested on his hips as a rage brewed inside him that he didn't know how to control. He grabbed his phone again, clicked open the CCTV app for the hospital and waited for the images to load.

Hill Top should be quiet at this time of night, especially the psychiatric wing where he worked the most. He made sure that each patient was sufficiently sedated when he left for the night, so that they would need little to no care. He lived a mile away, on the finer side of Wymere, so if he saw anything he didn't like, it was a five-minute drive, three minutes if he put his foot down, and he'd be there to put a stop to it.

On the screen of his phone, he saw a woman, slim, dressed in black, slowly walking down the hall, keeping her back pressed against the wall. She looked over her shoulder and almost made eye contact with the camera.

"Lucy," Mahone said under his breath. He watched as she scurried toward the end of the hall.

She'd been to see Laura, and Laura had told Lucy her wild fantasies. They were all bullshit, of course, but Mahone would rather have someone believe that he was using experimental drugs on patients than find out the truth.

His shirt flapped in the night air as he ran to his car, looking like the wings of an angel. Or a demon.

CHAPTER 63

Lucy laid the bolt cutters on the floor and crept into the room. It smelt stale and musty like a cupboard that rarely got an influx of fresh air. It was dark; only a small emergency light glowed, making every wall a dark shade of green. There were no windows, only solid walls, some of which were covered in handprints and smears that looked black in the green light.

"What the fuck is this place?" Lucy looked around. This was supposed to be a storage room, she had expected to find boxes of different kinds of restraints, paperwork, files, documents. Yet, what it actually looked like was a patient's room.

It had a sink on the left-hand wall, with a soap and paper towel dispenser above it. Along the back wall was a small bed, the length of a standard single but narrower, like a prison bed, Lucy thought. Then, she thought about how this place was nothing more than a prison for some of the patients that were here.

There was something on the bed, something wrapped in a blanket with black straps. She stepped closer to it, her heart

253

beating rapidly now, the hairs on the back of her neck stood on end, not knowing what she would uncover when she reached out and touched it. She reached out her shaking hand and stopped just short of touching whatever lay there. It moved. Then it made a pitiful sound, low and weak, not quite words but as if it were trying to communicate.

Lucy's breathing was loud and hurried, the fear that gripped her throat made her want to run away. This isn't what she came here to see, she was here to collect documents, evidence that Mahone had been testing illegal drugs.

She steadied herself. The thing on the bed moaned once more. Lucy outstretched a hand and touched it. It began to cry. Lucy didn't feel fear anymore, she felt a resounding pity for the thing that laid on the bed. She gently squeezed the thing's upper arm; it was so thin Lucy could almost grip her hand all the way around it. She pulled to turn the thing over, see who or what it was.

Lucy gasped and stepped back a few paces, almost back to the door she came in, hoping she'd be able to make more sense of what it was she had seen the first time. It was a woman. Her back faced toward Lucy. A row of brown leather straps that kept her locked in her straitjacket, were buckled up to the last hole. She was breathing, heavily, it seemed to Lucy.

The door was nestled gently in its casing but the latch didn't catch. Lucy walked back toward the woman; but didn't speak as she didn't want to startle her. In the dark, Lucy tripped over something and fell to the floor, landing against the hard tile with enough force that all the air was knocked out of her. She laid there, trying to get her breath back. She looked toward the bed, it looked strange seeing it upside down; stranger still, the woman in bed hadn't reacted at all to Lucy's presence.

Lucy sat up, gasped two welcome breaths of air, and looked for what she had tripped over. A yellow hazardous waste bin was tipped on its side in the middle of the floor. Lucy grabbed it and put it back upright under the sink where it should have been. As she did, she saw a bunch of needles inside it. She thanked God for the small favour that the one-way lid was on, meaning the needles didn't spill out all over the floor for her to stick herself with as she tried to navigate through the dark. The needles had labels on them. It was impossible to read what was written, however, Lucy didn't need to see much of the label to figure out it was a strong sedative. The ones Mahone had taken from the medication trolley.

The woman in the bed was highly sedated; no wonder she couldn't form intelligible words.

"Shit," Lucy snapped under her breath.

The woman didn't look big, no bigger than herself, really, and thanks to what Lucy was sure would have been a rationed diet, the woman was extremely thin. None of that meant that she would have the strength to carry an adult woman down the corridors, out into the car park, and down the road to her car. Especially not without being caught.

Lucy stood and went over to the woman. She stood over her and rolled her onto her back. A fast panic shot through her then when she thought the woman was going to tumble straight off the bed and onto the floor. She didn't. Lucy managed to stop her and let her roll down gently onto her back.

"How are we going to do this?" Lucy said.

She looked around the room for inspiration, saw nothing but four green-tinged walls.

"Hheppp mmm." The woman was trying to speak, her eyes were closed but her dry, cracked lips moved, trying to form words.

She wasn't fully sedated, Lucy realised gratefully.

"Miss, I need you try and get up. I'm going to get you out of here, but I need you to try and walk. Can you do that?"

"Hrreeepp mmm," the woman said louder. Louder was good, Lucy thought; she had fight, determination. That was good. Lucy bent low to get her arms under the woman's back; she wanted to try get her sat upright, see if she could drink a bit of water. Lucy thought she could slap her, that might help, but the poor woman had been through enough. As she bent low, she looked straight at the woman and saw how beautiful she was, or could be once the bruises healed and the swelling went down. Her hair was matted and greasy, and the cut of it was uneven, as if Mahone had just hacked at it with blunt scissors.

"Come on, we're getting you out of here." Lucy, filled with a determination that burned from somewhere deep inside her, managed to get the woman sat upright in bed. As soon as she let go, the woman tried to flop back down. Lucy grabbed hold of her and almost screamed in her ear, "Get up! Come on!"

"Heepp mee," the woman mumbled.

"Help you?" Lucy said. "I'm trying to help you." Lucy looked and saw the belts buckled at the back of her strait-jacket. "Let me get these off." Lucy began fumbling with each buckle, the first came off easily, the last two held more strain now that the woman was beginning to use what little strength she had to try and force her way out of it. Lucy did the last two and the woman's arms flopped down in front of her. She sighed with relief and Lucy thought she saw a tear roll down the woman's face.

Lucy finished removing the straitjacket by unfastening more straps and belts and a zip that ran all the way up the woman's spine.

"Okay, you're out," Lucy said. She peeled the straitjacket from the woman. She was naked underneath, her ribs covered in discoloured patches, bruises and healed cuts. Mahone had been torturing this woman for a long time. Lucy felt sick.

The woman was sitting up by herself now and her eyes had started to open. Lucy took off her own jumper and gave it to the woman. She put the jumper over the woman's head gingerly and helped her feed her arms through.

"Right, we need to go, if someone spots us, Mahone will be here and we'll both be fucked."

The woman was able to get up from the bed with Lucy's support. Her arm wrapped around Lucy's neck. They shuffled slowly toward the door. They could do this, Lucy thought, but it was going to be arduous.

They reached the door; Lucy pulled it open and poked her head into the corridor.

"All clear," she was about to say, when she saw Mahone turn the corner at the top of the hall. His feet thundered on the hard floor as he walked with menace toward her. She got her head back in and shut the door.

"He's coming." Lucy ushered the woman back toward the bed. She had fifteen seconds to think of a way out. There were no windows, nowhere to hide; it was a narrow room with a bed, a sink, and a bin.

Lucy felt the sweat trickle down her back; her black under-shirt clung to her skin and her pulse thumped loudly in her ears. She had jumped straight in and not thought of an escape plan.

Lucy looked around for the bolt cutters, but the green shade of the emergency light made it hard to focus. "Where are they –"Then she remembered. "Fuck!" She'd left them outside in the corridor. Desperate and doing her best not to panic, she bent, picked up the first thing that came to hand, and hid against the wall, so when the door opened, she would be stood behind it.

She tried to control her breathing. It was so heavy and loud, she was sure Mahone would have been able to hear her over his clomping footsteps that grew closer and closer – until they stopped dead.

He was at the door.

The door opened slowly. Lucy clutched what she had grabbed from the floor and held it to her chest. It was the hazard waste bin; she felt stupid for grabbing it, but it was all she had available. A long, thin, Mahone-shaped shadow stretched out on to the floor.

He stepped in; the sound echoed in the dark room. He took two more steps, then stopped and swung the door closed behind him. He was facing the woman. This was Lucy's chance. She could hit him, hopefully she had enough force to knock him down, then she could hit him over and over again until he was out cold. Giving them chance to escape.

Lucy raised the bin; it felt pathetically light. Mahone stepped forward, which meant Lucy had to take a step closer to be able to reach him.

She drew in a deep breath and swung the bin at the back of his head. It connected with a loud, hollow *thwack.*

He didn't fall. He turned around with one hand on the back of his head and lunged at her. She dropped the bin and crashed against the wall. The wind was knocked out of her. He raised a hand and punched her, sending the green room into a swirl of white spots and black shapes. She was on her back now, looking up at the ceiling. She lifted her hands to protect herself, but Mahone lifted them up over her head and straddled her, using his knees to hold her arms down. He sat on her chest, stopping her from getting any air into her lungs.

"You meddlesome bitch!" Mahone grunted as his hands clasped around Lucy's throat. "After you, I'll deal with Laura. No one tries to take me down and get away with it, nobody!"

He squeezed harder. Lucy felt the tendons in her neck strain and creak against the strength of his grip. She managed to pry a finger between his hand and her neck, which allowed two small life-saving breaths to enter her lungs and keep the darkness at bay for what would be a very precious ten more seconds.

The woman Lucy had been trying to save appeared behind Mahone. She was stumbling, but her eyes were wide and her mouth curled in a sneer. In her hand, she held a hypodermic needle. Lucy saw the hazardous waste bucket was on the floor with the lid torn off. The sedative had worn off enough that the woman could attack, but she was doing it so slowly, Lucy didn't think the woman would strike in time to save her.

Just as everything started to turn black, the woman fell on top of Mahone. The shock made him release his grip on Lucy's neck and they tumbled to the side. Lucy rolled over and sucked air into her lungs, air that felt like napalm as it burnt her throat. She coughed and wheezed, felt at her neck where the marks were already starting to show in thick red lines that would one day soon turn to purple and black.

She looked over to the woman and Mahone, then smiled at what she saw. Mahone was on his back, desperately trying to block the woman's frantic attacks. She stabbed him with the needle countless times in the chest, the face, neck, arms, hands. Every time one of the needles snapped in his flesh she reached down and grabbed another and began stabbing again. She was screaming, and the sound filled the room with such a deafeningly sharp quality that Lucy's ears rang.

Lucy got to her feet. Her legs were wobbly, but adrenaline powered her through.

The woman began to tire, and Mahone took his chance. He pushed the woman off, swung a clumsy fist but it caught her hard enough in the temple to send her into a daze. Lucy grabbed her arm. "Come on, we need to get out of here!"

Lucy dragged the woman to the door. Mahone writhed around on the floor, wincing and groaning in pain. Blood covered his white shirt; red spots dotted his face and torso.

"Get back here!" His shouts were laboured, and Lucy realised that there might have been some sedative left in that needle. "You take her, I'll fucking kill you!" Mahone screamed. But Lucy was already out the door, and the woman was with her.

CHAPTER 64

Josh Jones, or JJ to his friends, was hanging out with his gang of fellow fifteen-year-olds in the skate park. Tim had brought a couple of joints worth of weed, so JJ skinned up two fat ones underneath the half pipe and passed them round. They had reached the stage where everything was so hilariously funny that they laughed until tears rolled from their eyes, and JJ's girlfriend, Gina, reached the status of legend because she had brought two share bags of Doritos in her backpack.

JJ had his fingers deep into the crevices of said Doritos bag – the dust at the bottom was the tastiest bit – and then sucked his fingers clean, when one of his friends shouted from the top side of the skate ramp: "Hey guys, check out this chick!"

They all jumped out from under the ramp and scurried up the smooth curve to get to the platform on top. When one of the guys shouted to look at a chick, it meant she was a hottie. Gina was not impressed.

JJ got up first. "Where, man?" he said.

"Look over there, JJ," Tim said, pointing out to the open

grassland of the park in front of the woods. The blood red moon sat over the trees, big and bright; it illuminated the park well enough so that JJ could make out a woman walking toward the woods. She looked late twenties, early thirties at the most, but it was hard to tell from a hundred yards away, even with the strange light cast down from the moon.

The strangest thing was that she was naked. From the angle they had, JJ could see her left breast bouncing as she walked across the grass. It was a hot evening, JJ couldn't remember the last time they'd had a cold evening, the heatwave had gone on so long, but for a woman to be out in the middle of the night, naked and alone? It didn't sit right. Something was going on, and JJ wanted no part of it.

"Hey baby, you look like you're after a good time. I've got a good time right here for ya!" Adam, the mouthy, always-gets-you-into-trouble member of the group, pulled out his cock and started whirling it around in the direction of the naked woman.

"Hey, stop screwing around. Maybe she's hurt?" JJ said, but the guys were laughing too hard for Adam to stop now. He was a performer, and now he had an extra member in the audience.

"Come on baby, you think you can handle this?! Let's put my good time in your fun zone, whaddya say?"

The naked woman stopped abruptly. She turned to face them, and as she did, JJ noticed that random parts of her body were covered in black shadow. It was the middle of the night, and she was stood a hundred yards away, but the big red moon cast enough light that the white fleshy patches of her skin were visible. The black patches of shadow made no sense. Her right breast wasn't visible, the area of stomach above her "fun zone" was black, as well as most of her right leg.

"Guys," JJ said. His voice shook with a fear he normally wouldn't want the other guys to notice, but right then he was too scared to think of hiding it. "Guys, I think something's wrong."

"Yeah." Tim laughed. "You don't say? Either that pot I got us was the strongest shit I've ever got my hands on, or there's some naked hottie walking right towards us. I think we're in for an unforgettable night."

"JJ, I don't like this." It was Gina; she stood at the bottom of the half pipe where the curve turned into flat ground. "I want to go home. Take me home?"

JJ looked at Gina and then back to the woman. The guys weren't laughing as hard now, and he could see why. The closer the woman got, the clearer it became what the spots of shadow on her body were.

Adam whirled his cock in the air doing his favourite helicopter impression, laughing wildly, until he saw it too.

"Dude, what the fuck is going on with this bitch?" Adam said.

The black spots weren't shadows at all, it was clear what they were… kind of. What wasn't clear was how this woman was walking around without any sign of pain or discomfort. Patches of her flesh were gone, but there was no blood. It wasn't as if they had been cut out or ripped out – more like the patches had started to decay. Like those parts of her were dead and rotting.

"JJ, I want to go home, now!" Gina sounded frantic, about as frantic as JJ felt. Only he couldn't voice it. He couldn't move; his legs had stiffened and his voice had frozen in his throat.

The woman reached the perimeter fence. The boys took a collective step backward, and JJ nearly fell down the ramp, which worked to jump start him out of his petrified stance. He jumped down to the ground; the impact sent a thud vibrating through the metal ramp that echoed around the park.

"Come on, let's get out of here." JJ grabbed Gina's hand, then she started to scream.

JJ turned to see what Gina had seen, and he saw the woman floating through the air, her arms spread wide, her feet close together, looking like the shape of a crucifix. She was five feet from the ground, and by the time she had floated toward the gang of stoned teenagers that stood on top of the ramp, she was eye to eye with Adam, who stood with his mouth open and his cock in his hands, his cock which had now shrivelled away to keep safe.

The woman was beautiful, the most beautiful woman JJ had ever seen, and also the most terrifying. A smile worked its way across her red lips as she surveyed every boy there.

"Come on," JJ whispered to Gina, trying to pull her away. It was as if Gina had now petrified where she stood. He managed to get himself and Gina hidden behind the flat bank ramp to the side of the half pipe, where he could watch the whole thing.

The flying woman's eyes turned red, as if small fires had been lit inside them. She slowly raised her hands and everyone that stood on top of that ramp began floating up into the air, like hot air balloons that had just been unhooked from their anchors.

They started to scream and beg for their lives, but their limbs looked to have been frozen stiff. JJ couldn't watch, yet couldn't take his eyes from it. It was the strangest thing he had ever seen.

That isn't a woman.

He said it over and over to himself. He couldn't figure out what it was. A demon? A ghost? A witch? Every film he had ever seen now seemed possible.

JJ watched as his friends floated over toward her, then something snapped, with a hard *crack,* like a branch snapping from a tree. Tim started screaming. Then they all started screaming. Their arms and legs bent and snapped into unnatural positions. There were multiple hard crack sounds now, one after the other, like a chain of firecrackers had been lit.

Their screams filled the night by the time their bodies were mangled and snapped into obscene shapes, floating in the air. The woman stopped torturing them. She opened her mouth wide and took several long, deep breaths.

JJ noticed then that his friends had stopped screaming. He could also see that their skin was shrinking to their bones, as if their insides were being sucked out of them.

A sort of steam – this was the way he would describe it to the officer he reported it to later that night – came out of the boys' mouths. Tim, Adam, Scott, Louie – the steam poured out of their mouths and the woman sucked it all in. When she was finished, she laughed loudly. It was an awful sound. High and shrill, with a rough quality that gave it a terrible croak.

"JJ, if we don't leave now, she's going to get us too," Gina pleaded. She was crying, and so was he, he realised.

"Wait, let her leave," JJ replied.

JJ and Gina sat behind the flat bank ramp and waited in silence, holding each other's hands and praying that they would see another hot day this summer.

The woman dropped down to the ground, groaning with pleasure, her fists clenched down by her sides as she shivered. The black patches of rot began to move, flesh started to knit together. New flesh, living flesh full of blood and life, grew where there had been none. When it was over, there wasn't a single patch of rot on her. She was complete.

Happy and whole after her meal, she turned back and carried on toward the woods, to do whatever it was she had started to do that night, before this gang of stoned teenagers thought it to be a good idea to shout after a woman in the park.

JJ and Gina waited until the woman disappeared into the

trees, and then ran for the nearest place they could find, that would have a police officer.

To their backs was the bright red moon, and the storm clouds that gathered beneath it.

CHAPTER 65

The paramedics were great. Despite all of his years of training and experience dealing with high intensity situations that could mean injury or death, Tony was a wreck. He had turned into the proverbial tits on a bull: useless. He watched on as the medics rushed Sarah down the corridors of the hospital to the emergency room. The damage looked minimal at first; they weren't sure how long her brain had been starved of oxygen, but the fact she was talking, or trying to talk initially, was an extremely positive sign. Albeit jumbled up nonsense.

Mahone... did it.

She had said that to Tony. At least that's what Tony thought she had said. It was hard to hear her over the sirens and the screaming voices in his head telling him this was all his fault.

The problem, they found as they approached the hospital, was that she had dropped with such force, that the sudden forceful jerk of the rope going taught around her neck looked to have broken or dislodged a couple of vertebrae, and an impact that severe could damage the carotid artery.

Tony was told this by a doctor, standing in the hospital corridor. Sarah had started seizing as they unloaded her from the ambulance; she was taken into emergency surgery.

"It's rare, but people who hang themselves, or attempt to hang themselves, can sometimes die as much as two months later if the damage to carotid artery isn't spotted. She's lucky, so to speak, that she seized. If she hadn't, we might not have realised. Some patients can go about their recovery as normal, walking and talking as they did before and then one day, just fall down dead."

Tony wasn't sure what to say. "Thank you" was all he could come up with.

The doctor sat him down in the waiting room, got him a fresh cup of coffee, and told him he'd be back with news as soon as he had any. "She's in the best place," he added before shutting the door.

Tony looked at the coffee and thought of how badly he'd treated Sarah. How selfish he'd been. That made him think of Sophie, who could be laid out on a slab down the hall being poked and prodded by Doctor Francis Moss. Although, he doubted Doctor Moss was still there. He'd have finished his shift by now.

Tony checked his watch and saw it was nearly one a.m. It was going to be a long night.

The truth was, it was going to be a much longer night than Tony realised.

SARAH WAS in surgery for half an hour. The damage to the artery was minimal, an 'easy fix,' the doctor who performed the surgery said.

Tony followed the directions given to him and walked through the wards full of the old and the sick. The smell was awful, the noises were worse. Puking, crying, screaming – it was intense. Tony hoped Sarah was somewhere else. She was. He ended up finding her on a mental health ward, standard practice after a suicide.

Thank God they didn't send her to Hill Top, he thought.

Her eyes were closed, dark semi-circles swollen beneath them. A white bandage was wrapped around her neck where the incision had been made and a nurse was fitting a foam brace. The nurse looked up at Tony and smiled thinly.

I bet this is your fault. I don't know how, but I bet it is, that smile seemed to say to him.

To Tony's relief, she left. He sat beside Sarah and held her hand.

"I'm so sorry, Sarah. I hope one day you can forgive me." He stood and kissed her forehead. She murmured and then winced as she tried to shuffle herself in the bed.

"Sarah?" Tony looked up for a nurse. He wasn't sure if he was supposed to do something or tell someone. In the end he opted to stand, looking back and forth between Sarah and the curtain, which was only halfway pulled round. Only halfway, so any passing doctor and nurse could check that Sarah was okay, and hadn't woken up with an urge to end her shitty life again.

Sarah mumbled something that Tony couldn't make out. He put his ear near her mouth.

"What is it, honey?" he said.

It was hard to be sure, because it made no sense. Not to Tony anyway.

"So-phie," Sarah whispered.

Tony stood up straight and tried his best to wrap his head around what it all meant.

Just then a nurse walked through the curtain, wheeling in a blood pressure monitor.

"I just need to check her vitals, is that okay?" He was a big guy, looked more like a wrestler than a nurse. Stood a good whole foot over Tony and about the same measurement wider. Yet, when he spoke his voice was warm and welcoming.

"That's fine, thank you," Tony said, moving out of the way so the nurse could get through.

"No problem," the nurse said. He wrapped the blood pressure cuff around Sarah's arm and slipped a heartbeat monitor onto the tip of her finger. The nurse put one hand on his hip and rested the other on the machine as he watched the numbers on the screen dance. He let out a tired sigh as the machine let out a whirring sound, filling the cuff with air.

"God, it has been a busy one tonight," the nurse said. Tony turned to face him and saw his badge said Chris Wool.

"It looks it. The wards seem packed."

Chris nodded enthusiastically. "It's the heat. It's either dehydrating people and making them ill, or is making them do crazy stuff like jumping in rivers, lakes, streams – they hurt themselves, or get some nasty infection from the water, urgh." He stuck out his tongue to show how gross that was.

"Should calm down at this time, though?"

"You'd think. Obviously, we've got your wife here, then a car crash came in from the 66, an old lady fell down a flight of stairs at her home and broke a hip, bless her, then we've just had two women running in screaming like a couple of witch's cats! Honest to God, what a palaver." Chris rolled his eyes and turned to look at the numbers. Happy with what he saw, he tore off the cuff, the Velcro giving a loud *thripp* sound as he did, then he wound up the heartbeat sensor and hung it on the machine.

"That all looks good. Press the buzzer if you need anything, and one of us will come running."

"You're a star."

"Oh, I know it," Chris said and winked.

Tony, processing everything the nurse had said, couldn't

help but focus on the last thing. He put his hand on Chris's shoulder before he got further than the curtain. "What were the two women screaming about? Had something happened?"

Chris rolled his eyes again; something told Tony that Chris did that a lot. "Oh, I dunno, it was hard to make sense of it really. One of the women was practically dead on her feet, looked to be nothing but skin and bone, could barely walk without being held up by the other one. The other one looked healthier, but in a right state, y'know, emotionally. She kept saying, 'Someone needs to call Thorne, I need Thorne. He has to stop Mahone.' Anyway, she's been taken to a quiet room whilst the other one gets treated."

Chris scrunched up his face then and looked at the chart in his hand. "Wait a second, is your name Thorne?"

AFTER BEING ASSURED that Sarah would be checked on regularly by the staff, Tony went to see what this woman wanted, and why she was screaming his name in the middle of the night in a hospital. And what the hell had Mahone done?

He was shown to a quiet room inside the A&E department.

"Thank you," Tony said to the doctor. "I'll take it from here."

Tony saw a woman, young, slim, dressed all in black. She had black hair and light brown skin. She looked tired and extremely agitated. He couldn't help but notice marks on her neck, like someone had tried to choke her.

"Hello, I'm Sergeant Thorne, I believe you wanted to see me?" Tony said and pulled a chair round to sit opposite her. She had an instant look of relief on her face that turned into crying.

She wiped the tears from her cheeks and steadied herself.

She took a deep breath and let it out slowly.

"What is it?" Tony asked, not wanting to press her, but sensing what she had to tell him was big.

"My name is Lucy Swindle, and I work at Hill Top Psychiatric Hospital. I suspected Doctor Mahone to be conducting tests using experimental drugs on the patients."

"What reason did you have to believe that?"

"That was just one of my theories. I've heard some stories by the patients and the staff in there, how he abuses patients, treats them like animals. I witnessed him nearly hit a severely troubled patient, an old woman. So, I did some digging and found that a former employee of the hospital tried to take him to court. They didn't know exactly what he was doing, but they knew that he was up to something. He's extremely secretive, keeps everything close to his chest, y'know? She hoped that if she could get an investigation into the welfare of the hospital, he would be fired and hopefully arrested."

"And what did you find out?"

"He wasn't testing drugs, at least, I don't think he was. But he was abusing his patients." Lucy started to cry. Tony wanted to reach out and hold her hand, but he kept it professional.

"The woman you brought in tonight, is she one of his patients?"

Lucy nodded and wiped the tears away, trying to gather herself again. "She was kept in a small room. She was restrained in a straitjacket. She had been heavily sedated. When I got the straitjacket off, she was just skin and bone, she was malnourished, covered in bruises, literally covered. Her arms aren't straight, like she's had her bones broken and not set right, so when they've healed, they've healed *off*. I don't know how she's still alive."

Tony felt sick. He'd always hated Mahone, had always thought he was an arrogant, ruthless bastard, but this? It seemed excessive. Although, lately, there seemed to be no boundaries on things that could happen.

Just then a doctor opened the door. "Sorry to interrupt, but the woman you brought in is asking for you," he said to Lucy.

Lucy nodded. "Will you come with me?"

"Sure." Tony stood and followed her out. They walked through the emergency room. Paramedics wheeled people through, doctors discussed X-rays behind the staff desk, and nurses ran around like blue-arse flies trying to see to everybody as quickly as possible.

"She's just through here, she wouldn't take a sedative through a needle, so we put a mild one into her drip. It'll help her sleep and maybe by the morning she'll be able to tell us a bit more about herself. She wasn't making any sense before, could barely form words, in fact."

"What do you think's wrong with her, Doctor?" Tony said.

"I'm heading in, see you in there?" Lucy interrupted.

"Sure, I'll just be two minutes."

Tony looked at the doctor, who scratched at the stubble on his chin. "Hard to say until we've run further tests. She's obviously malnourished. If you've ever seen a World War Two documentary, she looks like one of the prisoners of Auschwitz. Not an ounce of fat on her. It's as if she's been kept alive on nutrients through an intravenous drip and not much else. Her teeth are rotting, gums are infected so badly that when we press on them puss and blood oozes out from between her teeth. The ones she has left, anyway."

"Someone's done this to her? You're sure of that?"

The doctor pulled a face. "Without a doubt. This woman has been through severe torture for, *years,* I'd say. God knows how many. Her arms have been fractured, several times in different positions. They've healed without any splints or placement correction – even an idiot knows a bone break has to be realigned in order to heal properly. This has been intentional."

"Thanks, Doctor. I best go see her, see if she can tell me anything."

"As I said, you won't get anything from her until morning."

Tony grimaced and turned to walk through the door.

"Sergeant Thorne, one more thing?" The doctor stopped him.

"Yes?"

"If you catch the person who did this to her, I hope you throw away the key."

Tony felt a burning anger inside his stomach as he thought of putting cuffs on Mahone. "Oh, I will."

Tony walked into the room and saw Lucy holding the woman's hand.

Tony reached the end of the bed and stood completely still, staring at the woman. Her arms were as thin as twigs, every bone visible; her collarbones stuck out making her neck look like an empty hollow. Shaggy brown and greying hair sat uneven on her head where it had been hacked and chopped. Her eyes were closed, sat in sunken black sockets; deep wrinkles lined her mouth. Flaky skin covered her dry lips.

The rage he had felt burning inside him turned to a gut punch. His stomach twisted over and over on itself until his mouth filled with bile.

The face of the woman was a face that had been at the forefront of his mind for fifteen years. The face that had kept him separated from his wife, had kept him from starting a family, from leading a normal life. The face that he thought was gone and lost forever, was now laid before him in a hospital bed, tortured and skeletal.

It was Sophie Rose.

CHAPTER 66

Jane held a glass of water in her hands and lifted it to her mouth, drinking it down in one. The glass made small clinking noises against her teeth as her hand continued shaking. She'd told Matthew the whole story, just as Mrs. Leadley had told her it.

"And you think that it's true?" Matthew said, raising one eyebrow. She could tell by the look on his face that he was doing his best not to smile and dismiss what she said. Maybe it was because of how scared she looked. She certainly felt scared. She actually felt damn right terrified.

"What if it is, Matthew? I've been tossing it over and over in my head all night, and the more I do, the more I think that it's the only thing that makes sense."

"How the hell does this make sense, Jane?"

Jane closed her eyes and ran both hands over her face and through her hair. They were sat at the table in the kitchen. It was gone twelve and Tiffany had long since been put to bed. Jane looked out the window then and shivered when she saw the big red moon hanging over the woods.

"I saw that kid's body, not you. He'd been missing, what,

less than forty-eight hours? He was dried out like a prune, like everything he was had been sucked out of him. Nothing does that, nothing! If those..." – she paused before saying the word with force, as if making herself believe it to be true –"...*witches* are trying to come back from Hell or wherever, they're doing it by eating the souls of the innocent. And they're using the parents like some sick delivery system, as if feeding on their misery is a fucking snack between meals."

"Jane, come on –"

"Don't, Matthew, I don't need you to try and tell me how wrong I am, and all the reasons that what I'm saying is bull-shit, I just need you to listen to what I'm telling you and just try and open your mind to the possibility. If I'm wrong, fine, good, I hope I am, but if I'm right, we need to do something. Because those things will be getting stronger, and I'm sure as shit that fucking moon is a warning for shit to come."

Jane pointed to the window and Matthew looked out at it. For the first time, she thought that maybe she'd got through to him. Even if it was just a bit. In the distance, a flash of brilliant white filled the dark clouds.

"Okay. So what can we do?" Matthew said, and that made Jane smile.

"From what Mrs. Leadley told me, the head witch – is that what you call the leader of a coven?"

Matthew shrugged. "High... priestess?"

Jane waved it away. "Anyway, she had a daughter who they murdered and then the mayor took her away, so that's why she's doing all of this. She's killing the children of Wymere, and forcing their parents to do the killing."

"That's one hell of a way to get revenge." Matthew grimaced.

"They buried her daughter somewhere else. The town didn't want the girl's body in the cemetery in case she was a witch like her mother. So the Mayor took her away. Maybe if we found her remains and gave them back to the witch, she'd leave us alone?"

Matthew laughed. "I doubt it. The damage is done. If this witch is hell-bent on killing everyone in this town, she's not going to stop because we found her dead kid."

"I think we should still try". Jane was pretty sure Matthew was right, but it was all she had to go on.

Matthew stood up and got himself a glass of water. Unbelievingly, Jane noticed that his hand was shaking too. He drank a long glass. The break in conversation seemed to suck all the sound out of the room, all apart from the clock, gently ticking away on the wall.

"Okay," Matthew said, turning back to face Jane, the red moon outside the window hanging over his left shoulder. "Did you get any clues as to where they buried this kid?"

"All Mrs. Leadley said was that after they killed the witch's daughter, the mayor took her away."

Matthew scratched his chin and pushed his neck over to one side until it cracked loudly. Then he did the same on the other side.

"I don't even know where we'd start. How are we supposed to stumble upon a coffin that's over four hundred years old?"

Matthew looked at Jane with wide eyes.

"What?" Jane said, feeling her blood pumping in her temples.

"I think I know where it is. I think I've seen it."

"Seen what?" Jane stood from her stool but kept her hand on the table. Her knees felt weak.

"The little girl; I know where she's buried."

Matthew flicked on the basement light; a musty smell came from the freshly-plastered walls. He'd left the ceiling as it was; wooden beams ran the length of the ceiling in rows. Jane followed him. She'd not been down there much, didn't like basements from all the horror novels she'd read; thankfully Matthew had kitted this one out with what felt like a hundred site lights. No dark corners to be afraid of. That was good.

Along the back wall that he'd left as old stone was a work bench. Off cuts of timber, a hand saw, an axe, and a sledge-hammer were laid on the side with a number of other tools.

"Here," Matthew said, and there was excitement in his voice. He had gone from a non-believer to jumping in with both feet. He pointed to the plastered wall.

"What is it?"

"The other day I was down here finishing off the stud walls, getting ready for boarding and plastering, and I noticed that one of the stones was loose. I couldn't get it back in, so I took it out and found that inside was an old box. About three feet long and two feet wide. I tried to open it and just hurt myself and got frustrated, you know how I do, and I just got mad and threw it back in the hole and boarded over it. Remember when we were looking at this place, the estate agent told us that hundreds of years ago, this was the mayor of Wymere's house. I think he panicked. He didn't know what to do with the dead body of a witch's daughter, so he buried it in his walls."

"Why didn't you say anything before?"

Matthew looked at Jane like she was crazy. Amazingly, it was the first 'you're crazy' look he'd given her that night. "I didn't think an old box would be that important, and besides, I just forgot. I had so much to do down here, I was in the zone, tunnel vision. Poor Tiffany got bored after about four hours today and took herself off to watch Tom and Jerry cartoons."

Jane went over to the wall and touched it. "How are we going to get it out?" She knocked on the wall with the heel of her hand; the plaster was still drying but it had gone off enough for it to withstand her knocking.

"Stand aside."

Jane looked over her shoulder and saw Matthew stood with a sledgehammer in his hands. She skipped to one side and watched as her husband smashed a few hammer-sized holes in the wall, and then with an almighty crash, half the wall came tumbling down to the floor.

"It's alright, I like doing the same job twice." Matthew smiled at her. Beads of sweat were beginning to form on his brow. He made light work of the rest of the wall, and then went at the original stonework underneath. That was tougher. He swung again and again. Jane ducked and yelled when a big chunk of stone flew toward her, narrowly missing her face.

"Sorry," Matthew said, and carried on. He hit the giant stone that had once been loose before he recemented the thing, with something far superior, apparently, judging from how much effort it took to knock the fucking thing back out again.

When the stone finally fell to the floor with a loud thud that shook the ground under Jane's feet, she gave Matthew a hug, and felt the wetness on his back.

He reached in and pulled out the wooden box, then laid it on the worktable, pushing the handsaw and the axe to one side.

"Here," Jane said, passing him the claw hammer.

"Thanks, but I think I'll need the crowbar for this." Matthew went over to a stack of tool boxes and pulled out a mid-size crow bar. He jammed it into the crack between the lid and the body of the box. He tried to get leverage and couldn't.

"Second thoughts," he said, the strain in his face as well as his voice, "Pass me that hammer."

Jane put it in his hand. He used it to hammer the other end of the crowbar, forcing the thin wedged end into the crack. The wood groaned and splinted at the force of something penetrating it after hundreds of years of being closed.

Finally, with a huge effort, Matthew pried the box open.

A cloud of dust, likely as old as the small body that lay inside it, filled the air, making both Jane and Matthew cough and flap their hands to make the cloud disperse.

Jane looked at her husband.

"Go on, you do the honours," he said.

Jane looked inside and saw the bones of a small child folded in rags of cloth.

CHAPTER 67

The hospital lights were harsh; they forced Lucy to squint, her eyes stinging with tiredness. She didn't think she'd ever been so exhausted. Mentally or physically. She sat on the cushioned chair; it had seen better days, but it was better than standing. Her feet throbbed, as if they had their own painful heartbeat. She looked over at Sergeant Thorne, watched him as he approached the bed. Her heart skipped a beat when she saw the look on his face.

"Sergeant Thorne? What is it?"

Lucy held the hand of the woman that she had saved from Hill Top. It felt like small twigs in a bag of cold water. Sergeant Thorne had walked into the room and stood at the end of the bed. That was two minutes ago. The blood had drained from his face; his skin looked white as snow against his black beard. His hands gripped the end of the bed. He was shaking, Lucy was seriously concerned that he was about to collapse.

"Mister Thorne, do you need a doctor?" Lucy let go of the woman's hand and walked over to him. She touched his hand; the difference between his hand and the woman's was like night and day, only his skin felt as cold as hers.

"I…" Thorne tried to speak, only to then choke on his words.

"Sergeant Thorne, what is it? You're scaring me."

"I… I need to sit down." Thorne stumbled over to the padded chair and sat; air escaped from the holes created in the sides where the stitching had come undone.

Lucy looked at the woman and then back to Sergeant Thorne. She did this several times, noticing each time the look in Thorne's eyes. He was devastated, confused, shocked. His hands trembled as he held them over his mouth.

The machine beeped in the corner; the woman's heartbeat was fast, a lot faster than it should be. It felt like they had just been left to fend for themselves, but if Lucy knew the doctors and nurses like she thought she did, they'd be working on a plan of action right now. Figuring out what was best to do for this woman.

"Where's Mahone now?" Thorne said.

Lucy frowned. "I don't know. At Hill Top, I suppose." Lucy pointed at the woman in the bed. "She stabbed him, a lot, with some old syringes; I think one of them even had some tranquilizer left in it, so he could be out for the count."

Thorne's sad, shocked expression changed into a look of anger and fury. "If he isn't, I'll find him." Thorne stood with such force the chair flung backward; the legs screeched as they skidded along the linoleum floor.

"You know her, don't you?" Lucy said. She swallowed against a lump in her throat.

Thorne walked toward her; his eyes glistened with tears. "That is Sophie Rose. She's been missing for eighteen years. She has been locked away, kept prisoner by that sick cunt all this time."

Lucy recoiled, feeling, in that moment, more frightened of Sergeant Thorne than she was of anything else. "What are you going to do?"

Thorne looked her deep in the eyes, as if part of this was her fault.

"I'm gonna kill him."

———

EVERYTHING WAS RED. The hospital lights, the walls, the doctors, the nurses, the doors, the windows – it was as if a red filter had lowered over Tony's eyes. Rage clawed up from his guts, its nails digging into his throat, trying to escape from his mouth in a flurry of shouts and screams. His heart beat like a fucking jackhammer on speed. He could hear the blood whooshing around in his head; his pulse thumped behind his eyes, in his throat. He wanted to grab Mahone and pound his face into the ground until there was nothing left but mush. Doctors moved out of his way as he marched down the corridors; a nurse looked at his face and it was as if she wanted to scream. She cowered from him behind the clipboard she was carrying and tried to bury herself into the wall.

He was almost at the door, but he didn't have his car with him; that fact just dawned on him as the car park came into sight. He didn't give two shits. He'd run to Hill Top if he had to. As a police officer, he kept himself fit, he could run the two miles to the psychiatric hospital in fourteen minutes, twelve with the mood he was in.

What stopped him, or what snapped him out of his fury-induced semi-consciousness, was a desperate cry from a young girl that reminded him of Sophie when they were kids, a million years ago. He couldn't remember what exact memory it was; it was more the quality in this girl's voice.

He turned around and, as the girl in question became apparent, the memory of Sophie floated away like steam on the night air, and the sounds coming from the girl turned from blank noises into words.

"She killed them, she was flying! Fucking flying and she killed them all'" she screamed. There was a boy stood next to her, not saying much. Tony looked and saw that the boy was trying, and failing, to cover a dark patch on the crotch of his jeans.

"You need to call the police! Four people are dead!"

"Kid, you need to calm down," the nurse on the front desk told her, desperate to keep the girl from raising her voice any louder. The hospital was busy, but most of the patients were quiet and sombre, like drunks at a wake.

"You don't understand, it was as if she... she... drank them. Like their insides evaporated. You have to call the police!!"

Tony thought of Alfie Weeds and Freddie Houghton. They both looked like their insides had been evaporated, their skin dry and rescinded into deep folds.

He was left with a choice. He could go to Hill Top, beat the fuck out of Mahone. If he managed to stop before he killed him, he'd arrest him; if he didn't manage to stop, then fine. He was happy to serve time for murdering that piece of shit. Or he could go get those kids and tell them to explain everything. Go find this flying woman that drank the life out these kids and put a stop to her before she hurt anyone else. And Tony felt that she *would* hurt someone else, he felt that most strongly.

He debated it for what felt like hours but was only seconds. He decided to go against his heart. He had to do the right thing; Mahone wasn't going anywhere, he'd get him later. He had to stop this killer, whoever it was.

Tony pulled his phone from his trouser pocket, hit the screen a few times, and put the phone to his ear.

"Ruth, I need you. Get to the hospital. Now."

Chapter 68

Ragan had never felt so alive. So full of electricity, full of power, full of life. There was a magic in the world, a magic that was separated into good and bad. One of them was the stronger of the two, and she loved it. She had, in fact, hundreds of years ago, sold her soul for the ability to wield that black magic. And that was just fine by her.

The world had changed so much; she saw things that scared her, and she wondered if the magic in the world had somehow been made accessible to all humans, without the need for sacrifice or as a divine gift. Then she saw how easy it was to take their lives and harvest their souls and she knew that time had simply moved on, whilst she was imprisoned in the dirt, under the heavy, foul stench of holy water.

Ragan wandered through the woods, stroking the trees as she did, feeling the life inside them. An owl let out a warning hoot above her, and when its big yellow eyes looked down on her, it diverted and flapped hurriedly away.

The red moon filtered through the trees and she felt the tingle across her skin. "The time is now," she said in a voice full of anticipation and pleasure. She bit her lip; the magic was flowing through her, the souls of the innocent filled her with ecstasy, and she wanted more. She had promised death to all in this town, and the Dark Lord had blessed her with the time and the power to do it. But she needed her coven. Her witches that had spent more than four centuries buried underneath the dirt with her. They were as much her children as the young girl she had birthed. The young girl born of the evil that men can do.

She never asked for the child; she hadn't asked to be raped, either. Men who were supposed to be good, men who sat in their council and made decisions for the people, those who thought they had power because they could do what they liked and get away with it...they were the real monsters. They had raped her and then sentenced her to death when she fought for justice.

She doesn't know which of the five of them managed to put the child inside her, but when that child came, she loved her. Fed the babe from her breast, clothed her, taught her to read and write. How many times had she asked the Lord almighty, the God in heaven, to answer her prayers and gone unanswered? Satan had answered without hesitation. He told her he could feel the darkness and the pain inside her and it pulled him in. He would give her the power to avenge those that wronged her.

And now she had the chance.

With the help of her coven, she would find her little girl, and when she had gathered enough souls, she'd be able to do what the Dark Lord had promised her. She would kill every person in Wymere.

Ragan had waited for her revenge. She knew her time had come, and it was now.

She stood before the wall of thorns. She raised her arms

and moved them apart in the air. The thorns parted, making a walkway through to the empty pit, where her coven slept beneath the dead tree.

CHAPTER 69

Matthew walked up the basement stairs holding the box. The thought entered his mind that it was a coffin really, considering its contents were the bones of a young girl. The idea made a shiver roll so violently up his spine that he flicked his neck, sending out a crack so loud that Jane turned around to look at him as if he'd just clapped his hands.

"You okay?" she said.

"Yeah." Matthew grimaced. "Just my neck. Get into the kitchen so I can put this fucking thing down."

Jane hurried through and Matthew followed. He placed the coffin on the table, gingerly, and stepped away, rubbing at the back of his neck with his hand. The sunburn from that fateful day at the fete, that had been healing quite nicely, started to give off a strong burning sensation at his touch. He sucked his teeth and moved his hand away.

"Your neck still?"

Matthew nodded.

They stood looking at the coffin for a minute. The kitchen was quiet. The clock on the wall ticked and tocked; the red moon seemed to hang in the window like it had nowhere better to be. It was the middle of the night and yet, it felt as warm as a nice spring day. There was humidity in the air that felt thick and electric. Matthew could smell it as well as feel it.

A storm's coming, he thought, and just then a deep rumble shook the house with such ferocity it was as though an eighteen-wheeler just drove through the front door. Matthew and Jane simultaneously looked outside and caught a white crack appear in the blackening sky. The moon was circled by black clouds that glowed a dark red in its light. The storm was close.

"What are we going to do with it?" Matthew said. There was panic in his voice, a panic he didn't care for.

"We need to take it into the woods, take it to the tree. Maybe then they'll go back to where they came from."

Matthew shook his head. "Not we. *I* am doing this alone."

"Like fuck you are!" Jane shouted.

"I am not putting you in danger. If something is out there, something in those woods, I won't let it hurt you, Jane. Someone needs to be here for Tiffany."

Jane ran over to Matthew and put her arms around him. Her tears wet the front of his t-shirt. He hugged her for a minute; a part of him, a big part, wanted to say fuck it, let's put the coffin back and go back to bed, let some other poor bastard deal with the witches. A flash of lightning over the woods and another roar of thunder illuminated the trees outside. It could have been the dazzling light burning in his retinas, or it could be his fear-filled mind, whatever it was, he was sure as shit he'd just seen a naked woman in the woods.

He put his hands on Jane's shoulders and gently pushed her back. She opened her mouth to speak, but before she had a chance to get the words out, he planted a kiss on her lips.

"I love you," he said, pulling back. "Go upstairs and see if Tiffany's okay. I'll go get rid of this."

Jane nodded.

"But first, go downstairs, get a weapon. I have a hundred

tools down there that will work just fine. Grab something to protect yourself with. Understand?"

Jane looked more frightened at the idea of getting herself a weapon than anything else, but she nodded.

Matthew kissed her again. When he pulled back from her this time, she looked more determined, more confident.

"Go, now."

"Be careful," Jane said, before heading downstairs to get a weapon.

Matthew watched her go, then he took a deep breath.

They hadn't discussed it, but he knew that from the look in her eyes she had been thinking the same thing. Two men had gone into those woods alone in the past two days, and both had their minds taken over and used as a weapon to kill their children. If they were both naïve enough to think that it couldn't happen to Matthew, they might as well ask Santa for a genie to give them three wishes while they were at it.

Matthew had asked Jane to get a weapon, not because he feared one of the witches would try and get them in here, but because *he* might. And if he did succumb to the powers of the witches, then he wanted to know that Jane was ready to stop him. He could tell by the feel in her hug, in the way her nails dug into the scant flesh of his back, that she didn't want to do it. Then the steely look at the end showed that she understood the assignment, the way she always did. She would do what she had to, to keep Tiffany safe.

Matthew picked up the coffin, looked down at the skull with its yellowed teeth grinning back up at him, and walked out the back door.

JANE LOOKED FOR A WEAPON. She grabbed a claw hammer, but it felt too small. She wasn't a strong woman;

even if she managed to get a clean connection, she didn't think she'd be able to do much damage with it. She picked up a handsaw, good for sawing bits of two by four, but not so much for self-defence. Crow bars, spanners, screwdrivers – the latter of which she shoved into the back pocket of her jeans, for if all else failed.

Then she saw it, the perfect thing.

The axe wasn't too heavy for her to swing, maybe not great for close encounters, but if she knew where the target was coming from, she could get enough force to do a lot of damage. She ran her thumb over the edge of the axe head.

"Mother fucker!" she snapped, shoving her thumb into her mouth and tasting warm copper. The axe had been freshly sharpened.

A shadow grew long at the bottom of the basement stairs and Jane almost cried out. She held the axe tight to her chest and waited, ready to attack if needed.

"Mum? Are you down there?"

It was Tiffany.

Jane let out a shuddering breath of relief and called back: "I'm here, love. I'm coming up."

Jane walked up the stairs and saw Tiffany in her nightie that, once upon a time, would have trailed all the way down to her feet. Now it barely covered her knees. The girl rubbed her eyes tiredly, and her hair was a mess, all bunched up at the back where she had been laid.

"Mum?" Tiffany sounded startled. "What are you doing with an axe?"

Jane looked at it as if she had no idea what Tiffany was talking about, and then shook her head. "Oh, no reason. Listen, Dad's gone out to do something. There's a big storm coming, so why don't you come into my room with me?" Jane had a big smile on her face that she hoped didn't look as fake as it felt.

"Okay," Tiffany said, with an eyebrow raised. "I'm just going to get a glass of water."

"Okay, but hurry up, love," Jane said and looked out of the window. She saw Matthew enter the woods; he glowed red in the light of the moon.

"Please hurry."

<hr />

MATTHEW FOUND the footpath that Jane had described to him. It was dark out in the woods, the light from the red moon was almost non-existent once he got more than a few metres into the density of the trees. Tucking the coffin under one arm, with great difficulty, he managed to grab his phone from his pocket and turn on the torch function. It illuminated the path, giving him a clear view of the next few metres. The further he got into the woods, the more thankful he was he had remembered to put the phone in his pocket.

The overgrowth grew out of control in some areas; how the hell Jane and Tiffany got this far he had no idea. Brambles clawed at his trousers, thorns managed to cut and graze his leg through the fabric of his jeans, nettles whipped at him, low-hanging branches sprung out of the darkness, forcing him to duck and weave. One branch came at him so suddenly he dropped the box with the remains of the young girl. The phone dropped into the dirt, the torch facing down, turning the woods into almost complete darkness; a dim glow of red sky grinned through the black treetops.

"Fuck," he snapped, desperately searching through the mud for his phone. Dry dirt and a handful of nettles that sent small burning stings through his palm and up his forearm were all he could find. A bird cawed above him, making him jump. His balls shrank away and desperation seemed to claw in his throat like small sharp fingers.

"Where is it. Where the fuck is it?!"

The trees shook as a huge flock of birds burst through the trees, all of them cawing loudly. They sounded like a gang of screaming children, as terrified and desperate as he was to get away.

Finally, he felt the familiar cold hardness of a mobile phone in his hand. He grabbed it and held it to his chest like a child reunited with his favourite toy. He shone the torch at the path in front of him and was perplexed to see a thick high wall of thorns six feet in front of him.

Wasn't I following a path? he asked himself, turning around to see no path behind or to either side of him. Just trees and overgrown bushes, fallen branches, and the old rotten corpse of a fox or large cat.

Trying to gather himself, he pulled the box toward him and gathered up the bones that had fallen into the dirt. Small bones he took for ribs, a fibula, femur, and others he couldn't remember the names of right now.

"Where's the –"

He panned the torch along the ground and stopped when a pair of bare feet appeared in the light, not three feet in front of him. He took a split second to wonder how he hadn't heard them coming. They stood before a huge opening in the wall of thorns, an opening he hadn't noticed before. Slowly, and doing the best he could to keep the light steady, he raised the torch, taking in the woman that stood naked before him.

The woman's long black hair fell more than halfway down her back, her face, a picture of beauty like Matthew had never seen before, was lit up with a smile; her deep green eyes glistened like emeralds in the light of the torch. In her hand was a skull that she stroked and caressed with such care, it reminded him of the way a new mother looks when holding their newborn baby for the first time.

"My babe," the woman said softly. "My darling girl, you

are returned to me. Now we can wake our dark beauties from their graves and harvest the souls of those that hurt us. We will restore you to life, and the world will be yours."

Matthew stood with the box in hand. The sound of the bones rattling in their wooden container forced the woman to look over at him, as if she had no idea he was even there.

Matthew's eyes met hers and the moment they did, he was entranced. He stepped toward her, an urge, desire inside him so strong, burning in his guts. He wanted her, wanted to please her, kiss her, make love to her. He would do anything that she wanted. He realised then that all these things were being silently whispered in his head; the voice was so alien to his own, yet so comforting, he listened to its every word.

"Come to me," the woman said.

Matthew nodded and walked toward her, his feet lifting and dropping with all the grace of a drunk gorilla.

He stood in front of her, so close he could smell her breath; it smelt like earth, it smelt like death, and it was sweet and moreish. He wanted that, too.

She gently placed the skull back with its bones in the box and took the coffin from him. His arms were kept in the same rigid shape that held the box; the bright white light coming from his phone illuminated their faces and cast the surrounding forest into complete darkness. She leant forward and placed a kiss on his lips, before gently, agonisingly, moving her face to the side of his, allowing her nose to stroke the skin of his cheek. He felt her soft lips tickle his ear, and her cold breath spread over his skin, forcing the hairs there to stand up on end, and his skin to prickle into a thousand spots.

"Bring me more souls," she whispered. The words danced in his mind, and whatever light he had behind his eyes was snuffed out.

And just like Gareth Weeds and Alan Houghton before him, he followed his orders.

CHAPTER 70

Lucy sat for a while. The shock still buzzed around in her head. *Sophie Rose?* How could that be right? She looked at the woman in the bed. Lucy, like everyone in Wymere, had seen a thousand photos of Sophie Rose over the years. She was plastered in the papers every year when the anniversary came round. There was a rose garden dedicated to her in the town centre with a placard and several photos of her in a glass-panelled noticed board. Lucy always wondered if another missing person would get the same treatment, or if that honour was only reserved for the mayor's daughter.

She felt bad for thinking that now. Now that she was sat beside that same woman.

All those years everyone believed she was dead in the woods, and the whole time she was in the psychiatric hospital in a makeshift room, being tortured and abused by Doctor Mahone. Lucy looked at the woman and compared her face to the memorized photo Lucy had of her in her mind. She suppressed the sudden urge to vomit. The photo of Sophie Rose had been of a young woman full of life; her skin glowed, her eyes were wide and beautiful, her dimpled cheeks were to die for, she looked like an angel. How far this angel had fallen. All the way to Hell, and the devil had had his way with her.

A flash of images flipped through Lucy's mind then, all the things he must have done to her, all the pain and the torment. She could suppress the vomit no longer. Lucy retched into the bin by the sink. She had to get on her hands and knees. Not quite quick enough, she got the first half of the sick on the floor. It cleaned up easily with a paper towel.

Lucy walked out of the curtained cubicle and grabbed a cup of water from the cooler. She wiped the film of sweat that covered her brow with the back of her hand, and went back in.

Sophie looked at Lucy now, making Lucy's heart jump and start beating at a hundred miles an hour. Sophie began to cry. Lucy ran to her, perched on the side of the bed, and held Sophie's hand in hers. It was cold and small; the feel of it made Lucy want to cry.

"Thank you." Sophie managed to choke out the words through a hoarse sounding throat.

"You don't have to thank me. I'm sorry I didn't get you out earlier. If I'd had any idea you were in there, I'd have –"

Sophie squeezed Lucy's hand as hard as she could, which wasn't very hard at all.

"Tell Tony..."

Lucy rubbed Sophie's hand, hoping it would bring some warmth to it and make it feel less like the hand of a dead person. "Yes?"

"Tell Tony..." Sophie's lip began to tremble, her eyes rolled, the iris disappeared so only the whites were visible, then the irises came back. "Tell Tony, not to blame... himself."

Tears fell down Lucy's cheeks now. It was all she could do not to sob uncontrollably. "You'll be alright, Sophie. You'll be okay. You can tell him yourself."

Sophie barked a short, cracked laugh at that and shook her head slightly.

"I'm too tired... thank you for... getting me out. I didn't want... to die there."

With that, Sophie's head dropped to her shoulder and the heart monitor screeched out a warning. Red lights flashed on its screen as the jagged line turned flat.

"Sophie?" Lucy shook her, still gripping Sophie's hand in hers. "Sophie!!"

She craned her neck over her shoulder and shouted. "Help! Somebody, we need help in here!"

The doctors and nurses were already rushing in; the curtain was drawn back harshly, making a sharp *whooshing* sound.

They surrounded the bed quickly and purposefully; they looked like a well-drilled strategic team of life savers. Which Lucy supposed they were.

The room swam in the tears that fell uncontrollably from her eyes. A hand grabbed her shoulder, making her scream out. The last thing she saw of Sophie Rose was a doctor tearing the hospital gown she wore open, revealing Sophie's chest, every rib prominently visible thanks to the tight stretch of skin with no fat or muscle underneath it.

The hands that grabbed Lucy guided her from the room and spun her round.

She now faced a young nurse who had a forced smile below worried eyes. "We're going to help your friend now; I'm going to need you to come with me."

"Will she be okay?" Lucy said. As she did, the sound of a defibrillator charging came from behind the curtain, followed by a shout.

"Clear!"

"Come on, this way. I think an officer needs to take a state-ment from you anyway. Do that, and I'll keep you updated on your friend. Let the doctors do their job, okay?"

Lucy allowed herself to be escorted down the corridors.

People looked at her with sympathetic eyes, a look that said: 'Life's shit, and I'm sorry yours just got shittier.'

The sound of the defibrillator grew distant, and the doctor's cries of "Clear!" became muffled. Lucy took a moment to dab at the tears in her eyes when they stopped. The nurse was talking to someone. Lucy glanced up and saw it was an officer. Sergeant Thorne must have seen sense and called someone to come and take a statement from her whilst he went to arrest Doctor Mahone. She couldn't focus on the conversation; in truth, she couldn't focus on anything. She wasn't sure she'd be able to give a statement tonight, but she felt that she owed it to Sophie to try.

Before she knew what was happening, the nurse's hand on her shoulder had been replaced with the officer's, and he was guiding her out of the hospital toward a police car parked in front of the hospital steps.

"We're just going to take you down to the station to give a statement, then we'll give you a lift home," the officer said.

"Thank you," Lucy said absently. Then something twisted in her gut and all she wanted to do was turn and run. Her blurred vision and overwhelming fatigue from the day was clouding her mind. She was going into fight or flight and she wanted a one-way ticket to 'get the hell out of here.'

It made no sense why she felt like this, but as the officer opened the back door of the car, she felt the urge to run away even stronger. Why was he putting her in the back instead of the front? She couldn't work it out. The back was where the criminals go, where there's no handles on the inside so they can't get out.

Before the officer 'helped' Lucy to duck her head down, Lucy said: "Did Sergeant Thorne call you, Officer?"

"The name's Westlake. Officer Westlake. And no, baby, Thorne didn't call me. It was another friend o'mine. I think you might know him."

Westlake smiled an evil grin. He pushed her head down with one hand and shoved her body hard with the other so she fell sideways onto the back seat. Her screams were cut short by the slamming door and finally, the hand that covered her mouth. Another hand covered her eyes and pressed down hard. She was suffocating; she flapped her hands hard at her attacker but he was too strong for her.

The car engine roared into life and the tyres squealed as they raced out of the hospital car park.

The hand moved from her eyes but the one on her mouth stayed firm. Her eyes adjusted and she saw an upside-down face scowling at her, covered in dark red spots of blood where a needle had punctured it earlier that night.

"Hello, Lucy," Mahone snarled. "We're going on a drive."

CHAPTER 71

Tony got the kids calm. The girl was bordering on hysterics and the boy was in a kind of stunned silence. After the girl, Gina Burrow, had told him everything that happened in great detail, Tony asked her what they had been smoking.

"Nothing! Well, that's not strictly true, they were smoking weed, but I didn't touch any of it. It's not my scene but I understand that there's fuck all else for us to do round here."

Tony jotted it down in his notebook and looked over his shoulder. He could see through the windowed door straight to the front entrance. As soon as Ruth showed up, which should be in the next two minutes, he was going to get in the car and go straight to this park. See what truth there was to Gina's story. As farfetched as it was – a flying, half-decayed woman sucking the life out of four kids and regenerating – he couldn't help but see the truth in her eyes. As a police officer, and one with experience, he knew the signs of a lie. Gina wasn't showing any.

"I'll check it out. I have your details and I'm going to need you to come to the station tomorrow to give a statement. For now, just rest. You're safe here." Tony looked over at her boyfriend, who still hadn't found his tongue to be able to help Gina with the re-telling of their story. "And get him looked at by someone. I think he's in shock."

Gina dropped her head in tired relief. "Thank you, sir," she said, and then started crying. "I can't believe what we saw, it was awful, just awful." She wiped at her eyes with the sleeve of her jumper and something caught her eye over Tony's shoulder. "I think your partner is here."

Tony looked at where Gina pointed and saw Ruth. She had no make-up on and her hair was thrown up on top of her head in a messy bun. She wasn't wearing her full uniform, just a police polo shirt and trousers.

"Thank you, Gina. You get some rest now," Tony said and left the small waiting room.

"This better be important, Tony, I'm serious. I've worked the same sixteen-hour shifts as you have. I need some fucking sleep –"

"Sarah tried to kill herself." The sentence stopped Ruth dead in her tracks.

"What the fuck? When? How did –"

"That's not important right now. So much has happened, I'll tell you on the way. We need to go, now." Tony put a hand on Ruth's back and walked briskly toward the main door. Ruth complied easily and followed Tony's lead.

They reached the outside, Ruth got in the driver's side, and Tony jumped in the passenger seat.

"Where to?" Ruth said, buckling her seat belt.

"The skate park," Tony replied.

Ruth put the car in gear and tore out of the car park. The wheels let out a short but sharp screech as they spun on the tarmac. As they left, Tony noticed the police car driving in, but thought nothing of it.

"Sophie Rose is alive?!" Ruth almost drove off the side of the road after Tony told her what he had seen. "Why aren't you in there with her?"

Tony shook his head. "She's out for the count. She needs doctors, not the guy who gave up and abandoned her. We need to get Mahone, but first we need follow up on what those kids said. If it's true, I think we've found the reason Alan Houghton and Gareth Weeds killed their kids. This has to be connected."

"It sounds like what Gina told you was a bunch of doped-up, horror-film bullshit."

Tony grimaced. "I know what it sounds like, Ruth, but there's something in what she said. It sounds insane, all of it, but when I was younger, we were all told these stories of how witches were once tried and executed here in Wymere. They were all killed and buried in those woods. One of them made a vow that with the devil's help, she'd return and kill everyone. To be honest, I totally forgot about it. We didn't believe it when we were kids, but enjoyed the stories anyway."

"Witches?" Ruth raised that eyebrow of hers. "Seriously, Tony? You think fucking witches are responsible for this shit? I'll tell you what, Whitby isn't far, after this we can go find Dracula and arrest him too."

Tony sighed and laid his head back against the headrest. Thoughts buzzed around his head, crossing paths, messing things up. He had believed Sophie to be dead all this time, just for her to have been kept prisoner a couple of miles from his house. He didn't know what to believe anymore.

"I don't know if it is. Believe me, I know how mad it sounds, but right now, it's the only explanation I can think of that actually makes sense. Tell me you understand?"

Ruth barked a laugh. "If this turns out to be true, I don't think I'll ever fully understand anything ever again."

Ruth turned off the road. The headlights illuminated the metal skate park. She killed the engine and they both got out. Streetlights buzzed overhead, the red moon hung over the woods at the back of the park, dark clouds had started to form a ring around it. A flash of white filled the dark night sky, followed by a low rolling thunder.

"Holy shit!" Tony shouted and ran to the metal fence that bordered the skate park. He hurtled it in one jump, using his hands on the top rung for leverage.

Ruth followed, and when Tony heard her footsteps closing in on him, she screamed.

There were four kids; two of them Tony knew, had seen them at the fete just a few days ago. They were barely sixteen-years-old. He knew it wasn't their parents that had killed them, because there had been an actual witness to these murders to testify to it, but the cause of death looked to be the same. They were in a pile, one on top of the other. Their faces were lined with deep wrinkles, mouths drawn open in silent screams. Tongues black, eyes rolled into the back of their heads.

"Do we call it in?" Ruth said.

Tony stood, ran a hand through his hair, and looked at her. "Yeah. They'll think we're crazy, but do it, tell them four boys have been murdered and we need a team at the skate park, *now*."

Ruth nodded and ran back to the car. Tony looked over the four boys and wondered what the hell could do such a thing. The idea of a witch, or anything supernatural, was becoming all the more a reality. He hated the thought of it; it scrambled his brains as he tried to get his head around it all.

"Tony, come here, now!" Ruth shouted.

Tony turned on his heels and ran to the car. When he got

there, Ruth held up the radio. "Just been patched through," Ruth said.

A voice came through the radio, crackled and full of static.

"We need help. We think there's something in the woods. We might have found a way to stop it but we're scared. My husband has gone in to try and give it back the bones we found. Please come, I don't know what else to do. We live at the Old Stone Cottage on New Road."

Tony and Ruth looked at each other. "That's the Stanfords," Tony said.

"Right where that fucking body was found. Let's go, we can be there in fifteen."

CHAPTER 72

J ane hung up. The operator told her the police would be
fifteen minutes. She hoped to God that Matthew would
be back before then. Tiffany was drifting back to sleep.
She looked so small in their bed, curled up under the covers
where Matthew normally slept. Jane laid beside her, the phone
in her hand, the axe leant up against the wall where she could
jump up and grab it if she needed to.

The anxiety was killing her. It was almost too much to
bear. Laying on the bed felt ridiculous. Matthew was out
there, in those damned woods full of God-knows-what evil. It
felt wrong, so fucking wrong. She stood up, careful not to
wake Tiffany, and walked over to the window. She got a full
view of the tree line that backed up on the field behind her
house.

The red moon was circled by storm clouds now. Lightning
flashed and thunder rumbled. It was getting louder; the lightning was coming faster and with more ferocity with every
passing minute. No rain was falling yet in Wymere, but Jane
would bet everything she had that it was coming. And when it
did, it would be something big.

Her eyes scanned the tree line back and forth, back and forth, each time praying that that would be the time she would see Matthew running from the woods. When that time finally came, her first thought was that it was her eyes playing tricks on her. She smiled and felt a strange urge to cry. He was coming home, walking through the field in a straight line directly to the house. Jane looked back up to the tree line and saw a slim white figure in amongst the trees looking back at her. It waved a hand, then submerged itself back into the darkness.

Her heart sank like a rock in the ocean. Looking back down at Matthew as he approached the house, she noticed the way he walked was wrong; as he got closer and the outside light on the house illuminated his facial features, she saw how blank his expression was.

"Oh my God, no," she gasped. Now the tears fell.

Matthew disappeared from view, and the sound of the front door being kicked open downstairs rang loudly throughout the house.

"Mum?" Tiffany sat up in bed, rubbing her eyes. "Is Dad back?"

Jane locked the bedroom door slowly, not wanting the loud *click* to give away their position, and gestured with a flapping hand for Tiffany to get up out of bed. "Get behind me."

Tiffany did as she was told and didn't argue back. She grabbed hold of Jane's t-shirt and stayed silent behind her.

Jane picked up the axe slowly, trying to keep as quiet as possible. A droplet of sweat tickled her cheek. The axe felt heavier than before; she supposed that was because now she was going to have to use it, and with that knowledge came more weight.

Footsteps sounded on the stairs outside the door. Slow and steady, echoing throughout the old stone walls of the house.

Jane gulped. She winced against the scratch of Tiffany's nails as they dug into the flesh on her back. Her heart raced; the wooden grip of the axe felt slippery from the sweat oozing from her palm.

THUD THUD.

The footsteps were getting louder.

THUD THUD.

She couldn't do it. She watched the door and took a step further away. How could she swing an axe at her husband? They came here to settle into a new life, a quieter life. She looked at the axe head and saw Tiffany's reflection in the gleaming mirror of the steel. Tiffany was crying silently. Jane took a deep breath and let it out in a shudder that vibrated through her chest.

THUD THUD.

She had to do what she had to do to keep Tiffany safe. It was her job to protect her.

THUD.

He was at the top of the stairs now. No more footsteps followed. He was right outside her door. She could hear him breathing. It was a harsh sound, crackly, like a smoker fifty years into the habit.

The door handle shook softly. Jane reached a hand behind her and grabbed Tiffany's arm to make sure she was still there. Then she raised the axe up high, cocked like an American baseball player on two strikes ready for the last pitch.

The door was battered in its frame with a suddenness that made both Jane and Tiffany cry out. It rattled ceaselessly; Tiffany screamed behind Jane.

"Why's he doing this? Tell him to stop, Mum! Please!"

Jane held the axe up high, tightening her grip. She ground her teeth, swallowed the lump of fear, and forced herself to feel only anger.

The door burst open. There was a snap of metal, followed

by a clang as the hinge hit the floor. The door hung slanted against the back wall, only the top hinge stopping it from falling.

Matthew stood in the doorway, his hands curled into fists by his sides. His head hung low, but his eyes looked straight forward at Jane. She saw nothing of her husband in them.

"Get out of his head, you bitch!" Jane shouted.

Then Matthew smiled. He moved toward her. One laboured footstep after another, his feet pounded on the floorboards as if his shoes were made of concrete.

Tiffany started screaming, high-pitched sounds that filled the room, piercing Jane's ears.

"Leave us alone!" Jane swung the axe as a warning; it cut through the air two feet in front of Matthew's face, yet he paid it no heed. He carried on, that half smile still curled up on one side of his face.

Jane swung again; this time she almost caught him, and a panic filled her throat.

"Please, don't make me do this," she cried. The axe felt too heavy to lift now. It dangled in front of her.

Matthew continued moving forward.

One last time she raised the axe, ground her teeth together so hard she heard a crack on the right side of her face, and she swung. Quick as a flash, Matthew's hand reached out and grabbed the axe head. He avoided the sharp edge of the axe, or that's how it seemed at first, until two fingers dropped to the floor and blood started gushing from his hand. His face didn't change.

Jane screamed and Tiffany joined her, grabbing and pulling at Jane to try and take them further away from Matthew, but they had run out of room. The back wall had crept up behind them and now pressed against their backs.

"I'm so sorry, Tiff. I love you," Jane said. The axe fell to the floor and laid useless at Jane's feet.

"I can't do it," Jane sobbed and turned to hold Tiffany tight in her arms.

Matthew took a step forward. All he had to do was reach out and take them.

"If you can't do it, I can."

Jane snapped her head round at the voice. Matthew whirled on the spot, faster than Jane thought possible. Behind him stood Mrs, Leadley. She swung a lump hammer at Matthew; it connected with his temple, letting out a loud crunching sound. His eyes rolled into the back of his head as he pirouetted and fell face-first to the floorboards. Blood spilled from the wound on the side of his head into a dark pool beneath him.

Mrs. Leadley walked over to Jane and Tiffany and stuck her hand out. Her twisted foot landed carelessly in the growing pool of blood. "Get up, and get the hell out of here!"

Jane, stuck in a daze, could only look up at the old woman in shock. She had accepted her fate. She should be dead; Tiffany should be dead.

"What are you waiting for, a written invitation? Get the fuck out of here! He won't stop, as long as that bitch is out of her grave, he'll keep on coming until she has your souls!"

Jane grabbed Tiffany by the arm and ran across to the bedroom door. She wanted to look back at Matthew, but didn't think she could cope with what she knew she would see. Leaving a trail of red footprints in her wake, she ran down the stairs and out the back door.

MRS. LEADLEY SHUT the bedroom door. She was tired, every muscle in her body ached, her ankle screamed in agony with every step. She could feel the bones grinding against each other from the unnatural angle her foot bent at. She also had never felt more alive. She was ready to die, had been ready for years. She knew she had been waiting for this moment. She wished it was that evil bitch that tried to kill her when she was a child, but you take what you can get in this life.

The witch would see her through his eyes and Mrs. Leadley hoped she remembered her from that day all those years ago. And if they were able to send her back to hell, she hoped that it was her face that tormented her there.

Mrs. Leadley stood over Matthew's body. The pool of blood had stopped growing. His hand twitched, his neck cracked as he raised it from the floorboards and turned his face to look at her. He half smiled at her and pushed himself to his knees.

"Come on then, you bitch!" Mrs. Leadley swung the lump hammer; it connected with Matthew's head, but he didn't go down. She swung again, the effort making the muscles in her arm tire; this time the connection was nothing more than a passing glance. A cut opened up on his forehead above the right eye. The momentum of the four-pound lump hammer swung Mrs. Leadley round with such force she almost went down. Almost. Her twisted ankle struck the skirting board, keeping her upright. She let out a loud pain-filled scream at the impact. The pain was so hot and so sharp her fingers let go, and the hammer fell to the floor with a sobering thud.

She now had her back to the witch-possessed man who was twice her size, and she had no weapon.

"Please, Lord, grant them the strength to send those demon witches back to hell."

Mrs. Leadley could hear Matthew's footsteps as he moved on her. The red light of the moon cast his long shadow onto the wall in front of her.

With one final surge of hate-fuelled energy, she swung to face him and connected the palm of her left hand to his face, using all the strength she had left to her.

He hardly moved.

Mrs. Leadley looked Matthew up and down and saw the axe in his hand. She crossed herself, and prayed for it to be painless.

It wasn't.

In one swift movement, Matthew swung the axe up over his head and brought it down on Mrs. Leadley. It missed her head by an inch; she wished it hadn't. The blade buried itself deep in her shoulder, the strength he used pushed the axe head down as far as her breast. She felt the bones crunch and the flesh tear.

She screeched until her mouth filled with blood. Matthew yanked the axe from her chest so hard that she fell to the floor, her own blood pooling there with Matthew's. He raised the axe again and dropped it down on her back, followed by a final blow to her head.

Matthew laid onto the floor and put his mouth next to hers. He pursed his lips and breathed deeply. Steam drifted out from between Mrs. Leadley's lips and into Matthew's. He stood and dropped his head back. He opened his mouth wide and let the steam leave him. It travelled out of the window, floating on the air toward the woods.

CHAPTER 73

Ruth pulled onto New Road; the cottage was up on the left. A flash of lightning filled the sky. The world was filled with a red light, bright enough to see, despite it being the early hours of the morning.

"I don't like this, Tony," Ruth said.

"Neither do I." Tony had one hand on his belt buckle, ready to spring into action as soon as they pulled up.

Ruth turned the corner and drove on to the driveway. She stopped the engine and Tony was out before she had engaged the handbrake. Tony ran toward the cottage. He heard screams coming from the back of the house. He ran round; Ruth was close behind. He screamed when Jane and Tiffany almost collided headfirst into him. They were both crying and screaming manically.

"What's happened? Tell me!" Tony grabbed Jane by the shoulders and shook her.

"He's trying to kill us!" Jane screamed.

"Who? Who's trying to kill you?"

"Matthew. You'll think I'm crazy, but there're witches in those woods, and they've possessed him. He doesn't know what he's doing." She sobbed and fell into Tony's arms. He looked over at Ruth and they shared a look.

"Have you seen her? The witch in the woods?" There was no time for debating the existence of witches now. This was happening whether it felt real or not.

Jane pulled away from his chest and looked at him. "You believe me?"

Tony almost laughed. "Looks like I do, yeah."

Jane sniffed and gathered herself to speak, and pulled Tiffany in close to her. "We found a coffin in the walls of our basement. It had the body of a young girl in it. Mrs. Leadley told me the story that the witch's little girl was killed and taken away from her. We think we found her, so tried to give her back, hoping it would end it."

Jane paused and looked up at the top window of the house. "It didn't."

Tony looked over at Ruth; her eyes had gone wide and she was shaking her head.

"I think she's trying to bring all the dead witches back from the dead. Including her little girl. When she does that, she's going to kill the whole town," Tony said.

Jane's mouth opened wide, hung open like a giant O.

Lightning flashed above them and a loud crack of thunder shook the ground. When it stopped, they heard the screaming coming from the house.

"Who's up there?" Tony said, his hand moving to the taser on his belt.

"It's Mrs. Leadley, she saved us. Do you think he's…"

"We need to get in there." Tony started walking to the back of the house; he felt the first drop of rain land on his cheek. He touched his fingers to it like it was an alien thing. He looked up at the sky and saw the dense black and red clouds circling the moon. The storm was coming.

Tony stood with his back to the door that stood wide

open. The inside of the cottage looked like a deep black mouth with no teeth. "We're going inside to stop him. Go to Mrs. Leadley's cottage, get yourselves safe. After we've –"

Jane's face filled with terror and she pointed to something over his shoulder. "Look out!"

Tony spun and saw Matthew in mid-swing. He dodged to the left just in time, feeling the faint rush of wind from the axe head as it fell past his face and landed in the ground. Tony swung a right hand and caught Matthew's chin. Matthew's head snapped to the side and looked straight back at Tony.

"Run! Get to the cottage!" Tony shouted. He started walking backward. Matthew held the axe in front of his chest, readying to swing again. Tony felt for his taser and unholstered it from his belt. He levelled it at Matthew and waited for the right time. Firing a taser could be tricky; if he missed or caught the axe handle, he'd be dead.

"Go, go, go!" Ruth shouted at Jane and then stood beside Tony.

"Go with them, I've got this."

"Like fuck you have!"

Never taking his eyes from Matthew, Tony snapped, "Get them the fuck out of here, Ruth. Now!"

Ruth turned and ran, leaving Tony to face off with Matthew.

"Matthew, if there's anything left of you in there, you need to stop this," Tony said.

Matthew laughed; his voice started deep and then turned to a high-pitched cackling that seemed to echo in his throat.

"You can't stop us. You're too late!" the voice screeched with delight. "I'll use this body to take your soul, and then I'll take his. Soon, every soul will be ours. When I raise my dark beauties from the earth, they will give me the power I need to destroy you all." The witch's voice cackled loud into the night, in perfect timing with another fork of lightning and roll of deafening thunder.

Matthew lunged with the axe. Tony dodged and fired the taser. It struck but Matthew kept on moving. He staggered forward, raising the axe higher, the electricity pulsing through him jerking and twitching his muscles. The axe fell from his hands and landed on the ground. Tony ran toward him, was about to fire the second shot when Matthew lunged.

Tony pulled the trigger, but not before Matthew grabbed his hand, forcing the taser down. The electrodes landed in the dirt. Matthew gripped Tony by the throat and raised him up into the air. Looking at Matthew closely, Tony could see the huge divots in his head; it looked like that old lady had smashed his head up pretty good. Tony looked over at the cottage and saw Jane and Ruth stood there with Tiffany trying to get in the front door.

Matthew opened his mouth and put it toward Tony's, like a death's kiss. Tony kicked and kicked into Matthew's midriff to no avail.

Matthew stopped, as if distracted by something. He made a fist with his free hand and drove it into Tony's stomach, then dropped him to the ground. Tony wheezed as he tried to get the air back into his lungs. Rain was beginning to fall in spits now; the water felt cool as it soaked his skin.

Matthew stepped over him and ran toward the cottage.

THE DOOR to Mrs. Leadley's cottage wouldn't budge.

"Over here!" Ruth shouted and smashed the living room window. Jane grabbed Tiffany by the arm and ran over to Ruth, who systematically knocked out all the glass teeth from the frame.

"You first," Ruth said to Jane.

Jane hesitated.

"I need you to go in first so I can pass you the kid," Ruth explained. Jane nodded and clambered through. There was still a shard of glass or two, but Jane managed to avoid them without getting cut.

"Come on, Tiff, I got you," Jane said, holding out her hands for Tiffany to grab.

Tiffany looked unsure, but she did as she was told. Ruth gave her a foot up to the window ledge. Tiffany's fingertips had just brushed against Jane's when she was jerked backward. Tiffany cried out in shock; those cries stopped as soon as she hit the ground, headfirst. Matthew stood over Tiffany's unconscious body. Ruth hit him once, twice. Matthew hit Ruth; she fell back against the house in heap.

"Matthew! Don't hurt her! Please!" Jane screamed. Matthew picked Tiffany up from the floor and slung her over his shoulder.

Jane began to climb out of the living room window. Matthew was already running for the woods. In her desperation, Jane jumped without looking; her foot caught in a hole and twisted her ankle. She fell to the ground screaming.

"Matthew! Bring her back!"

Sergeant Thorne was running across the fields.

"We'll get her back, I promise," he said, helping Jane to her feet.

"That fucker knocked me out cold," Ruth said, getting up from the ground, rubbing her jaw.

"He's taken her, he's taken Tiff!"

Ruth looked down at the ground solemnly.

"We need to get in those woods and finish this. Whatever it is that's in there, we need to stop it."

Jane put her arm around Tony's shoulder. The three of them walked into the woods.

Chapter 74

Lucy kicked at the back door and screamed until her lungs burned. She opened her eyes and saw Mahone's snarling face, and then the fist. Mahone hit her twice; the first landed on her mouth, splitting her lip and loosening her two front teeth. The second landed on her forehead and sent vibrations through her neck and down her spine.

"You can shut up screaming, you meddlesome bitch! No one's going to save you now," Mahone said through gritted teeth. He pushed her against the door so she was sat upright.

Blood trickled down the back of her throat, making her cough; splatters of red covered the Perspex divide between the front and back of the car. She felt a sharp pain shoot up into her gum. She leaned forward and spat into her hand. Half of a white tooth drenched in blood landed in her palm.

"Fuck you!" she screamed and threw the tooth at him.

Mahone raised his hand. "Ah, ah, ah. Don't make me knock more of those pretty little teeth out your head."

Lucy calmed and slunk back into her seat.

Mahone cut a frustrated figure. He looked like a man on the edge, desperate and lost for ideas. Lucy doubted that this was something Mahone had felt before. His leg shook; he gripped his hand into a tight fist and chewed on his knuckles as he watched the hedgerows pass by as they drove down winding roads.

"Where are you taking me?" Lucy asked. It felt strange when her tongue found the unusual gap in her teeth as she spoke.

Mahone shook his head. "I'm taking you where I took her." He grimaced and clenched his eyes shut. "Why did you have to push it? Huh? Why did you have to go digging around in places that don't concern you?"

"You kept a woman prisoner for eighteen years."

Mahone shook his head. Not in denial, but as if she just didn't understand him.

"Sophie Rose was the town sweetheart. I loved her from the moment I laid eyes on her, and what did she do? She laughed at me. She told me to take a photo of her so I had something to wank off over, because that was the closest I'd ever get to a girl like her. That fucking bitch!" Mahone screamed.

"She humiliated me in front of everyone. No one says no to me, no one! She made me a laughingstock. I didn't want to kidnap her, that was never the plan. Sarah wanted Sophie out of the picture too, because she had eyes for Tony Thorne. Only problem was, Tony and Sophie were inseparable. I said I'd kill Sophie in return for something that Sarah could offer me. That was all I wanted, that and knowing that I got rid of that prissy little cunt. Only, when it came down to it, it didn't feel like enough."

Lucy watched on, amazed. Mahone was so wired, so frantic and out of control, he was spilling everything. Like he'd had it bottled up for so long and now the lid was off, he couldn't help pouring it all out.

"When she first saw it was me, she told me to piss off. She underestimated me, that was a big mistake. I hit her, knocked her out. Dragged her through the woods until I found this wall of thorn bushes. I got us through to the other side; it was completely encircled, the perfect place to dump a body. I knew about the old reservoir but had never been before so wasn't sure exactly where to take her. We stumbled upon it without even really trying. I found a rock and beat her over and over. There was so much blood. I was going to finish her off and dump her in the water, but something came over me. I realised it wasn't enough. A voice spoke in my head, it told me that she deserved more pain, more suffering because of what she had done to me."

"So you kept her as your prisoner, your little plaything you could just torture and rape whenever you felt like it?" Lucy snapped; her voice was harsh with venom.

Mahone smiled at that.

"After the first few years, she stopped begging to be let go. All hope had left her, and all she'd ever say to me was that she wished she were dead. She begged me to kill her. You know what I told her? I told her that I'd kill her as soon as she said she loved me." Mahone's eyes shimmered with wetness and his lip quivered.

"She never said it, did she?" Lucy wanted to smile but held it in.

Mahone shook his head and then laughed loudly. "If she wanted to be a stubborn cunt, well, that suited me fine. I carried on doing whatever I pleased with her, and nobody would ever have found out if it weren't for you."

Lucy had a flash of memory; with it came that deep, sick feeling she had when she opened the door and found Sophie in that room, completely emaciated, trapped in those restraints. Only, now she imagined herself being the one tied up in that room.

"You're too late. You can't hurt me because the police already know," Lucy said, doing her best to sound confident.

Mahone raised his eyebrows in a sarcastic *oh really, you don't say?* expression. "You think I'm going to try and escape this? Carry on as I was?" He laughed so loud it hurt Lucy's ears. "Oh, you stupid, stupid girl. I know this is the end for me, but if I'm going down, I'm taking you with me."

Lucy looked forward to see where they were heading. The car lurched as Officer Westlake drove up a kerb and directly onto the grass of the park, toward the trees. Lucy recognised it as the place she helped the search for Alfie Weeds, a time that felt like a whole lifetime ago. She looked at Westlake; his face seemed to be frowned with confusion, she wasn't sure at what, but guessed that it was probably at what Mahone just said. Lucy didn't think Mahone had run that part of the plan past Westlake.

"Sir," Westlake said, his voice not half as strong as it was when he threw Lucy into the back seat of his car.

"Yes, anywhere here. I remember the way –"

"No, not that." Westlake stopped the car, the headlights lighting up the trees in front of them, taking away that strange redness that covered them before. A spot of rain splattered on the windshield. "If you're not expecting to get away with this, how are you going to give me a recommendation for a promotion? That was the deal in me helping you." Westlake turned to face Mahone through the Perspex divider.

Mahone scratched at his head in frustration. "Oh, for God's sake, Westlake! I have a plan, trust me, I always have a plan. Now get out and open this fucking door!" Mahone smacked the window hard with his fist. Lucy tried to move further away from him but found she was as far as she could go.

Westlake hesitated, but only for a second, then he got out and let Mahone out of his door. Mahone slammed the door and then walked round to Lucy's. She scurried across the back seat to the other side, but found Westlake out of that window.

Despite Mahone being the doctor and Westlake being an officer, she fancied her chances of escape more favourable at Westlake's side. She laid on to her back and raised her legs so they were poised and ready.

"Get her the fuck out of the car, Westlake!" Mahone shouted.

Westlake nodded and opened the door. As soon as he reached in for Lucy, she kicked out with her right leg; the heel of her trainer landed square in the centre of his face. Blood escaped either side of her foot in a messy explosion.

"Argh!" he squealed, falling backward, cupping his face with both hands. "You fucking bitch! You broke my nose."

Lucy couldn't help it. She laughed. It came from fear and adrenaline, but the laughter didn't last long. She hurried out of the car, giving Westlake a swift kick between the legs for good measure. He dropped to his knees, giving a silent scream.

Lucy started running. She got fifty yards before Mahone's hand gripped her hair and yanked so hard she thought she felt her scalp tear open. She screamed until the blows started coming. He kicked her in the stomach and ribs until all the air had escaped her lungs. The last kick landed on her already busted lip and broken teeth.

The world spun. The bright red moon overhead, encircled with black and red storm clouds, pulled in and out of focus. She thought she was going to pass out. Pass out and throw up. She retched into the grass. Things felt a little clearer after that. The world stopped spinning, but she couldn't stop the incessant ringing in her ears.

She raised her head and saw Westlake catching them up. He was talking to Mahone; their conversation was growing heated, but Lucy couldn't make out the words. Their voices were nothing more than muffled murmurings, like when the people in the flat next door had a late-night argument. Her hands gripped the warm dry grass and pushed against the ground. Her body rose until her elbows started to shake and her upper arms gave out. She collapsed back into the dirt.

Mahone and Westlake were fighting, grappling with each other now. They fell to the ground several feet in front of her. Mahone got the better of Westlake, spun him round and straddled over him. He reached down to somewhere out of sight and pulled out a gun, put the barrel of it into Westlake's stomach, and fired.

Mahone stood from Westlake's now motionless body and walked over to Lucy. He grabbed her by the hair and lifted her up. Lucy struggled until Mahone punched her in the jaw with the butt of the gun. Then things went dark.

CHAPTER 75

Tony, Jane, and Ruth all walked through the woods. They kept their voices low as they talked. The silence in the woods made anything they said seem to echo and project through the trees. Tony had a high-powered torch on his belt. It showed them the beaten dirt footpath they had to navigate.

"So, how are we going to stop her?" Jane asked.

Tony shook his head. The beam of light from his torch was big and strong enough to illuminate the forest around them. "I don't know. But they managed it once, right?"

"The story Mrs. Leadley told us." Jane thought of Mrs. Leadley then and felt a huge wave of guilt and sadness. "Sorry, I need to get a grip."

Jane wiped at her eyes and then continued. "The witch cursed the town when they killed her daughter, promising she would return and the whole town would pay for what they had done. They crucified her, buried her with the other witches, and then filled the pit with water."

Tony nodded. "The story goes that the devil promised her the power to get her revenge. Every soul she takes is for him, and he uses them to regenerate her. Now she has enough souls, she's going to try and bring them all back. Starting with her daughter. When they're all back from the dead, they'll kill everyone who stands in their way."

"Since when did you know all this shit?" Ruth said from the rear.

"I've always known it. These were the stories told to us growing up, we just thought of them as old scary stories brought out for Halloween."

Jane furrowed her brow and stopped in her tracks. "So, when she's brought all of the witches back from the dead, the whole town will die?" She winced at the pain that shot up through her leg. Her ankle was holding up well, but anytime it rolled on a stone or a dead tree branch, it stung like a mother fucker.

"That's how the story goes. She needs them. Together, their magic is stronger." Tony put a hand on Jane's shoulder and told her to walk on.

"How can she have survived being under there for so long? Wouldn't being buried under holy water be torture enough to kill her?"

Tony shrugged. "She must've found a way to survive."

The walk was longer than they thought; it came to a point where they thought they must have walked right past it. Then they saw it, as if it appeared out of nowhere. Suddenly, the wall of thorns was before them, only now it had a huge gap to walk through. The red glow from the moon lit up the whole pit; the dead tree stood in the distance.

"Holy shit," Ruth said.

"We need a plan." Tony looked at Jane and Ruth. He flicked off the torch; he didn't want to let the witch know they were there, although part of him thought she already knew.

Ruth was carrying the axe that Matthew had dropped. "We can't just go straight in and attack her head on, she's too strong. She's taken the lives of five more people tonight."

Jane put a hand over her mouth.

"We need to find a way of taking her powers away. Something has kept her alive all this time. We need to find out what it is and destroy it," Tony said. He looked between Ruth and Jane, hoping one would have an answer.

"What, like some sort of evil magic generator?" Ruth said.

"I don't fucking know, do I – "

"It's the tree," Jane said, her voice clear and certain.

"What do you mean?"

"It's like this episode of Tom and Jerry I watched with Tiffany. Tom is looking for Jerry, so Jerry jumps into a pond and grabs a reed to breathe through so he can stay under water for as long as he wants. They've been buried under the holy water for hundreds of years, so there was nowhere for their evil to go if they wanted to survive. They're using that tree to grow their magic. That tree is their reed. It's kept them alive and it's harboured all of their power."

Jane grew more animated as she spoke; her eyes were wide as if she had just cracked all of the world's secrets. "Get rid of that, and they'll be powerless. Then we can kill them."

Tony turned around to look through the gap in the wall of thorns and saw the tree. It stood, glowing in the red light of the moon. He had seen it move and twist before, had seen faces appear in its branches. It all made sense. He extended his hand to Ruth.

"What?" she said.

"Axe."

Ruth gave it to him.

"Okay," Tony said quietly, scared that someone might hear. "This is what we're going to do."

CHAPTER 76

S he should be nervous; she should be fucking terrified. But all Jane could feel was fury. The fear of death had gone. If Tiffany was by her side, she'd have left. Tiffany's safety was all that mattered. But that bitch had taken her, and Jane would do anything to get Tiffany back. As she walked, Jane stroked the handle of the screwdriver she had in her back pocket, the screwdriver she had taken from the basement.

Rain came in a steady flow now, and when the empty reservoir came into view Jane could see the mud at the bed of the pit was growing sludgy. The redness that seemed to fill the air like a thick mist, made it hard to see. Jane looked constantly over her shoulder, sure that someone or something was going to sneak up on her.

They slipped down the embankment; the slickness of the wet mud made it easy to slide to the bottom.

The long, slim branches of the tree were visible in the red air. The thickness lifted, and visibility improved. Whether that was because they were in the pit or not, Jane didn't know. She just focused on what was in front of her.

The witch was by the mound of the tree, down on her

hands and knees, frantically assembling something on the ground in front of her. Tied to the tree, sobbing and begging to be let go, was Tiffany.

A shout of *I'm coming* was on the tip of Jane's tongue, only Ruth put a hand on Jane's shoulder, then put a finger to her lips. Jane nodded reluctantly.

Matthew stood motionless to the side of the witch, like a robot that had been set to sleep mode. The witch moved to the side as she scurried about in the mound of dirt. It was the bones, Jane saw, the bones from the wooden chest they had found in the basement walls. She was assembling them, sticking them in the dirt that the tree grew from. The skull was set into the sodden earth, the arms, spine, ribs, legs, all placed so they were anatomically correct.

"Bring her back to me!" the witch cried. "Bring them all back to me!" She was screaming at the tree. Its branches moved in the still air; its skeletal limbs appeared to form sneering, evil faces with smiles full of teeth.

Jane and Ruth continued forward. The closer they got to the tree, the harder it became to walk. The sludge stuck to their shoes, making horrid *slurping* and *sucking* sounds.

"I hope this works," Ruth said under her breath.

Jane didn't reply. Didn't need to. They were all hoping that.

As the tree started to tower above them, Jane held up a hand for them both to stop. Tiffany was squirming; she looked dazed, blood poured over her face from a wound underneath her hair.

"Give them the power you have given me and we will gather the souls of the living, my lord. Grant me –" The witch stopped. She didn't turn to look at them, but she knew they were there. Jane was sure of it.

"It's funny," the witch said. Her voice was low and had an edge of amusement to it, a sharp edge. "You seem to know what I am, the power I have been given, and yet, you come straight to me. Tell me, do you wish to die?" She stood and turned, a wicked smile across her face.

"We gave you back your daughter," Jane cried. "Now give me back mine!"

"Your daughter will be the perfect sacrifice. Using her soul, I will bring my darling back from the dead." The witch laughed. "And when I have brought all of my dark beauties back from the earth, we shall bring death to you all."

"You touch her and I'll fucking kill you."

The witch's smile faded. "You stupid woman. I can't be killed. They have tried to kill me. They have kept me buried for hundreds of years, and still, the Dark Lord grants me the power to withstand it all."

"Then I'll just have to fucking bury you deeper!"

Jane lunged for the witch with all that she had. She screamed as she charged. Her legs ached from the effort it took to run in the sloppy mud, the pain in her ankle burned like it was bathed in hot coals, but her focus was only on the witch. She believed that she would get to her, and when she was only a foot away, she truly believed that she was going to be able to drive the screwdriver into the witch's heart and kill her.

Then, all of her muscles grew stiff, and she found she was frozen in mid-stride. The pain was immense. She screamed without moving her mouth.

"Fucking bitch!" Ruth charged from the side but the same happened to her.

The witch cackled, high into the night, lifting Jane and Ruth into the air. "I am Ragan, Bride of Satan, the most powerful sorceress sent from hell. I –"

The witch's eyes shot open wide, and she shrieked. A shriek that echoed in deep and high tones as if she had the voices of three different beings inside her. Jane and Ruth dropped to the ground, splashing into the mud.

The witch turned; the rain started to pour down and lightning flashed overhead. Thunder roared to match the witch's screams. Stood on the mound by the tree was Tony. The axe was buried deep in its trunk.

TONY PULLED the axe from the tree trunk; with it came a black sludge that oozed and spurted from the gash. The witch cried out in pain once more as if *she* had been hit with the axe.

The ropes tying Tiffany to the tree fell. Tiffany dropped to the ground. She frantically removed the ropes from her wrists and ankles; the soft skin on the inside of her wrist had torn from the friction of the rope.

"Go, run!" Tony shouted.

Tiffany looked around and slid down the mound through the sloppy mud and ran toward Jane, who stood with her arms spread wide open, beckoning Tiffany to her.

"Get back here!" the witch screamed.

Tony swung the axe again, the blade buried deep into the dead wood of the tree; more black sludge poured out. It was bleeding, Tony realised. He pulled the axe out and swung again.

This time, the witch flung her hand up toward him. An invisible fist punched deep into his guts and he flew through the air. He landed with an almighty thud into the boggy mud at the base of the mound, knocking all the wind from his lungs.

The witch appeared from the side of the mud hill and walked toward him. Tony reached for the axe by his side and found it wasn't there. It was still buried in the tree trunk. He rolled to his side and tried desperately to get to his feet. He got halfway to upright before the witch raised him up into the air. His legs kicked like he was riding an invisible bike.

"I'll enjoy taking your soul," the witch snarled and put her face to his. Tony could feel a pull somewhere inside him; it felt as though all of his insides were being vacuumed out of his mouth.

"Get off him!" Ruth jumped and wrapped her arm around the witch's throat. Tony dropped from the air and landed in the gathering water that broke his fall.

A flash of lightning, followed by more thunder, cracked overhead.

Ragan and Ruth grappled by the foot of the tree. Behind them, Jane and Tiffany climbed the muddy hill where the tree grew. They struggled to get a foot hold, their feet and hands sliding in the dirt. Another flash of lightning, this one dazzling, made Tony sees spots of bright stars in his vision.

He got to his knees; the water level had risen enough to cover his feet. He had been about to jump in to help Ruth when something in the dirt mound caught his eye. The white tree roots, or what he had thought were tree roots, were waving from the dirt, trying to get at Jane and Tiffany as they climbed.

They were bones. The bones of the dead witches that had been laid there for four centuries. They had been waiting for this day all that time, and they were doing what they could to stop Jane from getting to that tree. Dozens of arms protruded from the sopping wet sludge. Their long bony fingers scratched at Jane's leg, tearing at her jeans and taking a chunk of flesh with it. She screamed, then Tiffany kicked at the arm that had scratched her mother. It broke off, mid-forearm, and fell beneath the rising water.

Tony ran toward them to help. He heard Ruth cry out. He turned and saw that it was a cry of triumph. She had managed to get Ragan's face down in the water. She held desperately onto the back of her head.

It might not kill her, Tony thought, but it would keep her

busy whilst they destroyed that tree. He clambered up the mound, knocking away the arms of dead witches as he strode. He felt the claws swiping at him, tripping him, digging into the flesh of his calf muscle and tearing through the skin.

Jane had broken free from the hands that held her and was almost at the top. Tiffany stood by the tree, axe in hand. She would have swung it, Tony could see that in her face, but she wasn't strong enough.

"Give it to me!" Jane grabbed the axe, screaming over another loud crack of thunder. She swung the axe and buried it with a precision Tony wouldn't have expected. The axe head landed where he had already started. More black blood spurted out, and with it came a deep guttural roar. The arms in the dirt seemed to stiffen; wild screams of pain screeched from seemingly nowhere.

Jane hit the tree again, it tilted and a flat, dead crack sounded from the trunk.

"One more!" Tony screamed. He was on his stomach, dead hands and fingers scratching and tearing at his clothes. His blood trickled into the dirt, no doubt giving the witches beneath some gory pleasure.

Jane was breathing heavy, her hair slicked to her skin. Rain drenched her, droplets of water rounded her face and clung to her chin, ready to drop.

"Mummy!" Tiffany screamed, and Jane turned to look at where the scream had come from. Tiffany's legs had been pulled out from under her. She fell and tumbled down the mound.

———

TIFFANY LIFTED her head out of the water. She breathed deeply and got to her feet. The mound looked so high; the bones of the dead witches waved manically from the dirt. Her mum was looking down at her from up high, she was scream-ing, but Tiffany couldn't hear what she was saying.

A flash of lightning filled the sky and something caught Tiffany's eye. A skeleton was rising from the mound. It had no muscles and no flesh, but it staggered toward her, jolting and tripping with every step. It was the girl the witch had assem-bled. The witch's daughter.

Tiffany screamed.

The witch's daughter held her bony hands out in front of her, reaching for Tiffany. Tiffany tried to turn and run, but the skeleton's hands gripped the collar of her shirt. She hit the arms and heard a crack; she hit again and the right arm of the skeleton snapped in two.

It opened its mouth and its jaw clacked together, like it was laughing at her efforts. Its face moved toward hers, its jaws snapping, inches away from taking off her nose. Tiffany put her forearm into the thing's neck to try and force it back but it was strong. Too strong.

Tiffany heard shouting coming from the mound, and saw her mum raising the axe, ready to swing.

"THIS IS FOR MATTHEW!" Jane shouted, and swung the axe, screaming the whole time. The axe hit the spot and the tree began to fall. The trunk cracked and splintered; black blood erupted from the stump as it fell.

A terrible screech pierced the night. Tony put his hands to his ears; Jane and Tiffany did the same. The thing that had been attacking Tiffany collapsed into a pile of bones. The screech went on and on until it was on the verge of bursting ear drums. The hands from the dirt stopped clawing and retreated back into the earth. Lightning burst overhead. The tree laid dead and decapitated in the water. It seemed to make faces with its branches once more, only this time the faces were open mouthed, screaming in pain and terror... and defeat.

Tony got to his feet when the screeching stopped. He was sure he was deaf, until he heard it.

A gun shot.

BOOM.

It echoed around the forest. In the following silence, Tony looked down at his body; there was nothing. He felt no pain and saw no blood. He saw Tiffany had clawed her way back up the mound to Jane; they cowered together but were unharmed.

Tony felt his heart break, even before he turned around and saw the blood-red hole in Ruth's forehead.

"Nooo!" Tony screamed and ran to her. The witch raised her head from the water and took a huge breath, then clawed herself away toward where the tree once stood. Tony grasped Ruth in his arms. She had died instantly. Her eyes stared blankly up into the red moon in the sky above.

He looked up and saw Mahone walking toward them. He walked with a woman in front of him, the gun now pointed to her head. It was Lucy; Tony recognised her as soon as the lightning flashed again and her face became visible.

Tony got to his feet and stepped in the direction of Mahone. Mahone raised the gun. Hammering rain bounced off the barrel.

"Ah, ah, ah. Just you stay there, Sergeant Thorne."

Tony stopped still; the water was up to his knees.

"I don't know what you're doing here. I guess this is fate. My destiny."

"Why are you here, Mahone? I know about Sophie; I know what you did."

Mahone laughed loudly. "You know what I did," he said softly. "I take it you're going to arrest your wife when you get home to her?"

Tony's eyebrows closed in together. "What has Sarah got to do with this?"

Mahone laughed again. Lucy struggled in his arms and the laughter stopped. He swung the gun up and smashed her in the temple with the handle. She cried out but didn't struggle again. Tony stepped closer until the gun was pointed at him once more.

"She didn't tell you? She had been desperate to, but I told her not to." Mahone's smile turned into a sneer. "How do you think I managed to get Sophie to come to me, Tony? It was no secret that Sophie hated me. If it weren't for Sarah, I wouldn't have been able to get anywhere near her."

Something inside Tony's stomach twisted into a knot. A lump caught in his throat and the pulse of his heart pounded in his head.

"Sarah intercepted Sophie on her way home, told her that someone needed help in the woods. That they were screaming for help. Good girl Sophie Rose couldn't leave someone in need, could she? She was just too nice."

"You're lying!" Tony shouted.

Mahone shook his head, smiling. "Sarah led her right to me. I will admit, she had no idea that I didn't go through with killing her though, that was all me. The plan was to kill Sophie Rose so that you were a free agent, and, well, it worked for Sarah, didn't it? I was going to kill her; I was going to dump her in this reservoir, but a voice spoke to me. All this time I've believed that it was God, but now I'm not so sure. Not the God everyone prays to in church, anyway. It told me that killing her wasn't the right choice. That I deserved better, I deserved respect. Sophie always laughed at me, humiliated me. So I made her pay."

"You're a monster. You're more evil than –"Tony turned to look at Ragan. She was stood now, her head bent and her hair covering her face. One eye was visible through a parting in her hair. She raised her hand.

"You'll pay for what you've done!" she screamed at him and stepped forward.

Tony braced himself for the pain. And felt nothing. There was a small twinge somewhere in his chest, but nothing compared to what he had felt before when he thought his insides were being vacuumed out from his mouth.

Ragan put her hand down and held it in front of her. Her hair had parted more and a look of stunned shock spread over her face.

Tony laughed. "Your powers. They're gone. Without the power he gave you in that tree, you're nothing. Just a very old, powerless witch. Your great Dark Lord has left you to fend for yourself."

"No," she muttered and stretched her hand out again. "Noooo!!!" She ran for Tony. He braced himself for the melee when another deafeningly loud *bang* sounded.

Ragan fell sideways; a spray of blood and brain matter shot out a split second before she fell.

"I don't know who that cunt was, but if anyone's going to kill you tonight, it's me," Mahone said and cocked the hammer on his pistol.

"Let the girl go, Mahone." Tony looked around at the water that rose higher every second. He looked behind him at the feeder channel. It was pouring at a rapid pace now; the river Mere would be filling and flowing fast with this storm. "Let me and you end this tonight."

Mahone shook his head. "Nice try. But this bitch has to pay. I'd be sitting pretty if it weren't for her meddling."

"It's over, Mahone, do something good, for once in your life. Let her live."

There was movement behind Mahone, a dark shape emerging from the sheet of rain that pounded the rising water behind him.

"I think I'll just kill you all." Mahone levelled the gun at Tony. There was a *bang,* this one dulled by the heaviness of the rain. What followed was a loud scream.

Tony opened his eyes and saw Mahone had missed him. Matthew had crept up on Mahone and attacked him from behind. He was biting Mahone's neck, blood pouring down his chest and soaking into his shirt. Matthew gnawed and tore at the scant flesh of Mahone's neck and when he let go, there was a hole full of blood and gore. He had severed the artery; blood pulsed out, covering Lucy who screamed and ran toward Tony.

Mahone fell face first, where he floated in red water.

"Gurr dem serf!" Matthew shouted. His head was a mess; divots and lumps had been knocked out of his skull, the fact that he was still standing was a miracle.

"What?" Tony shouted.

Matthew raised a hand and pointed toward the mound where Jane and Tiffany stood.

"Gurr dem s-ayf," he said once more.

Get them safe.

Tony figured it out. "I will!" he said, and with that, Matthew fell into the water.

"Noooo!" Jane cried.

Lucy swam toward Tony, her neck only just above the water.

"Swim to the side, get yourself out!" Tony shouted at her.

Lucy nodded and changed direction, toward the embankment.

Tony waded through the water that was now up to his chest. "Come on!" he shouted. "We need to get out of here!"

Jane and Tiffany looked reluctant, but then they turned to

look at the feeder channel and saw the water pouring in like a waterfall. Jane nodded. She helped Tiffany into the water. The little girl wrapped her arms around Tony's neck and dug her nails into his back. Jane lowered herself in.

They swam together. Tony was the stronger swimmer, so he kept with Jane to make sure she didn't drop under at any point. She didn't. The drive to get back to safety was strong. Tiffany sobbed the entire time.

They reached the embankment where Lucy stood waiting.

"Give me your hand!" Lucy cried and pulled Tiffany from the water, then Jane.

Tony tried to climb out himself but the mud was too slippery. He fell back in; the water engulfed him. He opened his eyes and saw only darkness.

He tried to swim to the top, but his arms felt too heavy. He pulled and clawed at the water but didn't move. His air was running out; bubbles escaped his mouth as he tried not to panic. He had done a little training for these situations. The best advice for survival was DON'T PANIC. Which was easier to do in test scenarios than it was in real life. He flapped his arms and still the surface of the water came no closer.

He looked down into the water. There must have been a flash of lightning above him because, for a moment, he saw a hundred hands clawing at his legs, and one rotting face. Its yellowed teeth stuck out from its black gums; long black hair floated away from its peeling scalp. Its dark, decaying mouth opened wide as its eyeballs popped from their sockets. Tony kicked his feet desperately to free them from the hands. Lightning flashed again and the hands fell away; the face, nothing more than a skull now, disappeared into the darkness of the water.

He swam upward, and now the surface grew closer and closer until he burst out and sucked in huge gasps of air. He could hear the voices of the three people on the embankment screaming his name. He was close to passing out; using his last bout of energy he swam toward the sound of their voices. His vision was dark and spotted with white stars. He felt hands grabbing at his shirt and lifting him from the water.

"Tony? Tony!" a voice screamed. He pictured Sarah's face. Then another voice came. "Tony!" it spoke. Now he pictured Sophie's. Only hers was blurry.

CHAPTER 77

Outside the Stanford house, emergency vehicles gathered. Two ambulances and three cop cars. There was no one to arrest, not there anyway, but they created a crime scene around the reservoir, the now full reservoir. Divers were coming; sunlight was only a couple of hours away and they'd go in at first light to retrieve the bodies.

Tony couldn't give a statement; he had inhaled too much water. They got him in the back of the ambulance and Lucy went with him. She was okay, a few cuts and bruises, but the paramedics insisted she went in for scans. She could have a bad concussion.

Tiffany and Jane went in the other ambulance. Tiffany was okay, and despite a twisted ankle that would later turn out to be a broken ankle, Jane was okay too. Physically. The emotional pain would lessen over time, but it would never truly stop.

In the hospital, Tony was given an IV full of antibiotics; there was a risk of pneumonia amongst a whole host of other infections. He was semi-conscious. He remembered seeing Lucy's face, then a lot of faces that belonged to people he didn't know. They were like dreams. Then they were like nightmares. Every face he saw was shrunken, skin pulled tight and wrinkled with deep grooves. Rotten insides, black with decay.

That would have been the world, if they hadn't have done what they had done, the world would have rotted. Decayed into nothing but pain and darkness.

Then he slept.

WHEN HE CAME TO, Lucy was by his bedside. She was curled up on the chair in his cubicle, sleeping soundly. She had a paper bracelet with her details on. She must have had a shower because she looked clean. It made the bruises shine more. Beneath her eye was a deep purple, and her jaw was red where the smacks with the butt of the gun had scraped away the skin. Her lip had stitches in, his vision was blurry, so it was hard to see how many, but quite a few, he guessed, by the sight of it.

He used his arm to push himself upright, and winced at the sharp pain in his elbow. "Jesus, fuck," he said through gritted teeth. The location where the IV needle was implanted started bleeding slightly.

"Hey, you're awake." Lucy rubbed at her eyes. She looked tired.

"Yeah, I'm up. Can you get me a nurse? I need this thing taken out of my arm. I need to find Sarah; I have to talk to her about what Mahone said."

"It's true," Lucy said. There was a harsh, straight-to-the-point tone in her voice that Tony put down to her tiredness. "We spoke to the police and told them everything, the mayor was already in the building when we got here. He demanded Sarah be questioned in her bed."

"The mayor knows about Sophie, then?"

Lucy nodded. "I'm sorry, Tony, I know you probably didn't want to believe it, but Sarah admitted to everything. She's as guilty as Mahone. Just maybe not as twisted."

Tony laid his head back against the thin hospital pillows and closed his eyes. He had to bite his lip from crying. The exhaustion, the physical pain, the complete fuck-up that was that night had destroyed him. Ruth. He remembered seeing her face, blank of any life, the red hole in her forehead. It was all too much.

"There're officers with her now. She's been placed under arrest and moved to a private room."

Tony took a deep breath. "I wanna see her." He flipped the covers off and tore the IV needle from his arm. Lucy stood to stop him.

"Get out of my way, Lucy, I need to speak to her, hear it for myself."

"They won't let you, you're too close to this, Tony. The chief constable is taking charge of this."

Tony pulled at his hair. "Fuck!" he shouted. A nurse popped her head through the curtains.

"Everything okay in here?"

"No! It's not fucking okay," Tony said, more to himself than anyone else. He stopped pacing. "I'll go talk to Sophie then, she can tell me what she remembers from that night."

Lucy put her hands on his shoulders. She barely used any force, but something about that touch made him sit back down on the bed. "I'm so sorry, Tony, Sophie Rose died a few hours ago. Her body couldn't take anymore."

Right then, Tony felt his heart shatter all over again.

"Oh, God," He couldn't hold back the tears any longer.

Lucy sat beside him and nodded to the nurse that she had it under control. The nurse gave her a thin smile and left.

"The last thing she said to me was to tell you not to blame

yourself. I think she loved you to the last, Tony. She never blamed you for what happened to her, not once."

"How can I not?"

"You were little more than a kid, and you weren't the one in charge of finding her, Tony. There was a whole police unit looking for her, volunteers, fuck, basically the whole town. This isn't for you to feel guilty about. You did all you could."

They sat there together for a few hours. Tony drifted off after a new IV was fitted. Lucy was told she could go home and rest, but she insisted on staying. Tony was all alone now; it didn't feel right to leave him to wake up to an empty room.

Epilogue

A fter going so long with scorching sun and no rain, the whole of England suffered torrential downpours for the next three weeks. The dead and browning grass turned a lush green once more, the towns' reservoirs (the ones that didn't harbour a centuries-old witches grave) burst their banks. The rivers flowed deep and the smaller towns, villages, and hamlets suffered from flash flooding that destroyed homes, businesses, and bridges. People prayed for the sun to come back.

"Bring on the heatwave!"

"Where's this global warming?"

The sun came back and England had its mildest autumn. The river levels lowered, not as much as that summer though, so the reservoirs were kept at healthy levels without the need for an inconvenient hose pipe ban, or for bottled water to be bought and paid for at the government's (taxpayers') expense.

Jane and Tiffany decided to stay in their cottage. It was what Matthew would have wanted. He was cremated at the Wymere crematorium. They scattered his ashes on the acre of land they owned at the back of their house. In his memory, they planted dozens of fruit trees, an orchard that Jane and

Tiffany could enjoy. They wouldn't be able to eat all the fruit the trees would produce next season, so they decided they would box up what was left over and donate it to the church for the needy.

The second bout of hot temperatures began to subside and something resembling normal British weather resumed. It was ten degrees out, not too cold, but Tiffany and Jane both opted to wear light jackets for their walk.

"Are you sure you want to do this?" Jane asked.

Tiffany nodded. "I want to make sure. It'll help the nightmares stop."

Jane smiled and traced her finger around the outline of Tiffany's jaw. "I hope so, love. Come on then, let's get going."

They walked through the orchard of apple and pear trees and made their way into the woods.

The path was hardly visible thanks to the overgrowth of forest plants that had taken the mixture of tonnes of rain and loads of sun and run with it. They walked for a while before they reached it; that was good. Before, the wall of thorns had just appeared as if out of nowhere. If they had to pick out on a map roughly where it would be, Jane doubted that she could. The magic was gone, the magic that was used to confuse and disorientate them. The magic that no doubt stopped the police drones from working.

"What's happened, Mummy?" Tiffany reached out and grabbed a branch that protruded from the wall of brambles. It snapped off, a brittle crack followed by a cloud of dust.

Jane stepped up to it and did the same. "It's dying," she marvelled. Covering her hand with the sleeve of her coat, she pushed into the hedge and the branches simply disintegrated in front of their eyes.

Tiffany looked up at Jane and smiled.

They found the parting the witch had made and walked

through. In the dirt, small patches of green grass were growing; a few weeds, dandelions, and daisies grew in bunches.

"You see, Tiff, whatever had cursed this place is dead and gone."

Tiff walked down the side of the reservoir; the water was brimming all the way to the top. She stopped halfway and turned to look into the centre of the lake where the tree had once stood. There was nothing there. The water was still, the bright blue sky overhead reflected on the surface with perfect clarity. She saw black V-shaped birds as they flew across big white fluffy clouds. She turned to her mother. "I'm happy. We got rid of it, and it's never coming back."

Jane smiled. "We did, love. Your dad would be so proud of you."

Jane and Tiffany walked back to the path and went home, their hands entwined, and there was a small skip in their step.

In the water, a ripple appeared in the centre and spread out in tiny, almost invisible waves, which spread bigger and bigger until they reached the embankment.

From the centre of the reservoir, a small finger-size branch broke through the surface of the water, searching for the air above it.

Acknowledgments

First of all, I'd like to say thank you to everyone who has helped in the process of making this book what it is. Wicked house Publishing have a fantastic team, and working with them has been a pleasure.

Thank you to my wonderful wife, Haley. Without your support, I don't know where I'd be. You give me the strength to push on when I don't think I can. Any success I have is because of you.

And, of course, a big thank you to you - dear reader, for spending your time with my work. I hope you liked it.

Axl Malton

WICKED HOUSE PUBLISHING

Come find us!

Amazon: Wicked House Publishing
Mailing List: Sign Up Here!
Facebook Group: The Wicked House Cult of Slightly Insane
Readers

facebook.com/WickedHousePublishing
x.com/WickedHousePub
instagram.com/wicked_house_publishing

Printed in Great Britain
by Amazon

47137023R00202